Mrs. Chartwell
and the
Cat Burglar

ALSO BY PAMELA GOSSIAUX

Mrs. Chartwell and the Cat Burglar (A Russo Romantic Mystery: Book 1)

Trusting the Cat Burglar (A Russo Romantic Mystery: Book 2)

Romancing the Cat Burglar (A Russo Romantic Mystery: Book 3)

Good Enough

Why Is There a Lemon in My Fruit Salad? How to Stay Sweet When Life Turns Sour

A Kid at Heart: Becoming a Child of Our Heavenly Father

Six Steps to Successful Publication: Your Guide to Getting Published

Mrs. Chartwell

and the

Cat Burglar

pamela gossiaux

Tri-Cat Publishing

Scripture quotations are taken from The Holy Bible, New International Version, copyright 1973, 1978, 1984 by International Bible Society.

The author owes a debt of gratitude to William Shakespeare for his quotes and inspiration.

Visit the author's website at: www.PamelaGossiaux.com

First Printing, November 2017

ISBN 978-0-9976387-5-2 (paperback)
ISBN 978-0-9976387-6-9 (ebook)

Cover Design: Llewellen Designs
Editor: Erin Wolfe, WordWolfe Copy Editing
Formatting: Dallas Hodge, www.ebeetbee.com
Author Photo: Vera Davis Photography

Published in the United States by Tri-Cat Publishing

Tri-Cat Publishing

To Pam and Xanthe

Chapter One

Mrs. Abigail Chartwell filed away the last document in her stack and prepared to go home for the evening, but the gentleman at the counter kept *talking*. He was going on about some university course and how he was using certain historical documents to support his thesis, but she had stopped listening closely a while ago so she could leave the library before the weather got worse. There was a terrible snowstorm on its way. She checked the time on her phone.

"I need to leave now," she said, pushing her glasses up on the bridge of her nose and finally turning her full attention to the young man, who got flustered at the eye contact and choked on his words.

"Um…yes, of course. I'm sorry to have taken so much of your time." With flushed cheeks and ears quickly turning red, he exited the room, cutting through the Women's History section on his way out.

Abigail sighed. She was a beautiful woman, and most men couldn't meet her eyes for more than a few seconds before becoming tongue-tied. But she wasn't interested in flirting. She had experienced a brief marriage at the age of twenty-four, but her husband had died within months of their honeymoon, long before she had time to figure out how to navigate it. And that was some six long years ago.

She enjoyed her work at the library in the Ancient Maps and Documents department, and kept her thick red hair in a bun and her wide, beautiful eyes hidden behind glasses so as to discourage any interested potential courtiers.

Love wasn't even on her radar. Been there, done that.

Satisfied that her work area was tidy, she slipped out behind the Geography section, through Ancient Artifacts, and back to the break room to grab her coat. On her way, she set the alarms that secured the windows and central corridors, since it was her turn to close. She was the last to leave on Tuesdays. The collections of old books, maps and journals that the University's library housed were rare, and most were worth a fortune.

"Good night, Mrs. Chartwell," said the library's janitor, who had just pulled his bucket out of the closet. Bob had the security codes and could release them room by room as he worked.

"Good night, Bob," she said, waving her hand, which still bore her wedding ring. She made sure the light caught it. Bob had recently made some indirect moves that led her to believe he was taking an interest in her. She didn't have time for that.

Then she realized she was missing her gloves. She had pulled them on after lunch because it was cold in the stacks today and her hands were freezing. She had worn them all afternoon, so they must be back at her desk.

Bob disappeared on the elevator down to the basement. He always started at the bottom and worked his way up. Her department was on the second floor of the five-story building, and her desk was under a tall, domed skylight that let in the sunshine during the summer and an unpleasant draft during the winter.

She made her way back to her desk. There they were, on the floor under her chair. She bent down to pick the gloves up and noticed someone had knocked the Old Maps brochures off the desk at some point during the day and not bothered to pick them up. They lay scattered under the desk, out of reach. She got down on her knees, stretching her arm out as she tried to reach them. She had to crane her head to the side to get her arm that far under, but she managed to grasp most of them. She made another attempt, and when she had them all, she stacked them in a pile and stood up.

That's when she saw him.

He was dressed in black—some sort of tight outfit that looked like something a runner would wear. It covered his entire body, including his face, she noticed with a bit of fright. Only his eyes were showing.

He froze when he saw her. There was a long black rope hanging just above his head, threading its way up the three floors to the dome above them.

Abigail was about to scream when the man put his finger to his lips. Something about his movement stopped her.

"Good evening, ma'am," he said, and gave her a sweeping bow. "Welcome to the maps department."

That irked her. It was *her* maps department. And he was in it.

"If you move, I'll scream," she said, unsure as to why she hadn't already done so. Absurdly, she noticed he had amazing eyes. Dark brown. They twinkled as they gazed into hers.

"No reason to scream," he said. His voice was low, musical. "I'm not here to hurt you. I just wanted to check something out. Of the library." He pulled his hooded mask off, revealing thick, wavy black hair. "I'm Tony. Tony Russo. Pleased to meet you."

She reached behind her and pushed a button. It was a silent alarm they installed last year when they moved the classic maps in from France. She never thought she'd have to use it.

*Please God...*she prayed, not really sure how to finish the prayer.

He took a few steps closer to her.

If she could keep him talking, the police would be here soon. She wondered where Bob was.

"Russo? As in the famous painter?" She needed to kill time.

"Yes," he said, peering at her from under thick lashes. "I'm related."

"I don't believe you."

Antonio Russo was one of the world's most well known impressionists, with his works hanging in museums around the world, including the Louvre.

"Pity." He watched her calmly. "I just need one thing and then I'll leave."

She eyed the tube he was carrying. "You can come back during the day and check it out like a normal person. Instead of stealing it."

"You can't check this out."

He was right. The maps and documents in her department had to remain in the library.

"I'm here to *borrow* something. There's a difference. I plan to put it back."

Her eyes narrowed. "Is this a robbery?"

"This is most certainly *not* a robbery," he said, holding both hands up. "Robbers are armed. Thieves are not."

"I thought you said you weren't here to steal anything," she said. His lips twitched, as if he were about to laugh. Was he making fun of her? Her eyes traveled back to his and then to his hands, which were covered in black gloves. His skin-tight clothes, she noticed, outlined his body quite well. His *entire* body.

He took a few more steps toward her, and there was no longer a desk between them. The curls of his wavy black hair ended just above the nape of his neck. It was the type of hair you wanted to run your hands through.

She stared back at him. She felt her heart pounding in her chest.

"You won't get away with this," she said. "You're on camera."

"I disabled the cameras," he whispered. He was close enough now that she could smell his aftershave. Something a bit spicy. His breath was on her cheek and slightly minty. "And the security system. You usually leave promptly at 6 p.m. You're late tonight."

"So you *are* a thief."

"Maybe." He gently reached toward her cheek and behind her.

His hand slipped away from her face, and he held her hairpin between his fingers. She felt her hair fall down around her shoulders in a cascade of thick, soft, red waves. She smelled her lavender cream rinse and saw the thief swallow as his eyes traveled from her eyes to her hair. It was one of her best attributes, her hair. She had inherited it from her grandmother. Just like the pin.

"That's my grandmother's," she said, looking at the pin. "It's not worth anything."

Which was true. The jewels were fake, a 1940s costume jewelry piece. But it had sentimental value.

He looked at the pin in his hand and then back to her. He might be trying to charm her, but two could play at that game. She held his eyes.

"Did my heart love till now? Forswear it, sight! For I ne'er saw true beauty till this night," he whispered, his voice husky.

What? He was quoting Shakespeare at her? She held his gaze and frowned.

He seemed to gather himself. "At any rate, I've come to take what I need and I'll be going."

She wondered where the police were, or if he had also disabled the silent alarm system. She glanced at the clock. Bob was probably still in the basement.

"What are you looking for?" she asked, to keep him here. She wasn't about to let him get away with this...this...intrusion into her world.

He hesitated and then turned and walked a few steps away from her, twirling her hairpin between his fingers. His arms were strong, well muscled under his suit. "A map," he said. "There's an old Russo painting hidden in the city, and there's a map that leads there. I'm here to get that map."

"The portrait? That's a legend," she said. "It's not true. Treasure hunters would have found it years ago."

"But they don't have the information I have," he said. She noticed his cat-like steps as he paced around and how his body suit clung to him. He was in very good shape. Or maybe there was just a lot of spandex holding him together.

"What information?" She thought she heard sirens in the distance. But no, it was a silent alarm. They wouldn't put the sirens on.

"My great-great grandmother was rumored to have had an affair with Russo, and I am the descendant of that event. He couldn't marry her—because as you know from history, he was already married—but he painted a portrait of her and signed it with a heart next to his name. He called the painting 'Laurel,' after my great-grandmother. It was a nickname he had for her. Nobody knew who she was because back in that day to be pregnant out of wedlock was to be shamed."

5

"Nobody has ever proved that painting exists," Abigail said.

"Ahhh...but it does."

Abigail crossed her arms and sat down on her chair. "So you're telling me that you are related to Russo—the famous painter—by virtue of an affair and that you know where this world-famous painting is? The painting that every treasure hunter has been looking for for the past seventy years? The painting of the Mystery Woman?"

He turned to look at her. She had crossed her legs and taken off her glasses to chew on the frame, a nervous habit of hers. Her green eyes caught his dark ones. "Yes," he said simply.

She cleared her throat. "Well, go at it then. Go find your map."

He stood there, looking at her.

"What's your name?" he asked.

"Don't you know? I thought you had been stalking me."

"I don't know," he said. "I only watched to see who left the library and when. I don't *stalk*."

"Mrs. Chartwell," she said out of habit.

"Mrs.?"

She fingered her ring. "He died." She didn't usually share that information.

"Oh. I'm sorry."

"Yes."

"What's your first name?"

"That's none of your business."

"But I told you mine."

"Which was foolish. I'll use it to track you down once the police get here."

"The police aren't coming. I told you I disabled the alarms. We have time for some tea." He gave her a charming smile. She noticed he had a very nice mouth, with a shadow of a beard beginning.

They heard a crash as a door burst open somewhere.

"They're here," she said. "I have a secondary alarm, a silent alarm. I pushed it."

He swallowed hard and then met her eyes.

"You're beautiful."

She looked behind her. They'd be coming through that door.

"Go," she said, nodding toward his rope, suddenly wanting to keep him safe. "Go."

She turned her back to him, as the police burst through, guns out.

"Abby!" said the cop in the front. It was Jimmy Stout, an older policeman whom she knew. He had two others with him. He nodded to them, and they separated to right and left, guns ready.

"He's not armed," Abigail said.

"Who?" Jimmy asked.

"The thief," she said, turning back. "Don't shoot him."

But he was gone. There was nothing where he had been just a moment ago. She glanced at the dome and didn't see any sign of the rope. He had simply disappeared.

"Where is he?" Jimmy asked her. He followed her eyes overhead but she quickly looked down the stack, toward the Women's History section. She pointed. "He went that way. But he's gone."

"Clear," said one of the officers.

The other cleared his area and then they took to the stairs. "We'll cut him off below."

"Be careful," she shouted after them. "You'll scare Bob. He has no idea."

She could picture Bob mopping, humming along with his earbuds in.

"What happened?" Jimmy asked her. "Are you okay?"

"I'm fine," she said. "There was...there was a man. Here." She pointed to the floor in front of her. "I don't know where he went. He came to steal a map."

"A map?"

"That's what he said."

"Can you give me a description of him?"

She thought about it. His taut body leaning near hers, the dark eyes hidden under long lashes, the masculine mouth and strong hands. He was Italian, definitely, or of Italian descent.

His hair was thick, like hers. And wavy. And his eyes were kind. Mischievous, but kind. He had meant her no harm.

"I didn't get a good look at him," she said. "He had a suit on. It was black. Like a cat burglar."

"And he wasn't armed?"

She pictured his tight suit, outlining...well, everything.

"No."

"You're sure?"

"Pretty sure."

"Did he steal what he came for?"

"I don't think so. You got here in time." There was no way he would have been able to get the map, which was locked up, and get out in seconds.

Jimmy's men came in then. "It's all clear. We don't see any sign of an intruder. Or of how he got in here. But somebody disabled the cameras and perimeter alarms."

Jimmy relaxed and holstered his gun. "Abby? You sure you're okay?"

Jimmy had been the cop who came to her house with the news the night her husband died. She had been alone, no family, and he had taken her to his home shortly after she collapsed, weeping. Jimmy's wife had made her hot tea and put a cold washcloth on her forehead and later made up the guest room bed for her. They were in their fifties with no kids of their own. Jimmy had checked on her regularly the first year, and his wife had made her meals for a while. After six years, Jimmy still stopped in to catch up with her, and she frequented their house for Sunday dinners.

"I'm okay," she said, but she was trembling.

"At least let us drive you home."

She nodded and closed her coat around her. Jimmy had to stay and finish up, but his younger partner drove her home and walked her up to the door. She was glad of the thick boots she wore, as the snow was quickly accumulating on the sidewalk.

"We'll catch him," he told her just before she went inside. "He won't bother you anymore."

"I don't think he's dangerous," she said. "I think he just wanted a map."

"Jimmy will call you tomorrow for some more details. You may have to come down to the station." He tipped his hat. "Good night, ma'am."

"Good night."

She turned the key in her ancient, three-story home on Blossom Street. She had inherited it from her aunt, and its many cozy rooms and twisty staircases appealed to the bookworm in her. Indeed, she had outfitted nearly every room with bookcases, which were mostly full.

She closed and locked the door, greeted her cat, and sat down to pull off her boots. She thunked the snow off them, shook the snow out of her hair, and tossed her glasses on the side table.

She went into her bedroom and opened her laptop, typing "Tony Russo" into a search engine. Nothing came up that looked like him. She looked under the White Pages. Nothing. She tried Anthony. Then she searched simply "Russo." About a hundred entries popped up under the name of the famous Italian painter. She scanned down and read an article about the "lost" painting.

Russo's "Mystery Woman" was rumored to be a portrait of his lover. Its whereabouts have never been discovered and historians and collectors wonder if it hangs in the home of Russo's illegitimate relatives or is hidden in the hands of a collector. Or, for that matter, if it even exists.

She closed her laptop and sat there, thinking about Tony. She hadn't been interested in a man since her husband and had never even thought about dating again. She was finished.

She touched her hair where his hand had lifted the hairpin out and closed her eyes, remembering his softly spicy cologne and those amazing eyes. She had felt something.

"It's ridiculous," she said to her cat. Cocoa, a petite tortoiseshell, rubbed up against her hand, wanting more attention and petting. "He's a thief. He doesn't even exist, according to the Internet."

Why was she protecting him? Why hadn't she been honest with Jimmy?

She ran her hand down the back of her hair, remembering his soft touch as he had quickly pulled the hairpin from it. And then the look in his eyes as he had watched her tresses

9

fall. So he was enraptured by her beauty; most men were. So what? It didn't mean anything.

"I'm being stupid," she said, rubbing Cocoa behind the ears.

She went to fix herself a bowl of cereal for dinner. "After all, he's a thief." She thought she heard a window scrape open and went to check in the living room. It was only the wind outside blowing a branch against the house. The snow was falling harder now. It wasn't fit for man nor beast out there. She wondered if Tony had gotten home safe, wherever home was, or if Jimmy had found him. Surely they could track him in the snow.

She went to bed at 9:30, curled up in her big canopy bed under thick covers, but lay there long into the night thinking about the mysterious man who came to steal her map and quoted Shakespeare love lines. She finally fell asleep with a slight smile on her face.

Chapter Two

"You're late."

Tony gave his boss his most charming smile. "I'm sorry Mr. Poundstone. With the weather and all..."

"Which is why I gave everyone an 11 a.m. start time. Late is late, and it's 11:15." He glanced at his watch. "I've given you six good years with this company. The least you could do is show up on time. There's a score of boys out there who'd give their right arm to work as a painter for me."

"I'm sorry sir."

Tony looked over at the van. His co-worker, George, had already loaded the gallons of paint into the back. George was busy using a large broom to sweep the snow off the side to reveal Poundstone Professional Painters in large blue letters with a cartoon rendering of Picasso holding a dripping brush.

"I'll drive," Tony said, grabbing the keys off a peg from inside the building. He tipped his painter's cap at his boss. "I'm sorry, sir. It won't happen again."

Mr. Poundstone made a grunting sound and frowned. Tony hopped in behind the steering wheel, and George got in the other side.

"How are the roads?" George asked. He lived within walking distance.

"They're fine." And they were. That wasn't the reason Tony was late. It was the girl. The beautiful girl he had met last night. She had messed his head up.

"We're nearly out of gas," George said. Tony looked over at his friend. George nodded toward the gauge.

"Oh, yeah, okay." Tony made a turn into the gas station. George jumped out to pump the gas.

They headed over to the Dewey Science Museum. They unloaded their paint at the back door, and Tony went to park the van. Parking was awful, with huge piles of snow taking up half the street. He had to park clear down on Crescent Street and walk three blocks. By the time he got to the site, George had the drop cloths down and the ladders set up.

Tony grabbed a brush and dipped it in the cobalt blue, which he thought was too dark for this wall. An image of the girl came to mind. Woman, actually. She had been wearing a blue sweater. He frowned. He had never let a woman get to him like that. He had no idea what had happened. He was usually so professional.

"Tony, you're head's in the clouds today."

Tony looked over at his friend. They were painting the walls near the Sounds and Sonics display of the museum. He was standing on the splatter cloth, brush in hand, but hadn't made a move to make any strokes. A bit of paint had dropped on his shoe. George, on the other hand, had a good start on his half of the wall.

"I guess I didn't sleep well last night."

"You should have slept in," said George, "with an 11 a.m. start time. I'm surprised we even had to come in today with the snow and all."

Thirteen inches had fallen overnight, but it stopped around 4 a.m., giving the road crews plenty of time to clear the streets. Tony's boss had told them to come in late. He was a cantankerous old man, grouchy as heck, but he was good to them.

Tony couldn't keep his mind on his work. Her face kept swimming up in his mind. Mrs. Chartwell, she had called herself. She didn't look like a "Mrs." at all. She looked...well, she looked like a goddess. She was hands down the most beautiful woman he had ever seen.

But it was more than that. She hadn't reacted with fear when she saw him, and he was sure she had felt what he felt when their eyes met. He shook his head and dipped his brush in the paint, making long blue strokes on the wall.

"You got a girl?"

"What?" Tony frowned at George, who at thirty-seven was five years his senior.

"A girl," George repeated. "That's the only thing I know that can make a man so la-la in the head. This morning you forgot your coffee, and then in the van you turned left instead of right, even though we've been coming here for two weeks. Now you're just standing there with a brush in your hand like you haven't ever painted a wall before."

Tony sighed and dipped his brush in the paint again. "No, it's not a girl."

George lifted an eyebrow.

Tony ignored him and kept painting. He was disappointed in himself. If he had gotten what he came for last night instead of chatting with her, he'd be done with the job. As it was, his chances of getting back in there and getting the map now were zero to none.

The truth is, she had surprised him. He thought he saw her leave the area and was pretty sure everyone was gone except the janitor. He knew he had a good hour before the janitor reached the floor he was on. It was supposed to be an easy job, in and out, but then she had been there when he dropped in and messed up the whole thing.

With her huge green eyes and all that thick, long, red hair.

He wondered why she was hiding behind a wedding ring and big glasses. She was drop-dead gorgeous. She could have any man she wanted, but she was trying to look twenty years older than she was.

He shook his head, trying to clear it, but he couldn't get her out of his mind. He had thought about her all night long, tossing and turning in bed until the covers were all tangled up around his legs. And he had thought about her all morning, which is why he was so addle-brained.

"A woman will mess you up," George said.

"It's not a woman. I told you I didn't sleep well."

Tony worked as a contract painter by day. It got him into buildings and gave him a good chance to scope them out. Like this one, for instance. The Dewey Science Museum had a sub-par security system, and the cameras near the genetics display were pointed at the wrong angles, leaving a pretty good gap near the north windows. Anybody with half a brain could get in, dodge the camera in the north lobby, and be in Subterranean Refuge in less than five minutes flat. But none of that mattered because there was literally nothing to steal in the Dewey Science Museum, unless you wanted sonic glass, whatever that was.

Last month, he had done some trim work in Waldorf Jewelers. Now *there* was a find. Security was tight, but he figured he could hack his way in and pinch the rose diamond pendant he saw in the center display. Only he'd have to wait a few months so they didn't make the connection with Poundstone Professional Painters. Not that they could find him. He didn't exist outside of this job. He was Anthony (Tony) Venezio to the world beyond his door. His birth records, driver's license, and social security number were all under that name. His father's name.

Tony Russo was fiction.

He wondered what her first name was. He tried to imagine it and went through several lists in his head. Finally, after about an hour of silence, he decided to enlist George after all.

"I didn't get her name," he said.

"Whose?" George had apparently been lost in his own thoughts.

"The girl's."

"I thought you said there wasn't any girl."

"I lied."

George grinned. "Was she hot?"

"Yes," Tony said. "And I have no idea what her name is."

"Amy."

"Who?"

"Diane?" George smiled. "Delilah?"

"Maria?"

The two men laughed. "Do you know where she works?" George asked.

"Umm...yes. I do."

"Then you can find her, you idiot."

"I'm not sure she would want to see me again. I don't think I made the best impression."

"Tony, with that charming smile of yours, you can turn the head of any girl you want. The guys and I would kill to be you. We go out to lunch, the waitress hits on you. We stop to buy gas for the van, the woman pumping gas a lane over turns to check you out." He lowered his voice to a whisper. "Even Ms. Solomon, the museum director here...wants your body."

Tony laughed. It was true. Ms. Solomon, a full twenty years older than he was, had more than hinted that she'd like him to work some late hours. Alone.

"Cougar," said George.

"I like to think of her as experienced," said Tony.

Tony liked women, but he hadn't ever *liked* a woman before. Except that once, but he tried not to think about that. He didn't let pleasure get in the way of his work. At thirty-two, he wasn't ready to settle down, and at any rate, his lifestyle wouldn't allow it. He didn't do exclusive.

"Whoever she is, she's got you good," said George.

Tony had to agree. He couldn't get her out of his mind. Her smell, her eyes, her full lips. And her fearless attitude. Not that he was anything to fear. He never hurt anyone and wouldn't dream of entering a place for a job where people were. Last night was just a mistake.

A mistake he'd have to put out of his mind.

But he needed that map. He had promised his great-grandmother on her deathbed that he would track down the painting. That was ten years ago, and he had finally found a solid lead after years of research. After hearing stories about it his entire life, he wanted to find that painting and confirm if he was really, indeed, an heir of the famous Russo. He just wanted to know.

That, and it was worth millions.

The only way back to that map was through Mrs. Chartwell. He thought he saw a glimmer in her eyes when she looked at him. George was right: most women were entranced with him on sight.Maybe he could use that to his advantage and win her over. Just long enough to get his hands on that map.

He was slightly nervous that he had told her his real first name. Okay, more than slightly. It was an arrogant mistake, brought on by his hormones kicking in when she looked at him. There was no other reason for it. And bragging that he was a Russo, like an amateur. Now the authorities would be looking for Tony Russo, instead of a random thief. If they put the name together with the map and she told them the story about the painting...

He shook his head. What an idiot he had been. He had to find that map and get his hands on it and find the painting fast, before someone else did. She was right. Treasure hunters had been looking for it for years. But they didn't have his grandma and her stories to help them out.

He would find out where the girl lived tonight after work, and then he would find her. He'd win her over, and he'd get that map, one way or another.

He had to.

Chapter Three

Abigail sat up straight in the chair at the police precinct, her hands in her lap. Or at least as straight as she could. She wondered why, if they planned on keeping you waiting, they couldn't find a more comfortable chair than the cold metal folding one they directed her to. She frowned.

"Everything okay, Abby?" Jimmy pulled out his chair and handed her a coffee from across his desk. "I'm sorry to keep you waiting. There was a break on another case, and I had to consult."

The coffee felt good in her hands. They were cold.

"I'm fine," she said. "I'm just late for work is all."

She tried to give Jimmy a smile, but it felt fake. He returned it, warmly. "The wife invited you over for dinner tonight. Beef stew." He raised an eyebrow.

Her smile was more genuine then. "I'd love to, but maybe another time. Thank her for me."

She couldn't imagine sitting across the table from Jimmy and Martha and not telling them about Tony. This was going to be hard enough.

"Okay, let's get to work." Jimmy pulled out a notebook and grabbed a pen. "So tell me exactly what happened last night."

She hesitated. He wanted a statement from her and she was torn between lying to a dear friend and protecting...whom? A man she was infatuated with?

"At what time did the attempted robbery take place?"

"It wasn't an attempted robbery," she explained. "Robberies involve weapons or the use of force. He was unarmed."

Jimmy looked across his desk at her. She took a sip of her coffee, hiding her face behind the cup.

"Librarians." Jimmy shook his head. "You all know too much."

"Reading is fundamental," she said. Jimmy smiled. "I told you everything I know."

"Did you see his eyes?"

Dark. Long lashes. A twinkle, like laughter, boiling up from deep inside. The type of eyes you wanted to spend more time looking into.

"It was pretty dark in there. I was locking up." She took another sip of her coffee.

"Did he have an accent or speak a certain way?"

Deep voice. Very…attractive. Abigail took a deep breath and let it out in a long exhale, trying to clear her head.

"We thought maybe you'd want to work with a sketch artist," Jimmy said.

She shook her head. "He had a mask on. There's nothing to sketch.

Until he took the mask off, she thought.

"So he said he was there after a map?" Jimmy was making some notes.

"Yes."

"Did he say why he wanted a map, or what map he wanted?"

She took a sip of her coffee to buy some time. She hated lying to Jimmy, but for some reason she wanted to protect this man. She couldn't justify why. She just knew she didn't want him to be turned in. The truth was, when Jimmy called her this morning to come down to the station, she had been relieved that they hadn't found Tony.

"No tracks in sight. Nothing. It's like he was never there." That's what Jimmy had said on the phone.

I don't exist. She remembered Tony's words last night.

"Abby?" Jimmy's voice brought her back.

"Um...no. He didn't say what he wanted the map for." She glanced at her watch. "It's really not that big of a deal. I didn't get hurt. He didn't get what he came for. I need to get to work."

"The Library Board thinks it's a big deal," said Jimmy. "If he was after one of the ancient French collection maps…"

"He wasn't."

Jimmy raised an eyebrow.

She realized her mistake. "He started off toward English Archives. Not French. I know where my maps are."

She took another long drink of her coffee. Jimmy sighed and closed his notebook.

"If anything else comes to mind you'll call, right?"

"Of course. Thank you, Jimmy."

"Abby, I was scared to death when I heard the call come in last night. I knew you were there late on Tuesdays. If anything had happened...after all you've already been through..."

Abigail smiled. "I'm fine, Jimmy. Really."

He looked at her for a long moment. "Okay. Call me if you remember anything else."

She couldn't get on the bus fast enough. Her stomach was churning the coffee. She had lied to Jimmy and he had been so good to her all these years. But it didn't really hurt anything. The thief hadn't gotten what he came for, as she told Jimmy. It would be okay. She swallowed the guilt back down and was glad when the bus finally pulled up to her stop. She'd distract herself with her job.

But at work, she had to endure all the questions of her co-workers.

"Were you afraid?" asked Pauline, a good friend who worked over in microfilm. They hadn't completely gone digital yet.

"Did he have a gun?" asked Ross, an older man over in accounting.

The questions popped around her all morning. She smiled and answered politely. No, she wasn't afraid, and no, he wasn't armed. That's all she really knew. But when things got quiet and she was filing her maps, her mind drifted to him and she got a tickly little feeling in her belly. The only other time she had ever felt that way was with her husband. With that memory came a great pain. She tried to push it aside.

New shelves had been installed at the back of her section, and she spent a large part of the afternoon standing on a ladder shelving books. Her feet hurt, and she was tired, but she told Pauline that she had a bit more filing to do so would stay after and close up again.

"But it's not your day," Pauline said.

"Still, I don't have anybody to go home to. You do."

"Won't you be afraid?"

"No. The janitor will be here soon."

"A lot of help he was last night," said Pauline, but she went to get her coat. With two young children at home, she was always ready to get out early if she could.

Abigail told herself she wanted to get ahead on tomorrow's filing, but the truth was she was hoping he'd show up. She stayed until 7 p.m., an hour past her quitting time. Once she heard a scrape and looked above her, but it was only a branch on the north window.

She shook her head and closed up, saying goodnight to Bob. She set the alarms, which had new codes tonight, and said goodnight to the new guard. He was stationed at the lobby entrance until they could upgrade the security system.

It was cold and dark as she hopped on the bus and headed to her house. Cocoa greeted her with a meow and rubbed against her legs as she pulled her boots off. She let her hair down and set her glasses on the table.

"Let's have stir fry tonight," she told Cocoa, pulling some vegetables out of the fridge. She made brown rice, trying to forget about Tony. She would probably never see him again.

She wondered about the map he came after, the map that supposedly led to a painting, the map that was in her library. If only she knew which one out of the thousands.

After dinner, she took a long bath and put on her fluffy robe. She towel dried her hair and curled up on the couch to read. She was halfway through *A Little Princess* and wanted to finish it.

Cocoa was curled at her feet and purring, and she felt herself drifting off. It was past 11 p.m. and she knew she should be in bed, but there was something about sitting by the fire with a cat and a good book.

"Mrs. Chartwell."

She jumped up, dropping the book and knocking the cat to the floor. It was him, Tony Russo, standing in the doorway between her living room and kitchen, once again clad in his tight-fitting black suit.

"The cat burglar," she said, gathering herself.

"I'm sorry I scared you."

"How did you get in here?"

"The third-floor window. It was a bit stuck, but nothing a file and a few tools couldn't handle."

"Did you close it? I don't want the cat to get out."

He smiled, his eyes twinkling. "Of course, I closed it. Do you have any idea how cold it is out there?'

They stood, staring at one another. Finally he took his mask off, revealing the curly dark hair again.

"Why are you here?" she asked.

"I wanted to return this," he said. He held up her hairpin in his black-gloved hand. "I didn't want you to think I was a thief."

"Hmmmf." She walked over to him and plucked it out of his hand. "You can leave now."

"But I just got here."

She was close to him, and could hear him breathing in the quiet of the room. He gazed into her eyes, and she felt her stomach do that tingly thing. He slowly reached up with his gloved hand and touched her cheek.

"Where are your glasses?" he said.

"In the other room." She closed her eyes, feeling the soft, cool leather against her skin. She felt him move closer, and she opened her eyes. Their noses were nearly touching.

"Tell me why you want that map," she whispered.

"I did. That's the truth."

"You can't have it."

She heard the tremble in her voice. Cocoa had gotten brave and moved over to twine around Tony's legs.

"Are you sure?" His voice was a whisper as well.

She cleared her throat and stepped back, away from his touch. "Would you like something to drink? You mentioned tea the other night."

Tony blinked in surprised. "Yes. Tea would be great."

She brushed past him and went into the kitchen to put on the kettle. She needed to get some space between them. He was so...intoxicating.

After a minute, she turned to get some mugs. He was standing there in the kitchen, leaning against the doorframe and watching her. "Please...tell me your name."

He was quite possibly the most handsome man she had ever seen.

She reached for two mugs. "Earl Grey or Chamomile?"

"Chamomile. Caffeine keeps me up."

She put the teabags into the mugs. "It's Abigail," she said.

She turned to face him, and her hair fell across her shoulders. It was clean and soft against her face, and she was glad for the thick robe she had on. But she was still shivering.

"Abigail," he said. "I knew it must be something beautiful like that."

His dark eyes drew her in, and she couldn't resist their pull. She walked across the kitchen and took one of his gloved hands in hers.

"Tony," she said.

He raised an eyebrow. "Yes?"

"What are we doing?"

He pulled his gloves off and gently took hold of her hand. He caressed the smooth skin on the back, tracing his fingers along the fine lines and across her wrist. Then he grasped both her hands in his warm ones.

"I don't know." His voice was barely a whisper. He looked up, meeting her eyes and moved toward her. He gave her a gentle kiss, and she closed her eyes, moving into him. His breath came faster, and he put his hand on the back of her neck, drawing her closer to him. She didn't resist. That tingly feeling in her stomach grew, and she didn't want to fight it. She hadn't felt this alive in years.

He smelled like spice, maybe sandalwood, and when he pulled her against him, she felt the taught hardness of his muscles through his suit. His arms were strong, and for a moment, she was afraid, knowing nothing about this stranger who had stolen his way into her house. But then the fear was gone, as quickly as it had come, and she kissed him back, opening her mouth to him. He was awakening feelings that she thought long dormant.

The teakettle whistled and both of them jumped. She broke away from him to get it. The water was hot, and she splashed some on her arm but ignored the pain, setting the teakettle on another burner.

"Tony—" But when she turned back, he was gone.

"Tony?"

She walked into the living room, but there was no sign of him. She heard a soft thump above her and ran up the stairs to the third floor. The window was closed, but she could feel the remnants of the night air, which had recently blasted through. She ran to the window and looked out, and there, far below on the street, she saw a black-clad figure, sticking to the shadows and running far away from her house.

Chapter Four

Tony stopped in an alley, grasping the side of a brick building and panting. What had just happened? He went back to her house to use her to get to the map...and fallen in love?

He, Tony Russo, was in love? No. No way he would ever let that happen.

But there was no other explanation for it. He felt so alive when he was with her, so intoxicated. It scared him to death.

Was this love? He shook his head, trying to free himself from it. He couldn't afford anyone tying him down. Or worse, turning him in. He had a bitter memory from a time past, but he shook that aside too. He had promised himself never to trust a woman again, and yet here he was.

Tony jumped up on the fire escape ladder and climbed to the top of the brick building next to him. From here, he could see the entire city in its beautiful glory, a sprawl of university buildings encircled by the many shops and restaurants needed to support its students and staff. The buildings were old and tall, but no skyscrapers blocked the view. It was a city that was built before elevators were commonplace. Still, businesses thrived here, a large pharmaceutical company, many technology services, and the teaching hospital off in the distance across the river. There was river itself winding down to the small dam, creating a rush of frozen falls this time of year. The small white lights that went up on Main Street around Christmas and stayed up all winter, celebrating the snowy season. The windows, lit here and there, as university students studied or partied, neither of which he'd ever had a chance to do. His whole life had been about survival. From the time he left home at age seventeen, he hadn't the money to spend on learning or partying, not if he wanted to eat.

"You can have a better life," his grandmother had told him time and again as he was growing up. His mother had died when he was young, and his father hadn't taken it well.

He didn't want to remember what happened after that, so he walked across the roof, climbed down the other side, and took a few alleyways to his building. He climbed the fire escape, entering his apartment with the window key he kept around his neck.

Tony's apartment was far from Spartan. He took off his boots and walked barefoot across a thick, shaggy white rug to his overstuffed sofa. Springing over the back of it, he landed with a soft thud, put his feet up on the coffee table, and grabbed the remote for his flat screen. He flipped through channels.

Tony pulled off his gloves and his mask, catching a scent of her on his clothes. He went into the bedroom to change, trading in black spandex for sweat pants and a T-shirt. Then he grabbed a pop out of the fridge and went back to the sofa.

He needed that map. He wasn't poor, but he didn't want to spend the rest of his life stealing to make a living. If he could find that painting and prove his connection to it, there were a dozen museums he could legitimately sell it to. Then he'd be set for life. He could give up the life of crime.

After he showed the painting to his grandmother. She was his reason for finding it. She wanted to see it as badly as her mother had, as he did, maybe more.

This life wasn't what his grandmother had wanted for him. If she knew what he did, it would break her heart.

Tony's mind drifted back to Abigail. If he could quit stealing...

No. He wasn't going there. No more relationships for him. Not after what happened last time.

He was going to put Abigail Chartwell out of his mind. He'd figure out a way to get his hands on that map, and then he'd find his painting and settle down some place quiet. Maybe he'd go back to the town his grandmother came from. She always talked about it in a dreamy way, as if it were paradise.

Mind made up, he found an old movie on the Mystery Channel, and settled down for the night.

Abigail touched her lips where Tony had kissed her just moments earlier. She could smell his aftershave lingering in the air. What had just happened? There he was, pulling her in with his magnetic eyes, his touch, his smell, his words...

And now he was gone.

She pulled her robe tighter around her and then went back down to the kitchen and dumped the tea in the sink. She had been stupid to let another man get to her. Look what happened last time. She'd make sure all the windows and doors were locked, and then she'd go to bed. This was foolish.

Maybe she'd even report him in the morning.

She checked the doors and windows downstairs and got a board out of the basement. She took it upstairs and wedged it into the third floor widow so he wouldn't be able to open it again.

Then she went to bed.

It was late, she was tired, and she had to go to work in the morning.

Cocoa curled up by her feet and started to purr. The familiar comfort of her warmth, the sound of her little motor running, and the late hour lured Abigail to sleep.

In her dream, she saw her husband, Nick.

"Don't go," she said.

"It's not a problem," he said as he pulled his coat on.

"But the roads are bad."

He didn't say anything, just grabbed his wallet and left, shutting the door a little too firmly. She stood in the kitchen of their little apartment for a moment and then realized what was about to happen. She started to scream his name.

Abigail woke up, startled. She hadn't had that dream in years. She couldn't afford to go there again. She was finally settled and comfortable and able to sleep through the night. All of this stuff with Tony was messing her up.

"Please God, not again," she said. She had learned imagery from her counselor, and she decided to put it into use. She imagined a white clay jar. She took her worry, which at the moment was her dream about Nick, and put it in the jar.

Then she mentally handed it to God. She'd let God handle this one tonight. *I don't want it back,* she added for emphasis.

Then she turned her thoughts to her other problem, Tony. "I'm giving him to You, too," she said. She mentally reached over, put Tony in the jar, and put the lid on. *Take it, Lord. I need to sleep.*

"If I see him again, I'll tell him not to come back," she said to the cat. Cocoa came up close to her pillow, lay down, and began purring. She put her head on Abigail's hand. Abigail settled down into the soft linens and her feather pillow and felt sleep coming again. She didn't dream anymore, or wake, until morning.

Tony couldn't sleep. After watching *The Maltese Falcon* and *Woman in the Dark,* he thought he was tired enough to crawl into bed. It was late, and he did have to get to work in the morning.

But as soon as he lay down, his eyes popped open and he was wide awake.

He tried to fill his head with thoughts of how he would spend the money when he sold the painting. Moving away and finding a house in his grandma's childhood hometown was first and foremost on his list. He'd give her the house of her dreams and somebody to care for the lawn.

As for him, he'd hire an architect to design a house. Maybe on a lake. Then he'd retire...and do what?

He turned over and pulled the covers up around him. He could fish, except he had never fished in his life. Maybe he wouldn't move to a lake.

Tony flipped over again and looked at the clock. The numbers mocked him in the dark. He closed his eyes, and the first thing he saw was Abigail's face.

"Darn that woman!" He cursed and sat up, the covers spilling into a pool on the floor. He was hot now. He got up and went to the bathroom to splash his face. He looked at himself in the mirror. Thirty-two years old. What did he want in life? He was surprised to realize he had no idea. He was

27

like a boat without a rudder. (The lake image again? What was wrong with him?)

He went to look out his bedroom window at the city and the lights sparkling off the snow on the ground. Light flakes drifted down from the sky. It was beautiful outside. He stayed there a few moments, taking deep breaths and calming his mind.

He climbed back into bed and pulled the covers back up, now cold. He kept the thermostat really low in the house at night.

He closed his eyes again, and suddenly the image of Abigail was back. He decided to go with it this time and imagined himself with her, holding her hand, leaning into a kiss. Then he imagined her in his boat on the lake by his dream house. They were floating around, and she had packed sandwiches.

He laughed at himself. "George is right. I have it bad," he said out loud. There was no other choice. He would have to see her again.

Chapter Five

It was mid-morning on Thursday, and Abigail was filling out a form to buy a set of Great Lakes shipwreck maps from the Billingscreek Library. The library was closing and looking to place their maps in a new collection.

The form was tedious, and the back of her neck was starting to ache. She reached back and rubbed it.

Someone approached her desk just as she was trying to fit the library address into the unbelievably tiny line they gave her.

"I'm here to check out a map."

She kept writing. "You can't check *out* maps," she said. "You have to keep them here."

"But this is a special map."

Her brain registered something familiar with the voice. She looked up.

"Oh," she said.

There was a ray of sunlight shining down on him through the glass dome, and she saw dust motes dance around his wavy hair like tiny fairies. His dark eyes smiled out at her from under thick lashes, and his lips curved upward in response. "Hello again."

Tony was dressed in painter's clothes and had smudges of blue paint all over his outfit. She also noticed he had a streak of it on his cheek. She resisted the urge to touch it.

He glanced at his watch. "I'm kind of in a hurry. I'm here on my lunch hour."

She continued to look at him, unsure of what to do. An involuntary glance at the cameras confirmed to her that she finally had him on film.

"They're not working," he whispered. "They're in a continual loop for an hour. That's all I need. An hour."

She crossed her arms and frowned. "You can't have my map."

"Technically, it's not *your* map. And I just want to take a look at it. Is that a problem?"

"Abigail, is there a problem?" parroted Lulu Scott, the director of the library. She came up behind Abigail, causing her to jump.

"No, not at all." Abigail collected herself, taking in a deep breath and straightening her shoulders. "Right this way, sir."

She led him back into the stacks, out of sight.

"What are you doing here?" she hissed. "I could turn you in. Right now."

"But you won't."

His confidence made her angry. "How do you know?"

"You just proved it."

She frowned at him again. She remembered the touch of his lips on hers. "What do you want?"

"I told you. I just need to take a look at a map, the city map from 1904, the middle of town."

"Why 1904?"

"Get it for me, and I'll show you."

"We have it scanned in."

"I need the actual map, not a digital version." When she frowned yet again, he gave her his most charming smile. "Please?"

"Wait here." She didn't want him following her, which was silly because if he checked the electronic card catalog, he'd see where it was shelved. She reached the spot and pulled out the corresponding tray. Carefully, she lifted the document, which was in between archival-quality transparent paper.

She brought it to Tony and nodded for him to follow her to a long table at the back of the room. She glanced back at her desk. Nobody was there at the moment, so she took the time to spread out the map on the table. She had to admit, she was curious.

Tony sucked in his breath and leaned over the map, his hands spreading out the paper until it was flat. His eyes scanned it for a moment.

"There," he said, pointing to an area near the center. Abigail bent down. She could see a light-green pencil layout of brick buildings, mostly stores today, with blue lines running alongside, an underlay of what she thought might be an early sewer system.

"I don't see anything in particular," she said.

"Not now, you don't." His finger made a wide circle around the area in the center of town. "But here, somewhere in this area, is my painting."

The circumference he made covered several blocks.

"How big is this painting?" She was whispering, mostly out of habit because she worked in a library, but also because she felt she was doing something clandestine. "That's a lot of space to cover."

"There are clues drawn in a special ink. This map needs to be viewed under moonlight to reveal them."

Now she knew he was crazy. Invisible ink that only shows up at night?

"Our eyes have rods in them which work in low light situations," he explained. "The rods are basically colorblind, which is why we don't see a lot of color during the night time when we're outside. But they're very sensitive to blue-green light. They can pick that up."

He looked at Abigail. She realized how close they were standing.

"And?" she said.

"There are some lines on this map that we can't see during the day. We can only see them under moonlight, which is why I need to get this map outside."

"That sounds like a fairy tale," she said.

His eyes danced with excitement as he took hold of her hand. "But it isn't! My grandmother knew the story of the cartographer who made this map, and he made it for our family. He was working with the man who stole the painting, and he apparently wished for this painting to get back to its original owner."

"Which was your great-grandmother."

"Yes!" He gave her hand a little squeeze. His hand was warm and strong in hers, and she could feel his pulse. Why did he think he could touch her? And yet she didn't pull away.

"Can you help me do that?"

"Well...no," she said. How was she supposed to get a map outside into the moonlight? Nobody was allowed to check out these maps. Not even her. They had to be kept in this room, under certain conditions (right temperature, correct humidity, no direct sunlight) and there was no way—no *way*—anybody was going to let her take it outside. Even if she explained why. Well, if she explained *why*, some of the University's more curious archivists would probably jump at the chance. And then they'd find the painting. But was there really any such thing as ink that was visible only in moonlight?

"If I tell them why, they'll guess who you are," she said. Which was true. They all knew that the thief was looking for a map. They just didn't know who or why.

"I didn't plan on telling them," he said. "If you do, *they* will find the painting."

"Why are you telling *me?*"

He paused for a moment, considering. Then he gave her hand a little squeeze. "Because I trust you."

She drew in her breath and pulled her hand away, angry at herself for almost falling into his trap again. "You need to get going. It has been almost an hour. The cameras will be back on soon."

He glanced at his watch. "Think about it." Then he met her gaze.

"Abigail," he said, his voice growing serious. "About last night. I wanted to tell you..."

"It was a mistake," Abigail said.

Tony looked taken aback, but he recovered quickly. "Uh... yeah. That's what I was going to say. You're just so pretty. I guess I got carried away."

"You're a thief," she said. "You take things that don't belong to you." She knew the words were harsh.

"Yeah. I'm a thief," he said quietly.

"I should turn you in."

"You probably should."

He looked at her for a few seconds, and she swallowed, hard, fighting the feelings she had for him. "You need to go now."

"Abigail?" her boss said, coming over their way. "There's a woman at the desk who needs your assistance."

"Okay," Abigail said. "Are you finished here, sir?"

"Yes." He nodded his head. "Thank you for your help."

He gave her a little smile and walked out of her section, leaving the map on the table. She watched him disappear through the stacks on his way back to the front door.

Chapter Six

Tony pulled his black wool coat close around him and made his way back to work. He just had to see her today and thought the map would be a great excuse. Her words had hurt him, but at the end, when she told him to leave, he could see her fighting it. Her eyes were telling him what her words weren't. He was in no way about to give up on her.

He just didn't think now was the best time to get involved. He had a job to finish first.

For now, he'd concentrate on getting the map. Of course, he wouldn't be able to break in to take it anytime soon—they had beefed up security really good. But in a few months, things would settle down, and he could try again. It wasn't a very valuable map in itself, and only he (and his grandma) knew the secrets it contained. He guessed if somebody *did* know, then heck, the map would be worth millions only because it led to a valuable painting.

It had been so exciting to finally see it. As he traced his fingers across it, he was sure that the answers lay somewhere in it. That he was closer to finding that painting than he had ever been.

He was a bit surprised that he had told Abigail the family secret. He hadn't shared it with anybody, ever. Not even the woman he had almost married. Darci was beautiful, with the lithe body of a dancer, but after he proposed to her with a stolen ring, she had turned him in. He had no idea how she found out the ring was stolen—it was a beauty, it was—but when she did, she hightailed it away from him. She had a conscience, and while he loved her (or thought he did), he knew she would never be able to love a thief. She had proved that by betraying him.

It hadn't stuck. There was no proof it was stolen, no video footage, no claims at the police department. Probably because he had found it in the drawer of a society heiress (her house was huge and he had spent some time exploring) who had so many rings she didn't miss it. Darci probably guessed, because how could a painter afford such a ring? She never believed his aunt had given it to him.

So he decided at that point to never marry or become serious with anybody again.

But now, his feelings for Abigail had made him careless. He had never let a pretty head mess with his game before. He had even lied to Darci. So what on earth had made him expose himself so easily with Abigail? She not only knew what he did on the side, she now knew about the painting. She could take the map herself, find the painting, cash in, and run.

He remembered the smooth, warm feel of her skin when he took hold of her hand. What had made him touch her, anyway? He had felt her pulse beating quickly as if she were excited. Or afraid. Was she afraid of him?

He thought of the kiss in her kitchen last night. No, she wasn't afraid. And he suspected she was just as attracted to him as he was to her. He just didn't know what to do about it.

"You look happy," George said when Tony stepped inside the museum and shook his coat off at the door. George was pulling on his little paper shoe covers.

"Me?" Tony said as he fished his own shoe covers out of his pocket.

"You saw the girl."

"What? No."

"You're the worst liar ever."

"Okay," Tony said. "I saw her on my lunch hour."

"Did the second impression go better than the first?"

Tony thought about that. "Well, she didn't throw me out."

George smiled and started to whistle as he gathered up their paint buckets and went back to the Sounds and Sonics area. They were almost finished there. Tomorrow they'd be over in Storms.

"Did you ask her out?"

They were finished with the wall, and Tony was doing the trim work. "On a date?"

"No, you idiot, outside. Yes, on a date!"

"No."

"Why not?"

Tony sighed. How could he explain that just to be in the same room with her was enough? Just to smell her hair, touch her hands, breathe the same air she did...

"You've got it bad," George said.

Tony laughed. "Yeah. I guess I do."

"Ask her out. What do you have to lose?"

Tony went on dates, but that was all they were. Maybe once or twice with a girl, just to have some fun, and then he moved on. A heartbreaker, his co-workers called him.

"She's different. " Tony wasn't sure how to move with her. His body was telling him one thing, but his mind another. He had already shared enough with her. Enough so she could have him arrested. Part of him wanted to sidestep this and keep his distance, but he knew he couldn't do that. Not this time. Not with this woman. Honesty wasn't his thing, and it was making him uncomfortable. "This is different."

"I can see that. Already. Why don't you invite her out to dinner this Friday with the wife and me? We'll double date. That will keep it safe."

Tony thought about that. But no, if he went out, he wanted her all to himself.

"I'll think about it," he said, to keep George from asking again. Then he dipped his brush into the paint and started to whistle.

Chapter Seven

Abigail sat at her desk and tapped her pencil. After Tony left, she put the map away, helped the woman waiting at the desk, and had been sitting there since, thinking.

Her feelings for him were distracting. There was no doubt about it. Her heart did a little thing every time she saw him, and he made her feel alive. Nobody had been able to do that since...well, since Nick.

She fingered her wedding ring. She had pledged her love to Nick, and then he had died. When they had said, "'til death do us part," she hadn't expected it to mean months. She had been thinking more in terms of years. Decades. But then he had gone and gotten himself killed.

She still got angry at him when she thought of it, because it was his fault. She had told him not to go out that night. But then almost immediately, she felt guilty for getting angry. Her heart still hurt, even after all of these years. She had loved him so much. She felt a familiar panic rising at the memories, and she closed her eyes, willing it to pass.

Abigail heard the door open to her section, and a young man walked in. He looked like a graduate student. She looked up at him through her glasses.

"I'm here for a map," he said. "Um...ma'am."

She gave an uncharacteristic sigh. "I need more information than that."

"Um..."

It got on her nerves, this reaction of young men to her.

"Would you like to go out?"

Well, this one was direct. "No," she said. She waved her ring.

"I'm so sorry. I didn't see...I didn't realize..." he continued to stumble over his words.

"What type of map?" she asked. She clicked on her computer, taking her eyes off of the young man and giving him a chance to gather his wits about him. She brought up the index of maps they kept. "What year?"

"1966. Stockholm."

"History major?"

"Yes."

She helped him look up the map to be sure they had it and then took him to another computer and brought it up from their online database so he could look it over. As she walked back to her desk, she heard a few of her co-workers whispering in the stacks next to her.

"He asked her *out?*"

"Yes, I just saw it. Just now, at her desk."

"Does she know him?"

"Likely not. Men are always asking her out."

"Must be nice."

She recognized the voices as Pauline and Debbie. Obviously, they didn't realize she could hear them.

"Yeah…" That was Pauline's voice, wistful. She loved her husband, but was tired all the time from motherhood. "She'll never go out."

"Why?"

"She's still hurting from her husband's death."

"For goodness sakes, it has been six years!"

"Still…"

"That's just weird." Abigail frowned. She had never liked Debbie that much.

"I think it's romantic," said Pauline. "Imagine loving somebody that much."

" And the way she dresses…" Debbie's voice.

"She's fending off men the only way she knows how."

"So she's never going to date again? She's resigned herself to spinsterhood?"

"Maybe. Who knows. Don't let it worry you," said Pauline.

Pauline left and carried her stack of books up front. Abigail made sure she wasn't seen and then went back to her desk.

Is that what she was doing? Resigning herself to spinsterhood?

She couldn't think. The afternoon went by slowly. She got her work done, but not as effectively as she usually did.

Tony kept creeping into her thoughts. It was ridiculous. She would banish him from her mind. He was a thief. She had half a notion to go talk to Jimmy right now and tell him she knew where Tony worked.

There had been a name on his painter's uniform. Poundstone Professional Painters. She thought about that all day, wondering if she should tell Jimmy. Who knows how many other things Tony had stolen! The man was obviously a professional, the way he came down that rope and then disappeared so quickly. And he had the outfit and the tools. Metal files. The ability to turn cameras on and off at will.

She shuddered. What if he was watching her right now? She glanced up at the camera. But no, they just silently recorded, in case there was ever an incident. As far as she knew, nobody watched the film as it was recorded. There were no guards in the camera room, just the new one they had posted at the front door after the attempted theft. The room with the security camera computers was always kept locked. Wasn't it?

She took out her phone and did a search on Poundstone Professional Painters. Their website came up, with a cartoon Picasso holding a dripping paintbrush. "Let us color your world," read the caption. Tacky.

She dialed the number.

"I need to get my business painted," she said, when someone answered. "I was wondering if I could stop by and see their current project? I'd like to see some of their work before I hire you. I was looking for a particular painter my friend recommended. An Italian guy."

"That would be Tony," the woman said. The woman was friendly enough and told her they were currently working at the Dewey Science Museum and would be there until 5 p.m. Then she tried to get Abigail to come in for an estimate.

"Thank you, but I want to see their work first," Abigail said as she hung up. The Dewey Science Museum was walking distance from the library. She could be there in ten minutes.

She looked at the clock above her desk. It was 4:30. She picked up the phone and punched in Pauline's extension.

"Yes?" Pauline answered.

"I need to leave early today. Something has come up. Can you close up for me?"

"Everything okay?"

"Yes. Just something I need to take care of."

Pauline agreed. "I'll fill you in tomorrow," Abigail said and hung up. She grabbed her coat from the break room.

The sun was shining, but it was bitterly cold outside. By the time she got to the museum, her fingers were numb inside her gloves and her face hurt from the wind.

She walked into the quiet of the building and stood for a moment in the lobby, enjoying the warmth. Suddenly it filled with noise as a class of school children tumbled in, pulling on coats and getting into lines formed by their chaperones.

"The school bus will be here in three minutes!" someone said rather loudly to them. Abigail figured it must be their teacher.

"Can I help you?"

She turned to see a woman sitting at a desk. She explained why she was there and the woman pulled out a map and directed her to the Sounds and Sonics area on the second floor. The stairs were blocked off, so she had to take the elevator up.

The elevator door opened, and there he was. She knew him immediately from behind, even in his baggy painter's clothes. His wavy hair was covered by a cap, but black curls poked out around the nape of his neck. His well-muscled arm was holding a roller brush and expertly covering a wall in blue paint. There was a radio on the floor between him and another man, and Tony was whistling along with the tune.

She stood and watched him for a moment. Neither man had noticed her arrival, even though she thought they would have heard the elevator. Then the man next to him started singing along and Tony joined in. The two of them were pretty musical, but they were comical to watch as the blond man started to swing his hips. Tony laughed aloud, and the other man turned toward him and said, "We should go on tour." That's when he saw Abigail.

The name patch on his uniform read "George." He stared at her a moment, paint dripping from his brush. "Tony," he said finally. Tony turned and suddenly his smile faded and he stopped whistling.

"It's her?" George said. He turned off the radio.

Tony nodded. He recovered and flashed her that smile. "Abigail," he said.

She cleared her throat, uncertain as to what to say. Why had she come here? She had to see if he had a legitimate job. If there was anything he was telling her that was true. A famous relative. A day job as a painter. A night job as a thief. Maps that glowed in the dark.

Tony put his roller brush down and wiped his hands off on a rag. "It's a pleasure to see you."

She felt a bit awkward, standing there. She was usually so poised and sure of herself and felt a surge of anger that he could throw her so off balance. She pushed her glasses up on her nose and absently twisted her wedding ring.

Tony glanced at the man next to him. "George, this is Abigail. Abigail, George."

"It's a pleasure to meet you," George said, taking a few steps toward her and extending his arm and then pulling it back. "I'd shake your hand but mine is covered in paint."

She smiled at George, but her eyes went back to Tony.

"I thought I'd come see you at work. See what you do."

"I see," Tony said. He glanced at a clock on the wall. "George and I need to finish this up by five o'clock so we can get out of here. Come talk to me while I work."

Abigail suddenly felt foolish. What was she doing here? She didn't want to fall in love with anyone, most of all this... this...what was he? He was a thief. And she was aiding and abetting. She needed to turn him in.

"Would you and Tony like to go out to dinner tonight with me and my wife?" George said. Tony scowled.

"No." She said it too quickly. She didn't know these people. She suddenly didn't want them in her life. And what was that look on Tony's face? He was glaring at George. This had been a mistake.

"I just...I just wanted to see where you worked."

She turned and pushed the elevator door button.

"Abigail, wait." Tony was suddenly beside her. She pushed the button again.

"Abigail." His voice was soft, pleading. She turned and met his eyes. "Why did you come?"

She swallowed. "I don't know. I really don't. But I'm leaving now. Don't follow me."

The elevator door opened, and she got in. As the doors closed, she saw Tony standing there, looking bewildered. She felt a pang of guilt as the car lowered. She hurried out of the elevator and across the lobby floor toward the exit.

"Did you find what you were looking for, ma'am?" the woman at the desk called after her.

"Yes. Yes, I did, thank you." Abigail pushed through the door and nearly ran toward her bus stop and home.

"Well, that went well," George said.

Tony picked his roller up. "Which is why I never get involved."

"You're already involved with this one." George turned the radio back on. "I saw the look on your face when she walked in here. 'Of all the buildings in all the towns in all the world, she walks into mine,'" George misquoted Humphrey Bogart.

Just then, Tony's phone rang.

"She can't live without you," George said.

Tony answered and his eyes clouded. "Yes. I'll be right there."

He pocketed the phone. "Tell the boss I have to leave. I'll be in touch."

He ran for the stairs, and leaped over the tape blocking them, taking two at a time. George was left standing there, wondering what the emergency was and how far Tony would get without a coat on in this weather.

Chapter Eight

Abigail didn't sleep well that night. She tossed and turned, and her dreams were filled with a man in a black spandex suit reaching his hand out to her. "Come," he kept saying, but then she heard police sirens and woke up.

She stopped by the station the next morning on her way in to the library.

"Abigail," Jimmy said. "What brings you in? Did you remember something new about the case?"

"Have you found him yet?"

Jimmy shook his head and offered her some coffee, which she refused. "Not a trace. It's like he doesn't exist."

Abigail was there to tell him that he *did* exist and she knew exactly where he was.

"Jimmy…"

She paused, and he raised an eyebrow, waiting.

"I…"

"Are you okay?"

She swallowed. "I'll take you up on that dinner if it still stands."

Jimmy's face creased into a smile. "Sure. Come tonight. I'll call Martha and let her know."

Abigail nodded and fled the station back to the sanctuary of her maps.

"My grandmother's dying. I need that map."

Abigail looked up from the book she was reading. It was about the storage and care of ancient documents. She really needed to pay better attention to who walked up to her desk.

He was standing there, wearing jeans and a burgundy sweater, his hands gripping her desk.

"That's a terrible pick-up line," she said.

His eyes twinkled for a moment and then grew sober. "She really is dying. They put her in hospice last night. She doesn't have long."

Abigail stared at him for a moment, considering.

"Really," he said. "Come with me and see her. I'll show you."

His eyes were pleading, a side of him she hadn't seen before.

"Now?" She looked at the clock. It was late morning.

"Yes."

There was something about the look on his face that made her believe him. "Okay," she said quietly. Then a little louder, "Pauline?"

"Yes?" Pauline peeked out from behind a large filing cabinet near the back.

"Can you take over? I need to leave. Family emergency."

"Family?" Pauline stood up and brushed her skirt off.

"*His* family," Abigail said, reaching for her purse.

"Really?" Pauline raised an eyebrow, running her eyes up and down Tony.

Abigail took Tony's hand and pulled him away before Pauline could get more curious. "Let's go."

She grabbed her coat out of the workroom and left before anybody else could comment. Tony's car, a small non-descript blue sedan, was parked in the library lot. They got in, and he turned the heat on as she buckled up.

"This is ridiculous," Abigail said. "I'm running away from work in a car with a total stranger. You could be kidnapping me."

"I'm not a total stranger," said Tony. "You know my name."

"One of your names."

"Both now. And you know where I work…"

"Point taken."

Tony drove out of town and got on the freeway. "This is a really nice hospice. I thought she would be comfortable here. She wanted to die at home, but there really wasn't any way…"

His voice trailed off.

"Will your parents be here?" Abigail asked.

Tony's face darkened. "No. It's just me and her. She's all I have left."

"Oh. I'm sorry."

Tony kept looking straight ahead. He switched lanes and went around a truck. A light snow started up.

"What's wrong with her?"

"Cancer. It started off as a pain in her abdomen. They thought it was acid reflux, but it got worse. By the time they found the cause, she was stage four." He spoke matter-of-factly, but Abigail saw the muscle in his temple twitch.

"How long does she have?"

"Days. Maybe hours."

"I'm so sorry." She pulled her coat tighter around herself.

He exited the freeway and turned onto a side road. About a half mile down, Abigail saw a sign that said "Dove Hospice."

He parked, got out, and surprised her by coming around to open her door. He took her hand and then paused a moment after closing her door. "Thank you for coming with me." His eyes met hers.

"Of course," she said, because she wasn't sure what else to say. She still wasn't sure why she was here, why Tony had such a pull on her that she'd apparently follow him anywhere.

He checked in at the desk and led her back to a room where a small, frail woman lay in the bed, sleeping. The room was decorated in pinks, with a floral border across the top of the walls. Above the bed was a picture of a little girl picking flowers. On the nightstand sat a black and white photo of a much younger woman, Grandma in her twenties perhaps, holding the hand of a little girl.

"That's my mom," Tony whispered, pointing at the little girl in the photo. "Grandma's only child."

Abigail could see the resemblance to Tony. The same dark, curly hair. The same eyes.

"Grandma," Tony said quietly.

The woman in the bed stirred and opened her eyes.

"Hi, Grandma. I came for a visit."

"What time is it?" she said, so softly Abigail could barely hear her. "Shouldn't you be at work?"

"I've taken the day off to be with you," Tony said. "I brought a friend with me."

Grandma's eyes traveled across the bed to Abigail. "Who is this beautiful angel, Tony?"

"This is Abigail."

Grandma smiled and slowly reached a hand toward her. Abigail took it. It was warm, but the skin was thin, like paper. Grandma gave her hand a gentle squeeze.

"You take good care of my Tony," she said. "He's a great man."

Tony smiled at Abigail, who nodded and let go of his grandma's hand. What had she gotten herself into? Now she was making promises to a dying woman.

Still, she felt herself choking back tears and wondering at the life before her, the pains and fears that used to be this woman. She wondered if she ever had a dog, or rode a bike, or walked in the rain. What dreams had she had and had they been discovered, or buried? Did she have regrets?

Across the foot of the bed was a handmade quilt. The red and blue squares were worn and soft with age, and Abigail ran her hand across it.

"Did she make this?"

"Yes." Tony touched it.

"It's beautiful."

"There's not much she can't do," Tony said. "Quilting, canning, story-telling. And she makes a mean pan of lasagna. Right, Grandma?"

Grandma smiled, closing her eyes. "Long ago, Tony. It's time for me to rest now."

Tony took her hand. "Not yet, Grandma."

"The painting, Tony," Grandma said, just when Abigail thought she was asleep.

"Yes. I'll find it and bring it to you," Tony said.

"I think it's lost," she said. "Don't waste your time. It doesn't matter now. You know the story. That's all you need. It's in your heart."

Tony took a deep breath and let it out slowly. "I need to go now, Grandma," he said. "I'll be back later to visit."

Grandma reached for Abigail's hand again. She offered it. "I've been praying for my Tony for years," she said quietly. "That God would send someone to open his eyes. Maybe you're the answer to those prayers."

Abigail looked across the bed at Tony, who rolled his eyes a little.

"Grandma..." he said, turning a bit red.

Grandma smiled, closing her eyes again. "God knows, Tony. He has a plan." She seemed to drift off to sleep.

Tony held her hand for another minute, looking down at her and softly brushed her hair back off her forehead. Then he let go of her hand.

"Come on," he said to Abigail.

Abigail followed him out to the car. She was dabbing at her eyes.

"Not a pick-up line," he said.

"Apparently not."

He started up the car. "Can you help me get that map? The security is tight there now. I was planning to wait a few months until everything settled down, but I no longer have that kind of time."

"I could lose my job."

Tony didn't say anything. He just nodded. Then, "I know. You could." He thought for a moment. "If you can just distract the security guard, I can get in and get it. Probably take me five minutes, max."

"Tony, I can't do anything illegal."

He nodded. "I understand. I'm sorry I asked. I'll figure it out." They drove in silence for a while, and then he pulled up to the library. "Will I see you around?"

Abigail sat in the car and looked over at Tony. The snow had turned to sleet and was making little ticking sounds on the glass. She fingered her wedding ring.

"I can't do this. I can't get back into another relationship. I can't steal for you. I think we just need to..." She was going to say "not see each other again." But the words wouldn't come. She liked being with him. He did something to her that she

47

hadn't felt in a long time. And to see this latest tender side of him with his grandma softened her heart even more. But she would never admit it to him.

"I'll get you the map," she said. "Pick me up from work at 6 p.m. I'll have it for you."

"Abigail, you don't have to—"

She stopped him with a finger to his lips. "Just this once. Not for you. For your grandma," she said. And she got out of the car, not looking behind her again.

Chapter Nine

"You look awful," Pauline said. "Is everything okay?"

"Yes." Abigail rubbed her forehead. "No. His grandmother is dying. He took me to see her."

She couldn't lie to Pauline. They had worked together for eight years, and Pauline was sharp. She'd figure it out.

"Dying?"

"Cancer. She's in hospice."

"Oh." Pauline was uncharacteristically quiet. Finally, she said cautiously, "Who was that? I didn't realize you were dating someone. Or are you not?"

"No," she said. "We met, and I think he would like to date, but I'm just not...he's not...It's complicated."

"Abby, at some point you need to let go of Nick."

Abigail looked at Pauline and then fingered her ring again. "I found my soul mate once. I don't expect it to happen again."

"Do you think Nick would want you to be alone?"

Abigail sighed. "I think Nick would want me to be happy. I'm happy the way my life is right now."

"Are you?"

Abigail looked at her co-worker. Pauline never minced words.

"I'm just saying." Pauline tucked some hair behind her ear. It was forever falling in her face. She always seemed a bit harried. "You can't hide from life here in this library forever. You're young, you're pretty, you're smart. Live a little."

Abigail was starting to feel a bit irritated. "I'm fine."

"It was really bad...*really* bad...when Nick died," Pauline said softly. "And after. I remember because I was here. And then you closed off and never really came back. There are some things you never get over, but you can learn to live through and move on, despite the pain."

Abigail looked at her friend. She had a wonderful marriage and had just celebrated her tenth anniversary. They had two young children. Pauline loved her job, even if she was constantly exhausted by trying to balance work life and motherhood.

"How can you possibly know that?" she said. She didn't mean for it to sound cruel; she just didn't think Pauline would understand.

"Because." Pauline lowered her voice. "Because Drew cheated on me, and despite it all, we're still together."

The shock must have shown on Abigail's face.

"Yes, I know, we appear to be the 'perfect couple.'" She did air quotes with her fingers. "But four years ago he was on a work trip and had a brief affair with a co-worker he was traveling with."

Abigail mentally did the math. Their youngest was two.

"It only lasted about a month and then—"

"That's about the time he changed jobs."

"Yes. He realized he needed to break it off, so he told me what had happened and quit his job that same week. He found work somewhere else and asked me to forgive him. It took therapy and a lot of angst and was really, really hard, but we're okay now. And we have Sherry. If I had left him, she wouldn't have been born. But I chose to forgive him, and he was really repentant. Now it's better than it was before. But the pain is there. The pain will always be there. We've just learned to look at it through a different lens."

Abigail didn't know what to say. She obviously didn't know Pauline as well as she thought. But it was no wonder—she never joined her friends after work for drinks or went out with Pauline as a friend. She pretty much kept to herself, except for the occasional dinner with Jimmy and Martha.

She thought about that terrible night when Nick died. And what happened after.

"I'm not sure I can."

"Forgive Nick. More importantly, forgive yourself, Abigail," said Pauline. "Isn't that what Jesus teaches?"

She had her there. Abigail closed her eyes.

Then a patron walked over to her section. "I'm looking for a document from 1842."

Abigail looked at the patron, an older woman with a stack of books under her arm. "It's okay, I've got it," she said to Pauline. Pauline gave her a little smile.

"Okay. I'll be back in my section shelving if you need me."

Abigail offered to close up so Pauline could go home. It had been a busy afternoon, which was unusual for the library. Thursdays were usually slow. Ms. Scott stopped by on her way out. "You okay to lock up by yourself, Abigail?"

"Yes, I've done it a hundred times." Abigail smiled.

"But not since the burglary. Well, I guess now we have the guard."

"I know. I'll be fine."

Ms. Scott left, and Abigail filed the last of her maps away. Then she carefully pulled the map that Tony wanted from its drawer and took it out from between the archival quality paper. She had a sheet of acid-free parchment that she rolled it in and put it in a tube she had with her. Then she closed the drawer and locked it. She put the tube under the sweater she was wearing and secured it in the waistband of her skirt. She felt ridiculous. And also a little nervous. She could always check the map out as being cleaned, but she didn't want to draw any undue attention to it. It wasn't a popular map or one of great importance, so she figured it wouldn't even be missed.

She walked back toward her desk where she knew the camera could see her and was careful to keep the map hidden while she locked her desk drawer. Then she went to get her coat and left the building, setting the code as she walked out.

Tony was waiting for her at the curb, with his car running. She opened the door and got in.

"Is this the getaway car?" she said.

He laughed a little at that. "Are you sure you want to do this?"

"I'm sure. Drive before I change my mind."

He pulled out into the traffic. "I thought we'd go to my place first. I checked the weather forecast tonight, and it's supposed to be clear with a full moon."

Abigail hadn't even considered the problem of no moonlight.

"I can fix you some dinner first," he said. "We've got a few hours before the moon rises."

"Sure." She was in it this far. Why not have dinner with the criminal, too?

His apartment was on Fort Street, on the third floor of a five-story complex. It was in a nice neighborhood. When he opened the door and let her in, she was surprised at how neat he kept it. The white plush rug under her feet gave it an air of comfort, and the flat-screen TV and other electronics showed that he led a pretty good life. Probably all from stolen goods, sold for riches.

"Your secret lair," she said.

He laughed. "You do have a bad opinion of me." He took his coat off and offered to hang hers up. He was wearing jeans and a long-sleeve T-shirt. She realized she had on her green over-sized sweater and a gray skirt and felt a bit awkward and klutzy in it. She took off her glasses and put them in her purse.

He put on some soft music. Piano. Mozart, maybe.

"Do you like pasta?"

"Yes."

"Grandma made some lasagna last week while she was still on her feet. It was a huge pan. I froze some of it."

He washed his hands at the kitchen sink. He took the lasagna out of the freezer and put it in the oven to warm. Then he pulled out some vegetables from the fridge. "I'll make us a salad."

She walked around his apartment. He had two external computer hard drives, two separate monitors, and a lot of wires. On the other side of the room were several bookshelves, lined with books. Shakespeare, Dante, lots of recent best-sellers.

"You like to read," she said, pulling out a volume and leafing through it.

"Yes. We didn't have a television when I was growing up. Grandma preferred books."

"Your grandma lived with you?"

"She raised me."

Abigail put the book back. She walked over and leaned against the counter to watch him chop. "Do you want some help?"

"No, have a seat." He motioned to a chair at the counter, and as she sat down he got her a glass of water.

"Thanks." She took a sip.

"Sorry. I don't have any wine, and I drank the last of the pop yesterday."

"It's okay. I don't imagine you were expecting company."

"No." He looked up from the tomato he was dicing. "It's a pleasant surprise."

She traced her finger around her water glass, letting the music relax her. She hadn't realized how tense she was. Her life was so ordered, and she liked it that way. She knew what she was doing every day, and there were no surprises. Then Tony came into her life three days ago and now everything was…well, *different*.

Maybe that was a good thing.

"How's your grandma?"

"She's doing okay. Sleeping a lot. I sat with her most of the afternoon."

"So your grandma knows you're going to try to find the painting," Abigail said.

"She thinks I know an art historian who is searching for it for me. She doesn't know what I do on the side."

Abigail raised an eyebrow.

"She would never approve," Tony said. "She raised me better than that."

"Why did she raise you?" Abigail asked. She saw a shadow cross Tony's face. "I'm sorry. It's none of my business." The shadow passed.

"No," he said. "It's okay. I don't talk about it much. My mom died of cancer when I was eight, and after that, my dad started drinking. When I was ten, things got so bad that my grandma took me from my dad. I haven't seen him since. That was twenty-two years ago. In the beginning, Grandma tried to help him but he refused and she lost track of him.

We both just decided to move on with life. Last I heard, Dad died of pneumonia, homeless. There was no death certificate, just rumor. "

"So you had a good childhood with her?"

"She was—is—amazing. She has been wonderful to me. She knows I paint for a living, but I may have exaggerated my hourly wage a bit."

"Why did you start stealing?"

Tony smiled as he scraped the tomato into the salad bowl. He washed off a cucumber and started to peel it.

"Boredom at first. I couldn't afford college, so I started messing around on the computer. One day, I found out that I could hack into the high school security system. I was simply looking for an old friend that I wanted to get in touch with. But suddenly, there were all of our records and updated addresses. So just for fun, I tried hacking into the landlord's computer where Grandma lived. She was behind on her rent, and I "paid" the bill. Then I figured out I could control security systems and cameras, and I sort of went from there."

Abigail was sorry she asked. "So how many jobs have you done?"

Tony added the cucumber to the bowl and turned to wash his hands. She couldn't see his face. "I don't know. Enough. Enough to pay for hospice and my grandma's cancer treatments. And this stuff." He swept his arm to take in his apartment. "A painter's wages won't cover all of that."

"Your friend—George—seems to do well enough."

"George has a side job as a handyman. And his wife works."

They stood looking at each other for a moment.

"I'm sorry to disappoint you, but this is who I am," Tony said.

Her phone rang. She jumped and fished it out of her purse. "Crap!" she said, when she saw the caller ID.

"Jimmy!" she said answering it. "I'm so, so sorry! I completely forgot about dinner. I—" She looked across at Tony. "Something came up with a friend that I need to take care of. It's important, and I just forgot."

Jimmy was worried, she could tell by the tone of his voice. But he let it go. She reassured him again and apologized and promised to make it up to Martha, who had apparently cooked her favorite dinner.

After she hung up, Tony raised an eyebrow. "Boyfriend?"

Abigail laughed. "No! Not anything close. He and his wife are dear friends of mine, and I was supposed to have dinner with them tonight. I forgot."

"Jimmy?"

"He's the cop who nearly caught you the other night."

"You're best friends with a *cop*? Great." Tony shook his head and then laughed. "We make a great pair, don't we?"

The timer went off for the lasagna. He reached for some oven mitts and took it out of the oven. She found the dishes and set the table while he got her more water and warmed up some bread. He pulled out a chair for her, and she sat.

"You can't have a proper meal without bread, that's what Grandma says." He sat across from her.

Abigail watched him. His strong hands and long fingers were very deft at their work, and he sliced the bread easily.

"You love her very much, don't you?"

Tony swallowed, making himself busy with the bread. "Yes," he said quietly. "Yes, I do. She's all I have." He looked across the table at Abigail. Then his face brightened. "Let's eat! The moon will be up soon."

The lasagna was incredible, and Abigail found herself asking for a second helping.

"So how did you find out about this map?" she asked.

"Grandma knew about it. Apparently, whoever stole the painting wanted to be sure that it never got back into the hands of Russo's family. Rumor has it that Russo's wife and legitimate daughter wanted it destroyed, so hiding it was the only way to keep it safe. My own mom never believed that the painting existed, but Grandma was adamant that Russo was my great-grandma's lover. My mom thought they made the story up as a cover for a deserting husband. Grandma wanted to prove her wrong. She wanted to prove that Mom came from Russo."

"I'm confused," Abigail said. "So…your *great-grandma* was Russo's lover?"

"Yes. Her name was Margaret. But he called her Laurel."

"And their illegitimate daughter is your grandma, the woman I met?"

"Correct." Tony smiled.

"So that makes you Russo's great-grandson."

"That's right. And only surviving heir. His daughter died childless."

Abigail thought about that. "All of his money was given to the Louvre." She had read the plaque with his story on it in the University's own art museum many times.

"And his paintings dispersed."

So that explained why Tony's family wasn't wealthy. That, and the fact that there was no real proof that he was related. She remembered reading the date when Russo had died. It would have been a several years after his affair with Margaret and the birth of his illegitimate child.

"Russo committed suicide, right?"

"Yes, he was unhappy. He never contacted Great-Grandma (Margaret) again, not even after the baby was born. But every now and then, some money would appear in an envelope with no return address. That stopped, of course, after his death."

"Hmmmm."

Tony smiled. "Grandma just wanted to see the painting. I guess it was discovered while it was still drying. His wife found it in his studio and was going to destroy it, but he took it and ran. He hid it someplace, and it was discovered after his death and moved again. It was brought to the US to be given to his illegitimate heir and to be kept out of the hands of his daughter. But that never happened. Somebody stole it coming off the ship and hid it. The mapmaker, I'm told, was hired to build in clues to where it was hidden, but he made them tricky so the thief wouldn't be able to find them. The mapmaker wanted to return it to Margaret. But then the mapmaker and the man who stole the painting both died, or something else happened to them. My grandma thought we could find it. She just wants to see it, because it meant so much to her own mom."

"How did your grandma find out about it?"

"My great-grandma looked for it for years after she heard of Russo's death. She apparently spent a great deal of the family money trying to find it. But Margaret never found it. After her death, Grandma tried to locate it herself. Especially after she took me in. She said she'd sell it to a museum so she could send me to college. I ran across a small news story last year ago about a cartographer who in a drunken stupor in a bar one night, claimed he had made a treasure map to the lost painting of Russo. Nobody believed him. But I checked the dates and the timing was right. I took a chance it had to be hidden in the city and I figured it out."

"It's an amazing story," Abigail said.

"Hopefully, we can find it."

Tony watched Abigail pull on some gloves to wash the dishes. Even in the baggy sweater she was wearing, she was beautiful. He longed to reach over and touch her, run his hand along her hair, kiss her. Instead, he reached over her to wet a sponge. Their arms brushed, and he glanced up at her. Their eyes met and then he dropped his and squeezed out the sponge, focusing all of his attention on that. He felt himself turning warm.

He turned away from her before he made a move he'd regret. He wanted to respect her boundaries.

Thinking, or the lack of thinking, clearly got him in trouble, so he would focus on the map for the rest of the night. He wiped off the table and dried the few remaining dishes. Then he spread out the map on the table.

He loved old things, and he first ran his hand across the paper, just feeling it. He saw Abigail cringe, and it made him smile.

The map was old but in good condition, and the two of them bent over it, looking at all the old streets and buildings that used to be the city many years ago.

"You don't have your glasses on," Tony said. She looked up at him. Her eyes were a beautiful emerald green. There were a few tiny freckles across her nose.

"I don't really need them," she said, and bent her head back to the map.

She was a mystery to him, and he wondered what had hurt her so much that she chose to shut everyone out.

"It's old," he said. "Pre-twentieth century. Which means our cartographer got his hands on it later. How long has the library had it?"

"I don't know. I'd have to check. How do you know it's pre-twentieth century?"

He fingered the corner. "It's on linen. Most maps made around the mid-nineteenth century were on linen. So this was originally made earlier than its 1904 date and updated a few times." He used that bit of knowledge to impress her, he had to admit. It seemed to work.

"How do you know this?"

"I've been looking for this map for a while. I know everything there is to know about it."

He glanced up at her and saw a smile play at her lips.

He looked outside. "I think it's dark enough. Let's go," he said.

She pulled her coat and boots on.

He hesitated. "Can you climb a fire escape ladder?"

"Probably."

"Okay." He turned to go into his bedroom. "Follow me."

She hesitated for a moment and then followed him. He was glad he kept his room tidy, as his bed was made and his clothes were picked up. He put on his jacket and pulled open the window. It was large, made for a fire escape, and he took her hand and helped her out. Then he shut it and motioned for her to climb.

"We're going to the roof," he said. "Ladies first."

"No way," she said. "I have a skirt on."

It took him a moment to catch her meaning. Then he couldn't help but grin. "Okay," he said, and tucked the map storage tube into his jacket and started climbing up ahead of her.

It didn't take them long. The moon was full and bright, and they had no trouble making their way up the rungs of the ladder. He was impressed that she kept up with him.

"This is the moment I've been waiting for all my life," he said. Then, taking a deep breath, he pulled the map out of his jacket.

Chapter Ten

Abigail watched as Tony unrolled the map. It wasn't all that big, only about thirty-six inches square, and there was no wind. Once he got it unfurled, they stood looking at it. The moon was bright but not bright enough to make out much of the drawing.

"I don't see anything," Abigail said. She glanced at Tony and saw his eyes change. Disappointment, maybe?

Then he caught his breath. "Look."

She looked back down at the map, which had started to glow. Slowly, iridescent lines began to form over and under the existing drawings of streets and sewer lines.

"Ahhhhh," Tony breathed. "There it is."

Within seconds, the original map was overlaid with an entire second map in faintly glowing ink.

"Oh my gosh," Abigail said. It was like magic. She stared at it, marveling at the beauty in it.

"It's not in the heart of the city." Tony pointed, his hand trembling. "Look. It's here. In this building down this side street."

The glowing lines offered tiny arrows pointing north and then along the river. Coming in from the south, they entered an area around the Museum of Art and ended with an X.

"X marks the spot," said Abigail. "Just like a pirate map." She was grinning. She *loved* maps and old things!

"Look," she said, tracing her finger along the arrows, excited now. "That symbol means the site of a battle." It was two swords crossed. Then she pointed to a flower. "That's the symbol for an arboretum or garden."

"There's no garden there that I know of," Tony said. "And there wasn't one on this map when it was made."

"Maybe it means something else. Like a window garden."

"This is awesome," Tony said. "Incredible."

He was excited. He had that twinkle in his eyes, and his hands were trembling. "Let me see here…" She watched him work, his mind probably racing as he bent over the map and traced his fingers along some Latin letters and then the route. "I know the city pretty well. I think I can find this place. It's only about a mile from here."

He took her hand and pulled her over to the edge of the roof. "Look." He pointed. "There's the law school. Just down from that is the museum. But the map wants us to come in from the south, so over there." He pointed to his left. "Are you up to this?"

"Tonight?" She was wishing she had brought some other clothes.

"It has to be. I don't know how long my grandma has."

But she felt a thrill in her stomach. This is what she had studied for, what she did for a living, interpreting maps and old documents. Instead of doing it from behind a desk, she now got to enter the chase. How could she pass this up?

"Let's go," she said.

Tony stared at the map for another minute. "Okay, I think I've got it."

"Memorized?" she laughed.

"I have a photographic memory."

Back inside the apartment, Tony locked the window and they left through the door, like normal people. Tony gave her some heavy socks to pull on over her tights. Abigail was glad of the tall, thick boots she had worn. They were lined with fleece and should keep her feet warm.

They turned down a side street between two apartment buildings and then headed toward the river. The city looked different at night. Abigail didn't walk much in the dark, only as far as from the bus stop to her house. It was quiet, and there were a few stars out, their light twinkling off the snow on the ground. Rush hour was over and most of the people were inside, either at home or in restaurants, finishing up their day before heading to bed.

They half walked, half ran down Island Street. Abigail smiled at the name, which referred to a small bit of land sticking out of the river. Now, of course, the river was frozen, but in the summer, birds roosted on the "island," and sometimes a kayaker would stop there and sit for a bit, if they could find a clean spot among the bird droppings.

"So the X is here," Tony said. They had been walking about fifteen minutes when he stopped. They were at the side of a building, a set of apartments running along a side street with a view of the river. They looked around.

"There!" Abigail pointed. On the corner of an older-looking building was an imprint of two swords on their side, crossed. "Battle?"

Tony went over and traced his fingers along the swords. "Maybe they're pointing?"

"Let's see." Abigail grabbed his hand and pulled him in the direction of the sword tips, which were pointing northeast. It led them through an alley to another small street. She looked around.

Across from her was an old brick house with ornate flower designs in the scaffolding of the porch and eaves. Why hadn't she noticed the architecture before?

"A garden," she said. "It's just made of stone."

Tony looked around. "Is the painting in there, then?"

"Maybe."

They stood there in the cold, staring across the street at the house. Abigail noticed she was still holding Tony's hand and let go. There were lights on in the house, and through the window they could see someone setting a table and someone else strumming a guitar. Students, probably.

Suddenly she saw it. Each of the lampposts on this street had a circular pattern in the metal stems, similar to a flower. "Look."

They lined the street, starting at this house and heading north. She started walking, Tony right beside her.

The last lamppost stood in front of an old building. From the architecture, they could tell it used to be beautiful, but even in the dark they could see it was now a bit run-down. There was a sign, hanging slightly crooked, which read "Employ-U-Now Temp Agency."

"Classy," Tony said.

"This is the place," Abigail said, pointing up. Above the door, in stone, was a flower.

"A garden-y sort of street," Tony said. *"Here's flowers for you; Hot lavender, mints, savory, marjoram;"*

"The Winter's Tale," said Abigail. "More Shakespeare."

"Yes. I'm afraid I'm not very widely read." Tony walked over, ran his hand along the door, and then peeked under the doormat.

"You didn't think they'd leave a key?" Abigail said.

"You'd be surprised." He glanced around and then peeked through the windows. It was dark inside. "I don't see a camera. If I come back later, it should be an easy in."

"You're going to break in?" Abigail didn't know what else she had expected. Maybe for the place to be open so they could waltz in and ask to look for an old, stolen painting?

Tony looked at her. "That was the general idea."

She looked at the building and then glanced down the street. "When?"

"If I tell you that, you'll be an accessory."

"I think I already am." She wrapped her arms around her body, more from nerves than the cold.

The street was dark, the old lamps not putting out much light. There were no cars coming down it at the moment. Tony pulled something out of his pocket and bent over the door. Abigail heard a click.

He pushed the door open. "Coming?"

"Um…"

"Hurry. Before an alarm trips."

She ran inside and shut the door behind her. Tony ran his hands expertly around the doorframe and found a wire, which he pulled. Nothing happened. There were no lights, no sound, nothing.

"It's not even rigged up." He chuckled. "Apparently there's nothing here to steal."

He pulled Abigail to a back room. "I think I know where to look. At the bottom of the map were some words in Latin," he said.

"You know Latin?"

"The painting is upstairs, second floor, north wall. Come on." He turned on a penlight.

She followed him up a stairway with thin, industrial carpeting. There were a few rooms, one filled with file cabinets, the drawers all locked. (Tony checked.) The next one was some sort of break room and smelled of microwave popcorn. Across from that was a set of rooms running along the north side of the building. Tony walked into the biggest one.

"This is the room," he said.

Abigail looked at the north wall. There was a desk in front of it with a few chairs next to it. Probably the business manager, or owner, and probably someone who did a lot of interviews. Above it was a large painting. Tony shone his light on it. It was a bad rendition of a landscape, with a moose and some trees in fall colors.

"They didn't break the budget on decorating," Tony said. He removed the painting. Abigail expected to see something behind it, a safe or a faded spot or something. Anything. There was nothing. He set the painting on the desk and ran his hand along the wall.

"Plaster," he said.

"Is it buried in there?"

"Maybe." He unlocked his phone and opened an app. Abigail heard a soft beep.

"What's that?" Abigail whispered. They had been whispering, even though there was no one around to hear them.

"Its an app that uses sonic waves to tell me if there's anything behind the wall."

"I've never heard of that."

"It's not readily available to the public."

Abigail tried to see the screen on his phone. "Anything?"

"No," Tony said after a minute. "Nothing." He turned it off and sat down in the swivel chair. "I don't get it."

"Maybe the painting *used* to hang here?" Abigail said.

"Maybe. But not out in the open. Someone would have recognized it. How can the map be wrong?"

Abigail wanted to say that maybe it was all a made up story after all, but she didn't.

"What used to be here?" she said instead.

Tony took out his phone and did a search. "It doesn't say. We'd have to go down to the records office and check who the owners were before the temp agency moved in. "

"Let me come back on Monday and ask."

"For the painting?"

"No. I'll just casually find out what used to be here and who had this office last."

"Monday?" Tony studied her for a moment. She couldn't read what he was thinking. "Okay," he said finally. He stood up, picking up the painting to hang it back on the wall. "I guess we should get out of here."

Chapter Eleven

Tony checked on his grandma Saturday morning. She was sleeping. She was doing quite well, and it looked like she had more time than the doctors originally thought. That gave Tony some hope, but he stashed it away quickly, knowing that she was terminal.

Afterward, he met George at the Sounds and Sonics display, two coffees in hand. They spent the morning painting to an old Beach Boys CD that George played on the boombox he bought at a garage sale. Tony was restless and kept thinking about the map. What was he missing? He knew it was supposed to lead to the painting, but instead it had led him to a dead end.

What if it was so old that the painting was no longer where the cartographer had put it? Or worse, what if it never existed? Then why was the map even there?

He was also conflicted about Abigail. She was smart and beautiful and so sweet, and now she was leading a life of crime. He wondered what would happen to her if they found out that the map was missing. She'd lose her job, surely, if they traced it back to her. All the more reason to return the map quickly, hopefully over the weekend, before the library opened on Monday. He knew it was open this morning, but Abigail had this morning off. He didn't imagine anyone would wander in and ask for that specific map.

"Distracted again?"

Tony smiled at George. They needed to finish the job at the Dewey Science Museum. They were almost there—just some trim work left.

"Yes."

"The girl?"

"Woman," Tony corrected.

George laughed. "You must have gotten some."

"No. It's not like that this time."

Tony could feel George's eyes on him. "You really like her don't you? Especially if you haven't even slept with her yet."

Tony laughed to cover up his embarrassment. It was true, he had taken quite a few women home to bed in the past several years, but none of them had stuck around. All of his relationships except for Darci were short-lived, just-for-fun adventures. A cup of coffee, a movie, a night out on the town. Sometimes a roll in the sack. That was about it. And honestly, Darci had only lasted six weeks. A whirlwind romance, his grandma had called it. Lust, not love, she said.

But Abigail was different. She did something to him that he had never felt before. Ever. She was smart. She was pretty. But more than that—she fascinated him.

"Yeah, I guess I do," Tony admitted.

"Well, if you want my advice, don't let this one go." George dipped his brush again and climbed up the ladder to begin the trim along the ceiling.

"I'm not sure she feels the same way."

"Have you asked her?"

"No! We've only seen each other a few times."

"A few?"

"She was over for dinner last night. We had my grandma's lasagna."

George whistled. "You do have it bad if you're sharing the coveted lasagna with her."

Tony laughed. "And I took her to see Grandma."

"What does Grandma think?"

"I think she likes her. She said something akin to 'You'll straighten up my grandson.'"

George laughed. "Good luck to her with that!"

Tony laughed, but inside his gut was twisting a little bit. He was afraid he would get her in trouble. Heck, just *knowing* him could get her in trouble.

He thought about how she had told him she'd handle getting the information from the temp agency. He could think of at least a dozen ways to get the information fast—hacking into the city records, for one. It wouldn't take long, and her way, well, if he did it her way, he'd have to wait until the temp agency opened on Monday morning. That was a whole weekend he would lose.

She was stubborn and had been insistent that she could do this. He knew she would too, but he wasn't used to giving up control. So why was he? This had been his search for so long that it felt strange to have someone else in on it.

And yet...this was the first time he hadn't felt alone. He had plenty of friends, sure, that wasn't it. It was just that, even with Darci, he had never been honest with anyone before. No one. Ever. He had no idea why he told Abigail all the things he told her. They just came out.

She was probably going to be the undoing of him.

"Love goes by haps; Some Cupid kills with arrows, some with traps," he murmured.

"What?" George said.

"Nothing."

He wanted to talk to her again. He needed to hear her voice. When he was with her, she filled a void that he hadn't even known was there before he met her. Was it because he shared his secret with her? Or was it because she didn't judge him? Yes, she had called him a thief, which he was, and said hurtful words. But he could tell she didn't mean it. She was protecting herself, as well she should. But he didn't think she was just protecting herself from the dishonesty that was his job. It was something deeper. She was afraid to get close, and she wasn't about to let herself get close to him.

He dropped some paint on his cheek and wiped it off with the back of his hand.

She had been so excited last night about searching for the painting. He wondered how she felt about it all now. He needed to hear her voice.

"Tony, let's finish up this last bit and head out to the next job. I think we can get a good start on that place today," George said.

"Sure."

Maybe it was time he started trusting someone else. It felt good to have her in his corner. He'd call her tonight. He'd tell her he was going to do it her way, and let her get the information from the temp agency herself. It felt good not to be doing this alone.

———◇———————◇———

Abigail ran some errands, picking up stamps and groceries and then doing a bit of laundry back at her house. Saturdays were her day to get things done, and since Tony had to work, they couldn't do anything else. That evening he was going to visit his grandma and had invited her to go with him, but she figured she'd better go to Jimmy's for dinner.

She thought about Tony all day, even though she tried not to. She was thrilled about finding the map and the building. It was all like an adventure, and she had been so wound up last night that she hardly slept. Still, she felt great today, alive and full of energy.

She told Tony he could keep the map for a few days. He said he wanted to look over it more tonight and see if he could figure anything else out. It was supposed to be another clear night with a nearly full moon. She longed to see the secret map again under the moonlight, but she didn't want to let Jimmy and Martha down again. Maybe after dinner she'd go over to Tony's.

Jimmy picked her up in his cop car at 6 p.m. and drove her to his house. He only lived a few miles away. At the first stop sign, a car sped through.

"Hold on," Jimmy said. "I can't let this one go." He turned his light on and turned left after the car. He sounded his siren a few times, and the car pulled over.

Abigail had ridden with him several times over the years while he worked. It was usually small stuff—she had thankfully never witnessed anything violent while she was with him—or he just drove around with her when he was patrolling the city. Sometimes he had a partner with him, but he often worked alone and welcomed the company.

She watched him approach the car and talk to the driver. It gave her a mixed feeling of pride and fear to see him work. She wondered how Martha did it all these years. Any day a driver could pull a gun on Jimmy and that would be the end.

mrs. chartwell and the cat burglar

Or what if he responded to a robbery at a gas station and was shot? Abigail tried not to think about that.

The driver was handing over his credentials without incident, and soon Jimmy was back in the car to run the numbers.

He looked over at her.

"You okay?"

"Yes," Abigail said, giving him a smile and trying to shake off her bad thoughts. It was true that they lived in a pretty safe city. "I just think you look cool."

Jimmy grinned as he punched in the numbers on his keypad with his big, calloused fingers. He had never learned to type. The whole stop only took about ten minutes, and soon they were on their way again.

Their house was an old brownstone, and Martha kept it sparkling clean. She loved being a homemaker, she said, and despite Jimmy's tendencies to leave dirty socks lying around and a half-read paper open on his ottoman, she kept a tidy place. When she wasn't cleaning, she was canning food she bought at the farmer's market, making crafts for the ladies auxiliary craft show, and volunteering at the hospital. Abigail had no idea how she handled it all. She never seemed ruffled or out of breath. Just thinking of all Martha did exhausted Abigail.

"Hi, honey." Martha hugged her. "How are you? Jimmy told me of your scary run-in with a burglar on Tuesday night."

"I'm okay, Martha," Abigail said, hugging her back. "Really, I am. He wasn't armed or anything, and he was actually quite polite."

"I thought you said he didn't talk to you," Jimmy said.

"Well, he could have been shouting or swearing, isn't that right?" Abigail said, thinking fast. She felt her stomach tingle a little, only this time it wasn't good nerves. Why was she lying to these people she loved so much?

Because she had let Tony get under her skin. When he had approached her in the kitchen last night at the sink, she had almost kissed him.

No. She couldn't let herself think of him in that way.

70

"We're having spaghetti for dinner," Martha said. "I had a chicken pot pie made up for you last night."

"I know. I'm so sorry," Abigail said. "I had a friend who needed me, and I completely forgot. I'm *so* sorry."

"Oh, honey, it happens," said Martha. "Come into the kitchen with me and get some water glasses out."

Abigail was used to helping out when she came over. They treated her like family. They had no children of their own, and she suspected they were almost as grateful for her as she was for them.

She got some tumblers down and filled them with ice and water. Martha put the food on the table and the three of them sat down.

Jimmy cleared his throat and bowed his head. They held hands at the dinner table while they prayed, a custom that had made Abigail uncomfortable at first. Now she had grown to look forward to it. There was something warm and comfortable about it.

"So how's work going?" Jimmy asked as he handed her the salad. She told them about it and then Jimmy told them some funny stories about his job. He was always running across interesting characters out on the streets.

"Abigail, you are simply glowing tonight," Martha said. "What's up?"

Abigail felt herself blush. She wasn't planning to tell them about Tony. And what was he to her, anyway?

"Have you met someone?" Martha asked.

Abigail couldn't stop the smile but said, "No."

She heard Jimmy chuckle. "Lucky fellow. He'd better treat you right or I'll come after him."

"Jimmy!" Martha scolded. "Tell us about him, Abby. How'd you meet?"

"He's just a friend," she said. "Well, not even a friend. He's more of…" She paused. "An acquaintance."

"Apparently one you're smitten with," smiled Martha.

Abigail gave in and described his wavy black hair, well-muscled body, and beautiful eyes. She found she loved the chance to talk about him.

"Sounds Italian," Martha sighed. "They say that Italian men make the best lovers."

Jimmy raised an eyebrow. "I'm not Italian."

"It's what they say," Martha said. "I'll never know." She reached over and squeezed Jimmy's hand. "You're all the man I can handle, honey," she said.

"I'm not sure how to take that."

"Where'd you meet him?" Martha asked.

"He came into the library, looking for a map."

"There's been a lot of that going around lately," said Jimmy.

"It *is* my job," Abigail said.

"And...?" Martha said. Abigail laughed. Martha was like a young schoolgirl.

"And we started talking. And then I went over to his house for dinner. As a *friend.*"

Martha clapped her hands together and laughed. "I can't wait to meet him."

"We've only had one dinner together. I doubt he'll even call me again."

"He'd better call," said Jimmy in his rough voice.

"Jimmy!" Martha scolded again.

Abigail felt herself flush with happiness and put the napkin to her mouth to hide behind. When she had started talking about Tony, she got all happy on the inside. Why did she have to be infatuated with a thief? She would enjoy the feeling but not go with it. After all, she couldn't help how she felt, but she could control what she did. She'd remain friends with him. That was all.

"What's his name?" Martha asked. "What does he do?"

"I think that's enough talk about him tonight," Abigail said. "Maybe sometime I'll bring him around for you to meet. Honest. Like I said, we only had one dinner together." Then she emphasized. "He's just a friend."

"Well, if the way you light up when you talk about him is any indication, then I'd say you're in love," said Martha.

"I hope he's worthy of you," said Jimmy.

———◆——————◆———

pamela gossiaux

They played a few hands of Rummy and then Jimmy drove Abigail home. She was tired and was looking forward to a hot bath and a good book, but she also couldn't get her mind off Tony. She wondered if he was up on his roof with the map. She wished she had his cell number.

"I'll walk you in," Jimmy said, pulling up to the curb in front of her home.

"That's okay," Abigail said. "I'll be fine. I'll turn the lights on and wave to you from the window."

Jimmy smiled. "Okay, but I wish you'd get a timer on that front room light like I asked you to."

"Hey, at least I got the sensor on the porch light."

"No, *I'm* the one who put the sensor on the porch light."

"But I let you!" Abigail said.

They both laughed.

"And you have the gun," Jimmy said. Since she lived alone he had made her get one and taught her how to use it.

"Yes, I have the gun. It's in my underwear drawer."

"Good place." Jimmy laughed again.

Abigail reached over to hug him. "Thanks for a great evening, Jimmy. I really missed you and Martha."

"It has been a while since you've been over," Jimmy said.

"I know. I won't let it go so long next time."

She got her key out and trudged through the deep snow up to her door. She needed to shovel. Maybe tomorrow. She opened the door and stepped inside and turned the light on. Then she waved to Jimmy, as promised, from the window. Cocoa curled around her legs, happy she was home.

She watched Jimmy's car turn at the corner and then put her coat away in the closet and walked slowly up the stairs to her bedroom to run a bath. She was happy and relaxed after her evening with the Stouts, and her belly was still full from Martha's wonderful cooking. There had been apple pie with vanilla ice cream for dessert.

She was pulling a large, fluffy towel from the linen closet when her phone rang. The caller was "unknown."

"Hello?" she answered tentatively.

"Hi, Abigail. It's Tony."

She couldn't stop the smile that spread across her face.

"Tony," she said, sitting down on her bed. "How did you get my number?"

"I have ways," he said. She could hear the playful tone in his voice. "Is it okay that I called?"

"Yes," she said. "I was just…" thinking about you, was what she was going to say. Instead she said, "I just got home from Jimmy's house."

"How was dinner?"

"Delicious."

There was a long pause.

"How is your grandma?" Abigail asked.

"She's okay. No change since you saw her yesterday. She sat up while I was there and ate some dinner. Jell-O and mashed potatoes."

"That's good."

"Yes."

There was another long pause. Abigail realized the conversation had become awkward.

"Why are you calling?"

"I just wanted to let you know that Grandma is okay and I think we can wait until Monday and do it your way to get into the temp agency."

Abigail smiled. That's not why he was calling at all, but she didn't push him. She realized she was happy he had missed her.

"That's great," she said.

"Well, I should go," Tony said. He wasn't nearly as smooth on the phone as he was in real life.

"Do you want to come to church with me tomorrow?" Abigail asked, suddenly. She didn't want him to hang up, and that was the first thing that popped into her head.

"Church?"

"Yes, I go to the Presbyterian church over on Oak Street, where Jimmy and Martha go. It starts at 9 a.m. Service, that is. Or, maybe you have your own church."

"God shall be my hope, my stay, my guide and lantern to my feet."

"Is that *Lear*?"

"Henry VI."

She smiled. "A Shakespeare-quoting thief. You are an interesting man, Tony Russo."

"You miss me?"

She laughed. "Yes, Tony, I miss you, which is why I invited you to church in the morning."

She heard a sigh on the other end. "I can't," he said. His tone was more serious. "Honestly. I do want to go see my grandma, and then I'm meeting George at a customer's house to do some painting. I'm flexing my hours around a bit so I can spend more time with my grandma, and that entails working this Sunday. I'm free for dinner, though."

"Okay. No, wait! Oh drat it!"

"Drat it? Do people actually say that?"

"I already have plans. I've promised to attend a workshop on maps for work. Ms. Scott got me the ticket months ago. I have to go."

"Fun."

"Yeah." She twisted a strand of hair around her finger.

"No problem. I'll be in touch," Tony said.

"Okay. Good night."

There was a pause. "Abigail?"

"Yes?"

"I really appreciate you getting the map for me. I know you put your job in jeopardy. I'll get it back to you soon, I promise, and I'll take the rap if they find out. I can tell them I stole it that night I was in there."

She heard the sincerity in his voice. Maybe he wasn't the playboy she took him for.

"No, Tony. It's okay. It'll all work out."

He said goodbye, and she regretted when the call ended. She sat on her bed for while, hugging her towel and smiling. She had forgotten to ask him if he looked at the map. She hadn't been this happy in years. This strange man was so wrong for her, and yet he made her feel so right. He made her happy.

"Please God, protect me," she whispered the prayer. "Guide me. I think I'm getting in too deep."

Then she scratched Cocoa behind the ears and went to take her bath.

Tony had trouble sleeping. His mind kept drifting to Abigail and the map. He had spent quite a bit of time looking at it Friday night, and tonight was cloudy. He was restless and wanted to move on it. Waiting another day seemed like torture.

He reached over and turned on the light by his bed, thinking he would read. As he reached for the book on his nightstand, he knocked a picture on the floor. He picked it up, afraid it was broken. It wasn't. He held it for a moment. It was a photo of him and his parents when he was about three. His grandma had given it to him after his mom died.

He didn't have any other family. Once his grandma was gone, there was nobody left. He had friends, but no one who knew him well. He had to keep a lot hidden because of what he did. It had never bothered him before, but now that he was facing a future without his grandma, it suddenly seemed like there was no one else. For the first time, he found himself wishing he had a sibling to call. Who would he share childhood memories with?

He suddenly had a feeling something was wrong. He quickly got up, got dressed, and went outside into the snow, grabbing his keys on the way out. He drove to the hospice without thinking, going about five over the speed limit even though the roads were snowy.

"Alice," he said to the nurse at the front desk. "How is she?"

"She's fine, Tony," Alice said. A small woman in her late forties, Alice had a soft voice and kind eyes. "What's wrong?"

"I, uh, I don't know." He stopped and ran his hand through his hair, feeling his heart pounding. Suddenly, for some reason, he wanted to cry. He fought down the feeling. "I guess I just thought..."

His voice trailed off. He looked across the desk at Alice, who smiled.

"You thought you felt her leave," she said.

"Yes."

"That's normal," Alice said. "But she's still with us. Go see for yourself."

Tony walked down the hall, willing his heart rate back to normal. When he got to her room, it was dark. She was sleeping. He went in quietly and sat in the chair by her bed.

She was breathing comfortably, and he watched the rise and fall of her chest. She looked old and tired in the soft light from the hallway. The sounds in the hospice were quiet, almost comforting. There wasn't the beep of monitors like they had at the hospital. Instead, it was all soft colors, quilts, and no rush or hurry. Alice came in quietly and offered him a blanket straight from the blanket warmer. She put it across him and set a glass of water on the desk for him. He nodded a thank you. Then he sat in the chair, warmed, and watched his grandma breathe.

Chapter Twelve

Abigail pulled a green dress out of her closet. It was one of her favorites, and she knew she looked good in it. She was feeling pretty today, light on her feet, and wanted to dress the part. She glanced at some of her work clothes as she lifted a pink print scarf off of her shelf. They were a bit dowdy, and she did choose to dress that way to hide from and fend off men, as Pauline suspected.

She just had never been interested in getting married again. Or dating. Or even in going out.

She fingered the material of the dress after she slipped it over her head. It was soft and silky, a bit light for this time of the year, but with the scarf and some leather boots, it would be warm enough.

She loved her church and nobody ever bothered her there. None of the single men asked her out, and none of the ladies bothered trying to set her up. She suspected that was because Martha had made it clear not to, and she appreciated it.

She went over to her dresser and ran the brush through her thick, red hair. Then she put on some makeup and left her glasses in the dish on her dresser. She only wore them for work. They were fake; there wasn't even a prescription in them. They made her look more studious and hid her eyes.

"Am I hiding?" she asked the face in the mirror.

Cocoa answered her with a meow.

Things had just gotten so bad after Nick's death. She lost about a year of her life. Then Martha brought her to a grief counseling class at the church, and there she met people who were suffering like she was. Real people with real losses, not just a counselor spouting from a book. And she finally began to heal.

But not fully. Martha and Pauline and a few others kept telling her she had to take the walls down and quit protecting herself. She needed to love again. But she had no desire to do so. Or had never had. Until maybe now.

With Tony.

She felt her heart reaching for him, but then she got scared. What was it she wanted, anyway? Tony as a friend? As a lover? What?

Maybe she was just infatuated with him.

But she had made it clear she just wanted to be friends. So they would just be that. Tony seemed to be respecting that and keeping his distance.

She realized she had been twisting her wedding ring on her finger. She pulled it off and looked at it closely.

The diamond was small because they were in college when Nick bought it.

"I'll love you forever," he had said.

And then he had left her.

She fought back tears and put the ring back on.

Just then a text beeped in on her phone.

Beauty provoketh thieves sooner than gold.

She laughed out loud. She knew it was Shakespeare but had no idea from what play.

A poem? she texted back.

As You Like It.

Ahhh...a play. I need to brush up on my Shakespeare.

He texted her a smile emoji and then **I've got to go. TTYL.**

She texted **TTYL.** She looked in the mirror and another Shakespeare quote came to her mind.

God has given you one face, and you make yourself another.

She looked down at her hand, pulled her wedding ring off her finger, and put it in the bowl next to her glasses. Then she left for church.

Tony was regretting that he had to work on Sunday. He was tired from the lack of sleep and hadn't showered, only going home to brush his teeth and grab a bagel and some coffee. He had sent Abigail a quick text this morning and was wishing he could see her tonight.

George yawned. "It's gonna be a long day."

Tony put on his cap and pried open the can of paint. "Yeah."

"Laney is with her mother today. Somebody's baby shower for couples. At least I get out of that."

Tony stepped back to look at the wall. It was a large one. The owner needed the banquet room painted today so he could prepare it for a party next weekend.

"You got some tunes?"

"Yep." George popped a CD in his boombox, and Elvis poured out.

Tony glanced sideways at him. "Really?"

George frowned at him and cranked it up. "Yep. Start swinging those hips, dude. Next time you can bring your own music if you don't like mine."

Tony laughed. It beat thinking about his grandma and Abigail and how long it was going to be before he was back on the trail of the map. The two men started singing "Ain't Nothin' But a Hound Dog," and Tony pushed down all other thoughts of Abigail, concentrating on getting the words right.

"Your ring is missing."

"What?" Abigail looked up from the folders she was filing. It was early Monday morning, only 10 a.m. It had taken Pauline less than an hour to notice.

"Your wedding ring. It's missing."

She glanced down at her finger, where there was still a little indentation from where the ring had been. "Yes. I took it off."

Pauline stared at her. "You took it off."

"Yes, Pauline," she said irritably. Why didn't people leave her alone? "It's not like I'm married anymore."

"But..." Pauline stopped. Abigail avoided her eyes. "Okay," Pauline finally said and walked away.

Abigail sighed and put a file under the "B"s where it should go. Bismark. Why did they have a map of Bismark, anyway? The file contained all the information for the map, such as where they got it, when they got it, and more. She shifted on her knees on the floor.

"I just need to ask," Pauline said. She was back. Abigail looked up at her friend.

"What?" She tried to sound aggravated, but she felt like she owed Pauline some explanation. Pauline was one of her best friends. One of her only friends.

"Is it because of this guy?"

"What guy?"

"The guy who took you to see his dying grandmother."

"Tony."

"So he has a name," Pauline said. She smiled and knelt down beside Abigail. "Tell all."

Abigail smiled despite herself. "He's cute, he's funny, he quotes Shakespeare."

"Shakespeare? How cool!"

"And we're just friends."

"And yet you removed your ring for the first time in how many years? Six since Nick died? Wow." Pauline tucked her hair behind her ears. "I'm so happy for you!"

"We're just friends," Abigail repeated.

"So is he a good kisser?"

"Pauline!"

"Is he?"

Abigail felt herself blush. "Yes," she said. Both women giggled.

"Okay," Pauline said, getting to her feet. "Tell your 'just friend' that I'd like to meet him. Maybe we could double-date some time."

Abigail nodded. "Will do. Now will you leave me alone?"

"Certainly!" Pauline said, and walked back to her section, looking triumphant.

Abigail glanced at the clock. It was 10:15 a.m. Now was just as good a time as any to pay a visit to the temp agency.

She filed the last of her stack and stood, brushing off her skirt. She had worn a gray pencil skirt with a cream blouse because she wanted to look good for her visit to the temp agency.

"Pauline?" she called, walking back toward where her friend had disappeared.

"Yes?" Pauline came around a corner. "Wow! Look at you! All dressed up, too!"

"Shut up," Abigail said, trying to hide her grin again. "Look, I need to take an early lunch to run some errands. Can you cover for me until I get back?"

"Sure thing." Pauline smiled. "Tell Tony I said 'hi,'" she said over her shoulder as she walked away.

"I'm not going to see him!" Abigail said a little too loudly for the library. She saw Ms. Scott scowl at her from across the room.

Abigail smiled an apology and went to get her things. She figured she'd take a taxi instead of walking the twenty minutes there. It was cold outside, and she didn't want to be gone more than an hour.

The taxi pulled up in front of the brick building that she and Tony had broken into the other night. When she thought of the words "broken into," she got goose bumps, remembering the rush of adrenaline that went through her that night. But she knew it was wrong. What would Jimmy think of her if he found out?

She paid the taxi driver and went inside.

"May I help you?" said a young woman behind a desk. She was wearing an orange scarf that accentuated her coffee-colored skin, and her curly hair was cut short. She was very pretty.

"Yes." Abigail pulled out her tablet and a stylus. "I'm writing a story on some of the historical buildings in the area, and I'd like to know the history of this place. Can you tell me who owned it last?" She paused, stylus ready. She had come up with the story last night and thought it would help her get the information she needed.

"Oh, sure. Let me take you upstairs to talk to our owner," said the woman. She smiled and held out her hand. "I'm Skylar. Right this way."

Abigail shook her hand. "I'm Andi," she said. "Thank you."

She followed Skylar up the stairs and couldn't believe her luck when the young woman led her into the same office she and Tony had been in on Friday night. A woman in her fifties was entering some figures into a computer from a legal pad. She stopped when she saw them, and Skylar explained why Abigail was there.

The woman stretched her arms out and cracked her knuckles. "Come in, Andi, and have a seat," she said. "I'm ready for a break." She closed her laptop. "So what newspaper are you with?"

"It's more for a graduate thesis I'm working on," Abigail said. "The Historical Aptitudes of Architectural Rationales." Abigail had learned long ago that if you didn't want to talk, you just had to say something to confuse or bore whoever was listening.

"Oh. Wow. Sounds important," said the woman, and dropped the questioning. "I'm Connie Williams. I own the temp agency. We've been here for about six years, and before us, this was a law firm. As far as I can tell, it was always a law firm but they outgrew the building and built a new place over on Upton Street, across town."

"I see," said Abigail, jotting a few notes down on her tablet. "So have you remodeled the building, or is this the way it originally was?"

"We put in new carpet," said Connie. "But the structure is the same. This office belonged to the owner of the law firm, and I was told it belonged to his father before him, and his father before him. Probably because of the view." Connie pointed to the window, and Abigail could see the river behind the buildings across the street. "That building wasn't always there," said Connie, "so I imagine he once had a better view of the river. But this office is big, and I rather liked it. Since I'm the owner, I took it." She smiled.

Abigail scribbled some more notes down. "Do you know his name?"

"The last lawyer? Yes, I bought the building from him. John Stewart. He's a nice man, but very busy and a bit abrupt.

I don't have his phone number any longer, but you can find him online. His firm is pretty big and well known."

Abigail looked around the room. "I was told there used to be some nice paintings in here. Any idea if he had any in his office?"

Connie thought. "I don't remember anything that really stands out. He had a beautiful photograph of his wife and children hanging on that wall there." She pointed to the wall across from her desk. "I only remember that because the woman was very beautiful. Almost like a model. Oh, and he had some old lawyer-type of painting back here, behind his desk. It was his grandfather, I believe, the founder of the firm."

"Really?" Abigail said. "What did it look like?"

"Just some old stodgy guy standing in front of a bookcase."

"What happened to it? Maybe it has some architectural clues on it from the era when this building was built."

"I imagine he took it with him," said Connie. "I really don't know."

Abigail made a few more notes and then stood. "Thanks for your time, Connie. I'm sure I'll have more questions about the building as I research, but maybe Mr. Stewart can answer them." Abigail reached across the desk to shake her hand. "You've been a big help."

Abigail left without incident and hailed a cab. She texted Tony.

Mission accomplished. Let's meet to discuss.
She received a text back.
Roger. 7 p.m. tonight? My place?
Sure thing. I'll bring dinner.

She tucked her phone back in her purse and felt that familiar tingle in her tummy. She tried to stifle her excitement at seeing Tony again. *We're only friends*, she told herself. Still, it was okay to look forward to seeing a friend. Wasn't it?

Back at work, she ate her lunch at her desk. Ms. Scott frowned on that, but Ms. Scott was in a meeting until 2 p.m. Abigail wondered at herself, breaking so many rules lately.

"So?" Pauline was back from her lunch. "How's Tony?"

"I didn't go see Tony," Abigail said. "But I'm sure he's fine. I'll let you know. I'm having dinner with him tonight."

84

"Squeee!" Pauline said. "I'm so happy for you!"

"We're just—"

"Just friends," said Pauline. "But that's okay. At least you're going out."

Abigail munched on a potato chip and thought about that. She hadn't been social since Nick's death. Maybe this was a good thing. She just had to be careful or she'd end up in jail.

Tony put his phone away and smiled. It was good to hear from Abigail, and she obviously had good news to tell him tonight. He wondered what she had found out about the temp agency and what used to hang on the wall behind that desk.

"It's good to see a smile out of you," George said. They were working on a new project in a large home belonging to one of the deans at the University. He needed his whole house painted, but the vaulted ceiling and stairs were going to be tricky. They had just taken measurements and were sitting at the enormous dining room table calculating them out. The owner was gone. "That was your girl, wasn't it?"

"Yeah," Tony admitted. He tried to stifle his smile, but it wouldn't leave. "She's really something."

"She's good for you."

"So you keep saying."

"You've been down all morning. Is it your grandma?"

"That and the bills," Tony said. "I can't believe what her treatments cost. I have been working with a cancer strategist to give her more time—he's researching her tumor—but it's costing thousands. Insurance won't cover it, but it lengthened her life from what they originally told us she had. Looks like it has stopped working," Tony added, with a wry smile. "But on top of that, I got a bill on Saturday in the mail for her hospital stays last month and the month before. We've got quite a copay."

George shook his head. "What are you going to do?"

Tony sighed and ran his hand through his hair. "I don't know. I guess after she's gone I can sell some of her things," he said quietly. "She doesn't have much. She lived simply."

"You won't get much for the furniture," George said. "My mother-in-law had some vintage furniture, and people still didn't want to pay for it."

George's mother-in-law had died two years ago of cancer. He knew what Tony was going through.

"George?" Tony asked, hesitantly. He had been trying to put this conversation off, but he knew it was time.

"Yes?"

"I was wondering about, you know, funeral costs."

"It's expensive, Tony," George said. "Does she have life insurance?"

Tony shook his head.

"Figure on several thousand. Does she want to be cremated or buried? Does she have a plot?"

Tony shook his head. "I have never really asked her."

"That surprises me. Your grandma is really on top of things. I'm surprised she hasn't planned the whole thing out herself."

Tony felt a lump form in his throat. "She has always done things. I've never really had to worry about stuff like this. I'm finding that I'm not very good at it."

"I can give you information for the funeral home we used, and when the time comes, I'll go with you to get things set up. You have to, you know, pick out the coffin and stuff."

Tony put his head in his hands. He didn't even want to think that far ahead. He had never really had to make decisions other than how to pay his rent and what to eat. He kept his life simple. His grandma had done all the hard stuff when he was growing up. He couldn't imagine life without her.

"Man, I'm sorry. I don't know what to say," George said.

"It's okay." Tony sighed and lifted his head. "Sure. I'd like that. I'm going to need all the help I can get." He slid his chair back and stood up. "Let's head out and buy the paint."

Chapter Thirteen

Tony met her at the door with a deep theatrical bow.

"I would not wish any companion in the world but you," he said with a flourish.

"Shakespeare?"

"The Tempest," said Tony. "It's Miranda speaking to Ferdinand."

Abigail stepped in and shook the snow off her coat. It was forever snowing in this city, it seemed. Tony took her coat and hung it up on a peg by the door, and she noticed a table set with candles.

She raised an eyebrow.

"We're only friends," Tony said. "But I didn't see any reason why I couldn't set a nice table."

He had added a linen tablecloth and some pretty china. "Most of this is from my grandma's house," he said.

"Wow. It's beautiful. And probably not worthy of the fare I bring." She handed him a plastic bag. "I hope you like Chinese food."

"I love it," he said, setting the bag on the table and taking the little paper cartons out. "Did you get fortune cookies?"

"Of course! But no peeking at yours until after dinner."

"Come. Sit. Let's eat and talk."

Tony was wearing a blue cable knit sweater over some jeans. He looked very cozy and warm, and Abigail wondered what it would feel like to be wrapped in his arms.

"Is it okay if I say you look very nice tonight?" Tony asked.

"Yes," she said, feeling herself blush. She told herself she wasn't dressing up for Tony, but that wasn't really true. She had worn a pair of skinny jeans and a soft pink sweater that she knew she looked great in. She had brushed her hair out and left it down, falling loosely over her shoulders. "Thank you."

"Where are your glasses?"

"I left them at home."

If Tony noticed her ring was missing, he didn't say anything. She was grateful for that, as she was already starting to feel self-conscious.

Tony finished pulling the food out of the bag. "Won ton soup, too? Yum! You bought enough to feed a crowd!"

"I wasn't sure what you liked so I got a few things," Abigail said. She had ordered almond chicken, vegetarian fried rice, egg rolls, sweet and sour pork, shrimp lo mein, and the soup. She knew it was a lot of food, but she figured it was better to have too much than not enough.

"This is all perfect. Thank you." Tony pulled out her chair.

"Again?" Abigail said, accepting the chair and letting him help her in. "Such manners."

"My grandma insisted I treat a woman with a certain amount of respect," Tony said.

"I like this grandma of yours," Abigail said.

"It seems she likes you too. She has talked about you quite a bit since your visit."

"What did you tell her?" It pleased Abigail to think Tony had been talking about her.

"That you are wonderful at keeping maps safe, and that you have beautiful eyes."

Tony was gazing across the table at her.

"For a friend," he added.

Abigail smiled.

"So tell me what you learned today," Tony said eagerly, diving into the pork. Abigail had been about to ask him if he wanted to bless the meal. It seemed like something his grandma would do, but when he started dishing out food, she let it pass.

"Well, I know what our next move is," she said and told him everything she learned.

"A stodgy lawyer standing in front of a bookcase," Tony said. "Interesting. Even more interesting is that the map I have looked for for so long was only the first clue in a series. I think it's strange."

"So what are you going to do? I was thinking we could make an appointment with Mr. Stewart."

Tony raised an eyebrow as he popped a shrimp into his mouth. "An appointment? That will take way too long. I plan to break in and have a look. Probably tonight."

"Tony, you can't keep breaking into places. This is much different than the temp agency. This is a law firm. They're bound to have very good security, and you'll get in a lot of trouble if they catch you."

"I don't plan to get caught," Tony said.

"Thieves never do."

"There are really only a few basic security systems out there. Once you know how to break in to the basic three, it's more a matter of tweaking things for each individual case. I know what I'm doing."

"Would your grandma approve?"

"Leave my grandma out of this." His voice was firm. Abigail looked at him across the table. He had stopped eating and was looking at her. "My grandma doesn't need to know any of this, you understand?"

"I'm sorry," Abigail said, surprised at the change in him. "That was inappropriate. I know how much she means to you. I just don't want to see you arrested, Tony."

He put down his fork, and his face softened. "I'm sorry too. There's just so much going on. I'm not sure how long she has. I was talking to George today and he told me I should look into securing her a plot."

"Oh."

"I imagine it's expensive."

"It is," said Abigail. "Nick didn't have one. We hadn't even thought about life insurance yet. I was married for all of a few months and suddenly faced with all of these bills. His parents helped out, but still."

Tony took the rice and scooped some more out on his plate. Then he set it down. "What happened to Nick?"

Abigail moved her shrimp around her plate. Suddenly her finger felt naked, and she wished she had her ring back on. She also wanted to be wearing her glasses right about now. She felt exposed.

"He went out for milk," she said. She set her fork down. "We were both working a lot of hours at our jobs and with graduate studies. We were tired, and I asked him to pick up some groceries. He did. I got home late, around 11 p.m., and all I wanted was a bowl of cereal. But he had forgotten to buy milk. I was upset and asked him how hard was it to remember milk? Milk is a staple, like bread. He said he'd go get it, but it was icy out. I told him not to, just to go to bed and I'd have a piece of toast. I still remember thinking about the blueberry jam he had bought that afternoon and how it would taste good on some toast."

Abigail was looking down at her plate. She could remember that night as if it were yesterday. Her heart started to pound. "But he grabbed his keys and put his coat on. I told him not to be foolish, but I was still mad, and he knew it. And he left. I didn't even kiss him goodbye."

She realized, to her horror, that her hands were starting to shake. She hid them under the table and concentrated on her breathing.

"Abigail, I'm sorry. What happened? A car accident?"

"On his way back, a drunk driver ran a stop sign at a high speed and hit the driver's side of his car. They say it killed him instantly. Jimmy was the cop who came to give me the news."

Abigail got up. "I need more water. Do you want some?"

"No. I'm fine."

She stood at the sink, letting the water run until it got cold. With her back to Tony, she tried to compose herself. But she felt him next to her.

She turned.

"Come here," he said, and pulled her into a hug. She leaned her head on his chest and could hear his heart beating. She was right; the sweater was as soft and cozy as she'd expected, and she melted into his body as his arms wrapped around her. It had been so long since she had been held.

"Tony," she said, clutching the sides of his sweater in her hands. She turned her face up to him. "I can't do this."

"It's just a hug. I'm just comforting you. That's all. No strings."

She leaned her head against him again for a moment, trying to steady her breathing and then drew back. "Thanks. I'm fine." She picked up her water glass. "I should go. You have the information you need."

He put his hand on her wrist. "Wait," he said. "I'm sorry. Please stay. You don't need to be afraid."

"I'm not afraid."

"You are," he said. "But why? Because you blame yourself for Nick's death?"

Because I fell apart, Abigail thought. *Because I didn't handle it well and went away and almost didn't make it back. Because you're right—I'm scared.*

She pulled her wrist free and walked back over to the table and sat down. She wouldn't run, but it was his turn.

"What about you? Have you ever been in love?" she asked.

Tony sat back down, looking a little shaken. She had turned the conversation around quickly, she knew; she was good at deflecting questions. She had worked at it for years.

"Me?" he said. He sighed and seemed to resign himself. "Darci. Her name was Darci. I asked her to marry me."

"Marry you?" She glanced at his finger to make sure there wasn't a ring there.

He saw her look and waved his hand. "She refused. And she turned me in."

"Turned you in? As a thief?"

"Yes. I made the mistake of proposing to her with a stolen ring. Somehow she knew. I have no idea how, probably women's intuition." He laughed. "I took it from a woman I had painted a house for. Sometimes I take painting jobs on the side. She refused to pay me, saying she didn't like the color after it was dry. She was rich and I knew her schedule, so one night when she was out, I broke in and took the ring. It wasn't right, I know, but it was justified. However, it nearly got me caught."

"How did you get out of it?"

"The ring was never reported stolen. I don't know if she didn't notice it, or figured it out or what, but the owner never reported it so they had no proof. Only Darci's word, and she was hell bent on seeing me sent to jail."

"Hell hath no fury like a woman scorned."

Tony laughed. "True enough. She thought if I really loved her I'd have worked hard to pay for a ring. Oh well. Water under the bridge. That was four years ago."

"Has there been anyone else?"

"Nobody special. And I've never told another soul what I do. Except you."

"Why me?"

Tony shrugged. "I don't know." But his eyes locked on to hers. There was a beat of silence. She looked away and picked up her fortune cookie. "Here," she tossed his cookie to him. "Read yours." She cracked open her own.

"A smile is your ticket into another's life." Tony read. He flashed her his smile. She laughed and opened her cookie. "A good way to keep healthy is to eat more Chinese food," she read.

"Blatant marketing," Tony said. They ate their cookies.

By the time they got the table cleaned up, it was after 9 p.m. Tony pulled the curtain aside and peered into the darkness. "It has stopped snowing," he said. "I'm going after that painting. I need to see it."

"Now?"

"Sure. Or after you leave. I don't want you involved in this."

"I'm already involved," Abigail said quietly. She met Tony's eyes.

"This is a very risky job. If I get caught, I'll go to jail."

"Which is why you need me."

"You'll slow me down."

Abigail raised an eyebrow.

"What I meant was..." Tony realized the insult and tried to back peddle. "I just don't want you to get caught."

Abigail pulled the kitchen chair out and sat down again. She planted her elbows firmly on the table.

"Then let's hatch a plan. Tell me how we're going to do this."

For the next two hours, Abigail and Tony went over software and computer images of the building. She knew she was an accomplice, but she was caught up in the mystery and had to see that painting herself. He was able to pull up blueprints from the city and hack his way into their system from home. He figured out which type of security they had and where it was located and then used that information to figure out how to circumvent it. It was fascinating to watch him work. He had a quick mind, and his fingers flew across the keyboard effortlessly. Abigail found herself wondering why he really hadn't gone to college. Surely he could have gotten a scholarship.

"We can't cut the wires or it'll send a report to the security company," he explained. "So if you can't go through, you go around."

"How do we do that?"

He glanced at her jeans. "You have to climb," he said. "Did you wear good shoes?"

She had worn her hiking boots.

"Excellent," he said. "Let me get changed and we'll go."

A few minutes later, Tony emerged from his bedroom wearing black and carrying a zipped bag. He pulled a black jacket from his closet and zipped it closed around him.

Then, thinking again, he took out another jacket.

"This will be a bit big on you, but it's less bulky than your winter coat and very warm," he said, handing Abigail a black jacket like the one he was wearing. "You need to be able to move freely."

She put it on and zipped it up, and he gave her a black cap and some gloves. The gloves were too big.

"I can wear mine," she said, and dug them out of her coat pocket. They were brown leather and pretty supple.

Tony nodded. "Ready?"

"Yes." Abigail hoped she sounded more sure than she felt. Tony looked at her for a moment.

"Are you sure?"

In response, Abigail turned and opened his front door. If she hesitated now, she'd back out.

Tony drove across town and passed the law building. Then he turned the corner and parked the car about a block and a half away.

mrs. chartwell and the cat burglar

"Take these," he said, tossing her his keys. "If things get hairy, I want you to get out and go home. Meet me at my apartment. I'll find a way back."

Abigail pocketed the keys, hoping it wouldn't come to that.

They walked on the sidewalk until they came to the building. It had stopped snowing, and there was nobody out. Most people were probably sleeping at midnight on a Monday.

Tony stepped into the alley and looked up. "We're going in this way," he said. Abigail followed his gaze and saw the fire escape about a floor above her head.

"How are we going to reach the first level?" she whispered.

In response Tony pulled a rope out with a hook on the end of it, and swung it up. It caught on the first try and he gave it a tug. "Climb," he said.

Abigail was glad of the yoga class she had been taking. Her arms and shoulders were strong and she was able to shimmy up the rope, although she was out of breath by the time she got there.

"Impressive." Tony smiled, coming after her. He climbed it in seconds and wasn't even winded. Then they climbed a ladder up to the third floor.

Then he took his phone out and ran it around the edges of the windowpane. Some static lines showed on the screen.

"It's alarmed," he said. He pulled out a tool. Abigail watched as he started to carefully cut the glass inside the frame."

"What are you doing?" Abigail whispered. "I didn't think you were going to destroy property."

"It's the frame that's alarmed. As long as we don't open it, we're okay."

"What about the inside? Won't something catch us once we get in?"

"Only on the first and second floors. Remember the diagram we saw? The rest of the building is only alarmed at the perimeter. Foolish."

He placed a suction cup on the glass and as he finished cutting he carefully lifted it in his gloved hands and laid it on the fire escape. He stuck his head in and looked around.

Then he carefully climbed through and turned to reach a hand out for Abigail.

"You sure? As soon as you cross this threshold, you're breaking the law."

She took a deep breath and grabbed his hand.

"Don't jiggle the window frame," he said, as he helped her through.

They stood inside a room that seemed to be somebody's office. It was small and cluttered, and didn't look like part of a fancy law firm.

"Probably a grunt worker," said Tony.

Abigail felt her heart pounding. She was scared to death, although she'd never admit it to Tony. What was she doing here? They heard a noise and she jumped before she realized it was just a paper blowing off the desk. There was a cold breeze coming in through the open window.

Tony pulled out his penlight. "Stewart's office is upstairs, on the tenth floor."

Abigail silently followed him to the stairwell, and they started to climb. "Aren't these doors alarmed?" she asked.

"No. The stairwell is on the inside, so no reason to. Not a very good fire escape plan though."

They saw a sign reading 10 and went through the door. Tony shone his light around. They were in a plush foyer with a flat screen TV in the waiting area. It was surrounded by offices with glass fronts. The carpet was thick.

Tony whistled. "Mr. Stewart is doing pretty well for himself," he said. He shined his light on each door until he saw Stewart's nameplate.

"Here."

Abigail followed him in, her heart still pounding. Then she saw it.

The painting was hanging above his desk. It must have been about five feet tall and four feet wide. It was of a man with sandy colored hair, wearing a dark suit and standing in front of a bookcase full of books. He had a book in his hand.

"What's he holding?" Abigail asked, moving closer.

Tony pointed his light at the corners of the room.

"What are you doing?"

"Making sure we didn't trip any alarms."

Abigail felt her stomach clench. "Did we?"

"Not that I can see."

"A confident 'no' was more what I was hoping for."

Tony smiled. "Okay, no, then. We didn't. I do this all the time. We'll be fine."

"All the time?"

Tony ignored that, went closer to the painting, and shined his light on it. "It looks like just a law book," he said. "In his hand."

"But the clues must be in this painting, right?"

"That's what I would guess."

Abigail was scanning it, looking at the man, his clothes, the books behind him. "But where? It must be a puzzle."

Then she saw it—more floral patterns cut into the woodwork on the top of the bookcase. "Look."

Tony moved his light up. "The same flowers as were on the temp building." He looked around. "How fast can you run?"

"Why?"

"I think we're going to have to take the painting out the front door. It's not going to fit out that tiny window we came in. I don't think I can unarm the rest of the alarms. They're too sophisticated."

"You can't steal the painting!" Abigail said.

"Well, what do you expect me to do? We didn't come all this way just to look at it. We need it."

They gazed at each other for a moment. Abigail wondered again why she was here. He was a thief. He was about to take someone's painting of their grandfather, handed down over generations.

"It's his grandpa," she said.

Tony smiled. "You're sweet."

Abigail frowned. "Don't condescend. It's wrong to take it and you know it."

"There is nothing either good or bad, but thinking makes it so," Tony said quietly.

"Don't quote *Hamlet* to me. There is too such a thing as good and bad. The world isn't all gray, with morals to be determined by what you can justify. There's black and white too, and this is one of those times. It's simply wrong to steal."

"And break and enter. Yet here you are." Tony frowned, and Abigail could tell he was upset with her. "Your morals are a little mixed up, Abigail."

He did have a point.

"Do you have another plan?" he asked.

She thought for a moment. "Yes!" she said and pulled her phone out of her pocket. "We'll take a picture of it."

Tony raised an eyebrow. "Okay," he said. She was surprised he wasn't going to argue. "But wait a minute." He went over to the window and pulled a shade. "We don't want anybody to see the flash. It's brighter than my light."

She waited, focused on the painting, and took a few pictures. They all turned out really good, considering the lighting.

"Okay, let's get out of here," Tony said. But he stood there, staring at the painting.

"What?" Abigail asked.

"I want to look behind it. Just to be sure. Here, help me."

Abigail pulled a chair over and stood up on it, grabbing one side while Tony took the other. The painting was heavy and it took both of them to lift it up and off of what it was hanging from, which turned out to be a thick cord tied to the back. With some wires.

Abigail frowned. "I wonder what those wires are—"

Tony uttered a four-letter word.

"What?" Abigail said, even as the answer was dawning on her. Tony hefted the painting back up, and they quickly hung it on the wall.

"Run," he said, grabbing her hand.

"Wait! It's crooked!" Abigail straightened it, and they ran out of the room and into the stairwell. Abigail's heart was pounding.

"Was that an alarm?"

"Yes."

"I don't hear anything."

"It's silent. Hopefully that's the only one we tripped."

They heard police sirens in the distance.

"Here." Tony grabbed her hand and burst out of the stairwell.

"Where are we going?" Abigail said. "This isn't the floor we came in on. This is," she glanced wildly around and saw a number five on the door. "This is the fifth floor."

"We're out of time," said Tony. He was jimmying a knife around a window and it soon cracked open. Alarms burst out, so loud after the sudden quiet that Abigail was certain her heart stopped in fear.

She saw they were at the back of the building, over an alley. Tony threw his rope out the window, hooking one end to the sill. He crawled out then, hanging from the rope with one hand, and reached to help Abigail.

"Come on!" he said.

Abigail looked down. The ground was a long way away.

"I can't..." she said, but Tony reached through and hooked his arm around her waist, pulling her out. "Hold on to me," he said, and she had no choice, as she was already halfway out the window. Once her arms were securely around his neck, and he had his arm around her waist, he slid down the rope, landing lightly on his feet and setting her down next to him. He looked up, gave his rope a quick tug, and watched as it came down.

"Run," he said and took her hand once again as they raced down the alley and around a corner. Once out on the main street, Tony slowed to a walk and put the rope in his bag.

Then he entwined his fingers in hers. "Act casual," he said. But she was glancing wildly around her.

"Are we—I mean, did they—"

He squeezed her hand. "Abigail," he said, his voice soft.

"Tony, I—" She couldn't seem to finish a sentence. Her heart was about to burst out of her chest.

"Look at me," he said. She turned to meet his eyes. He gave her a little smile. "It's okay."

"Are you sure they didn't see us?"

Tony looked around. "Pretty sure. But we're not going to wait around to find out."

They were back at the car.

When they got inside, he locked the doors and drove away. As they got closer to home, Abigail began to feel herself relax. A little.

"Oh my gosh," she said, letting out a whoosh of air.

"Pretty exhilarating?" Tony asked.

"No. Terrifying!"

Her heart was still pounding, and she found herself remembering when he asked her to put her arms around him. He had effortlessly lifted her out that window and safely down the rope. He was so warm and strong, and his body heat had warmed the scent of his spicy aftershave. She didn't like that she was so distracted by him that she was forgetting she was probably going to jail.

They pulled into Tony's lot, and he parked the car.

"We made it," Tony said, shutting the engine off. "And we didn't have to steal anything."

He turned to her and smiled.

She looked over at him. He had pulled the hood of his jacket off, and his wavy black hair was all messed up, giving him the look of a little boy.

Her head was telling her to get out and run. To get away from him before she wound up in jail. But her heart was telling her differently.

For a few moments there in the law office, when he wanted to steal the painting, she saw him for what he was, a lowly thief. But when he pressed her up against him to rappel down from the window, when he opened her car door for her on the street, she couldn't help but feel how badly she wanted him.

He reached over, took her hand, and squeezed. "That was a brilliant idea to take a photo," he said.

She saw in the lights from the street that he had a slight beard started. She longed to reach over and touch it. She remembered how Nick's beard would always start coming out by dinnertime.

"Thanks," she said, pulling her hand out of his. She was tired and wanted to go home. The dashboard said it was 1:30 a.m. Morning would come way too soon.

mrs. chartwell and the cat burglar

Abigail came in only long enough to get her coat. Then she left, saying it was going to be hard to get up in the morning. He could tell she was really shaken, and her hands were trembling as she texted him the photos of the painting. He wanted to say something, to tell her again that it was okay, but he didn't want to push her boundaries. He had almost gotten them caught. It was a stupid mistake, one he wasn't usually so careless to make, and he was ashamed of himself.

He watched her car pull away, and then downloaded the photos to his computer so he could enlarge them. He looked at them for a few minutes, but it was 2 a.m. and he needed to get up for work. He was exhausted from not sleeping well, from the worry over his grandmother, and tonight from worrying about Abigail.

He almost declined to take her with him, but he found he couldn't refuse her anything. How could he live with himself, though, if she wound up in prison because of him?

He closed his eyes and remembered how it felt to have her up against him. He probably could have let her rappel down the rope by herself, but he wanted to get out of there quickly, and he admitted that the idea of having her against him had its appeal. She was beautiful, and the soft floral scent that she used on her hair was intoxicating.

He had been surprised when she showed up with her hair down, no glasses, and no wedding ring. What a change from just a few nights ago. He wondered why she was letting her guard down around him. Had he won her over, even if only as a friend? Tony didn't think he could just let it stay at friendship. His feelings were too strong for that. But when he had reached over to take her hand in the car, she had pulled away.

Tonight she was scared, but he was pretty sure she felt the same way about him as he did about her. Or at least had before he almost gotten her thrown in jail.

She was probably just being cautious. And why not? He was a criminal. What sort of life could he offer her? Hanging out with him was a one-way road to trouble.

Unless he could quit stealing.

100

If he found the painting, he'd settle down. He was sure of it.

He thought about what she had told him about her late husband, Nick. It sounded like she blamed herself for his death. No wonder she was hesitant to get in another relationship. She hadn't forgiven herself yet. Or Nick, Tony supposed.

Tony sighed and ran his hands through his hair. He had to get up in a few hours, and he couldn't seem to find any clues in the painting. He was too tired. He'd work on it tomorrow on his lunch hour. As he did every night now, he called the front desk at the hospice to check on his grandma on the twenty-four-hour line they had given him. They told him she was sleeping and had a good evening. He was grateful for that.

He shut down his computers, plugged in his phone, and went to bed. He was asleep within minutes.

Chapter Fourteen

Abigail carefully put away a document she had taken out earlier for a group of school kids. They were studying the city bylaws and wanted to see the very first draft that was written, which was before the university even existed.

"They're cute, aren't they?" Pauline said when Abigail returned to her desk.

"They?"

"The school children. Did you see how big their eyes got when you told them how old that document was?"

Abigail smiled. "It was cool. And yes, they're cute. You wonder how many of them will even remember this a year or two from now."

Pauline grabbed a file folder and put the handful of papers she was carrying inside it. "Do you think you ever want kids?" she asked casually.

"What? Me?" Abigail scowled. She pushed her glasses back up on the bridge of her nose. "That will be a bit hard without a man."

"They have ways. There are sperm banks."

"That still requires a man. I don't think I want to buy a child like I would a carton of milk."

"Hey," said Pauline. "That's unfair. My sister got her kids that way. Her husband is infertile."

"I'm sorry." Abigail instantly regretted the words. She had been antsy lately. She felt uncomfortable on the inside and couldn't quite put her finger on it. And last night had shaken her up. She had lain awake for a long time listening for sirens, certain Jimmy was going to come knocking on her door with handcuffs. She hadn't fallen asleep until 3 a.m. and was exhausted. Then she had dreamed about the painting of the lawyer.

"You and Tony would have beautiful kids," Pauline said. "All that thick hair. And you both have incredible eyes."

"Stop it!" Abigail threw a paper clip and hit her on the shoulder. "He's just a friend."

"So you say," said Pauline. "But I see the ring is still missing."

Abigail sighed. "He does have nice eyes."

Pauline smiled an "I told you so" smile and went back to her section. Abigail pinned up a stray hair from her bun and turned to her computer. She had data to enter.

But she got distracted after two entries and took her phone out. She went to her photos and brought up the picture of the lawyer. She had been staring at it all morning and still couldn't figure out the clues. She suspected it had to do with the books, but she couldn't figure out what. They were all academic books. Mostly law, but then some Jane Austin, Mary Shelley, Darwin, the plays of Shakespeare. She smiled at that last one, because it made her think of Tony and his quotations. But why those titles? The books were so random. Perhaps they were the favorites of the Stewart in the painting.

She took another look, sighed, and put it back in her pocket. She returned to her work. She was categorizing the maps they received this morning. Some were maritime maps and some were land maps. She had to designate which each was by labeling it a certain color and then putting it in a subcategory by age.

That's it! Categories! She pulled her phone back out and brought the picture in closer. The books were in categories. The books were all law-related except those on the bottom shelf, right behind the lawyer. On that shelf were several books of literature grouped together. Next to them were six science books. Then next to them some plays, and a book on Monet and Beethoven.

Literature, science and the arts.

There was one odd book out, sitting a bit crooked at the end of the shelf. It was on Italian architecture and had a floral symbol on the spine. She brought it in closer. It was a bit blurry, but she was pretty sure it was the same floral symbol they kept seeing. It was on the building at the temp agency, and here it was again.

Smiling, she called Tony.

"I figured it out!" she said without waiting for him to say "hello."

"Really?"

"Yes!"

"Hold on a minute." She could hear metal squeaking, as if Tony was descending a ladder, and then the creak of a door. "I wanted to find some place I could talk in private," he said. "So tell me!"

"The books are grouped into categories," she said excitedly. "There are books of great literature, science, and the arts. I think that's a clue that we're supposed to go to the LS&A building on campus! Then there's this last book, standing a bit alone on the shelf, on Italian architecture. It has a symbol on its spine, the same one that's on the map and the building. I think we're supposed to look for that symbol."

There was silence on the line. She could hear Tony breathing. "That's it!" he said finally. "Wow. Abigail, you're brilliant!" She heard him blow her a kiss over the phone. "Impressionate!" he said in Italian.

"When do you want to go?" she asked.

"I need to work. I've been missing a lot, and my boss isn't too happy. Then I need to visit my grandma after work. Can I pick you up and take you with me? We can check out the LS&A building after that. It's open late because of the students."

"Okay," Abigail said. "It's my night to close. Pick me up at seven o'clock?"

"I'll be there." Tony hung up.

"A date?"

Abigail jumped. Pauline had come out of nowhere. How much had she heard?

"No. He's taking me to see his grandma."

"Then why are you blushing?"

Abigail smiled. "Pauline, don't you have some work to do? Someplace else?"

"I just came to grab another file."

After Pauline left, Abigail forced herself back to her data entry. She could hardly wait until tonight.

Tony was whistling.

"I take it that was the girl," George said.

"Her name is Abigail."

George rolled his brush in some paint and started applying the cream paint to the wall. "You have another date?"

"I'm taking her to see Grandma."

"That's not a date!" George said.

Tony laughed. "We've had dinner together twice. She keeps insisting we're just friends."

"And yet she walked across campus to see where you work."

"And she took her wedding ring off."

"What?"

Tony explained what he knew about Nick.

"Hmmmmmmm."

"What do you mean 'hmmm'?"

George rolled his brush in the paint again. "There has to be more to the story. He died six years ago? And she's still not wanting to date? I don't think she's told you everything."

Tony thought about that. It did make sense that she was hiding something. The woman went through a great deal to make herself unavailable. It didn't seem like she had much of a social life or even cared for one. She dressed down. She hid behind those glasses and her ring. Or at least she *had* hidden behind the ring. Tony wondered if he was the reason she had finally removed it.

"Maybe you're right," he said.

"I'm sure it's not a big deal. You could always ask her."

"Yes. I guess I could."

The day couldn't move fast enough for Tony. At promptly 5:30 p.m. he started packing up. "George, dry your brushes. Let's get the van back to the office so I can get Abigail on time."

George dutifully obeyed, and Tony pulled into the library parking lot at 6 p.m. He was an hour early, but didn't care. He was excited to see Abigail and maybe talk about the picture some more.

Instead, there was another woman at her desk, a blonde, whom he remembered her calling...what was her name? Paula?

"Hi," she said when she saw him walk through. "I can go get Abigail. Our director has her working on a project in the back. I'm staying late to cover her desk."

Pauline, that was it. At least he was pretty sure that was it.

"Hi," he said, extending his hand to her. "I'm Tony."

"I remember," the woman said. She took his hand in hers. "Pauline."

"You don't have to go get her. I'm an hour early."

There was a brief, awkward silence. "So, are you two going out?" Pauline said with a little smile.

"Kind of." Tony wondered how much he should tell her. "We're having dinner, but afterward I'm going to see my grandma in hospice and Abigail's coming with me. It's not exactly what you would call fun."

Pauline's face creased into an expression of sadness. "I'm so sorry. She told me about your grandma. How is she doing?"

"She had a good night," he said. "Hopefully she had a good day. I called and checked on her at lunchtime, and she was sleeping then."

Pauline nodded and then took out a stack of papers and started sorting them.

Tony wanted to ask her about Abigail, but he didn't want to intrude. He stood there at the desk, fiddling with his fingers. Pauline finally looked back up at him. "Can I help you with something? Or if you want, there's a café down on the first floor. You could get something to drink."

She was trying to get rid of him. "Okay," he said. He turned to go.

"Tony?"

"Yes?" He stopped and looked at Pauline.

"Is there something you wanted to ask me?" she said.

"Um…no." Where had his smoothness gone? He was usually so suave with women. "I mean…" He sighed and walked back to the desk. "How long have you worked with Abigail?"

"Let's see…probably seven or eight years."

"So you knew Nick?"

He couldn't read Pauline's expression. She hesitated for a moment and then said, "Yes. I did."

"She really loved him, didn't she?"

"Very much."

Tony nodded. He had so many more questions, but he didn't want to intrude on Abigail's privacy.

"When he died, she took it really hard," Pauline said quietly. "If you're wondering if she's over him, I don't know. I don't think that's something you get over. I think you just learn to move on with the pain somewhere inside of you."

Tony nodded. He had been thinking about that a lot, with his grandma's death on his mind. There wasn't a day he could remember not talking to her.

"Is she letting you in?"

He was a little shocked at Pauline's straightforwardness. He shook his head. "Not really. Maybe a little."

"She hasn't let anyone in. Don't take it personally. Just be gentle with her, okay?"

Tony met Pauline's eyes. They were earnest. She really cared for her friend.

"Okay," he said. "Can you tell me what happened after?"

"After?"

"After Nick died."

Pauline gathered her stack of papers and glanced at her watch. "I'm sorry, Tony. I just saw the time. I really need to get these organized. Why don't you go get something to drink in the café, and I'll send Abigail down when she's finished. Okay?"

Now Tony knew for sure she was trying to get rid of him. He had pushed too far. "Okay. I'm sorry. I didn't mean to pry."

"It's okay. I just have to get this done."

Tony walked over to the elevator and took the car down to the first floor.

There was a man down there starting to mop the café floor. Bob, he remembered. He was the janitor on duty the night Tony broke in.

Tony nodded a hello and then went to the vending machine. The cashier had cashed out for the night and closed. He selected a cola and went to sit at a table to sip it.

A little after 7 p.m., Abigail came down. "Hi, Tony. Pauline told me you got here early."

He looked up. She was wearing a gray skirt and a black, close-fitting top that outlined her nicely. She had her hair up in a bun and her glasses on.

"Hi," he said, getting up. He pulled out a chair, and she sat down.

"Hi, Mrs. Chartwell," said Bob, pausing from his mopping. "I see you're staying late tonight."

"I've already closed up," she told him. "The alarms are set up on my floor. Don't set any of them off."

Bob laughed. "What? And spoil the fun?" He came over to their table. "Who's your friend?"

"This is Tony," Abigail said. "Tony, this is Bob."

The two men shook hands. "Tony and I have some things to discuss," Abigail said, when the other man didn't seem to be going anywhere.

"Okay. Back to work then," Bob said and put his earbuds in. He took his bucket and pushed the elevator button to move up to the second floor.

"He's got a thing for you," Tony said when Bob was gone.

"Just a bit. I keep discouraging it."

"Good," Tony said, reaching across the table and taking her hand in his. "So, you figured it out, did you? That was brilliant. The LS&A building!"

Abigail's eyes glowed with excitement. "Yes! And I had some time this afternoon to look over a few architecture books. That symbol wasn't used a lot during that era. It's pretty rare so should be easy to spot."

Her hand felt so warm in his. He found it difficult to concentrate when he touched her. She still wasn't wearing her ring, he saw. He absently rubbed the white mark on her finger where it had been.

108

She pulled her hand away. "Should we go?"

"Yes." He stood up, realizing the move had been too intimate. "Have you eaten?"

"I had dinner at my desk at five."

Tony had grabbed some pizza on his way across town after work and had eaten in the car. "I hope Pauline didn't notice. I told her I was taking you out to dinner." He needed to be more careful.

"No. She was downstairs then."

The drive to the hospice was uneventful. Tony always felt a little nervous when he first went in. What if she had died while he was away?

But the nurse greeted him at the front desk. "Hi, Tony," she said. "Your grandma is sitting up and waiting for you."

He was relieved and felt a rush of blood go through him. He didn't realize he had been holding his breath.

She was sitting up in bed, like the nurse said, reading from her Bible. She had some color to her and looked better than she had in a while.

"Tony," she said, holding out her arms. He bent down and gave her a hug. "And you brought that pretty girl back with you." She motioned for Abigail to come and get a hug too. It warmed Tony's heart to see his two favorite women hugging.

He smiled. "That's Abigail," he said.

"I remember her name, Tony. I'm dying, not daft."

He laughed. "I'm sorry, Grandma."

They made small talk about their day at work, and she told them she had eaten some green Jell-O for dinner.

"I think it's actually better than the red," she said. "Maybe because it's my favorite color. They all kind of taste the same, so I go by color."

She smiled. He was glad to see her in a good humor.

"What were you reading?" Abigail asked.

"The story of the prodigal son," Grandma said. "I always liked that story. Do you know it?"

Abigail nodded.

"Tony does too, but he has probably forgotten," Grandma teased and then patted him on the hand. "The prodigal son ran away and spent all his inheritance, but when he came back, his father welcomed him with open arms. That's my favorite part. Can you imagine having a child run away? You worry and worry and wonder and then suddenly he reappears! He comes home!" Grandma patted her Bible. "And his dad takes him back in. He's so excited he throws a party. I can see that. I was a parent too."

She closed her eyes for a bit. "But I always wondered about the other son, didn't you? He spent so many years working hard and then here comes his lousy brother, who gets the same treatment. No wonder he was mad. I think it's only human."

"I don't understand that part," Abigail said. "Doesn't it seem rather unfair that the younger brother spent all the money by partying, and the older brother was such a good son who worked hard, and the father treats them both the same?"

"But that's the beauty of the story," said Grandma. She opened her eyes again and faced Abigail. "No matter what he did, his father was willing to forgive him, simply because the prodigal son asked. His father was rejoicing that he was back. The son was humble. He came home and asked to just feed the pigs and sleep in the barn. He knew he was wrong. But his father saw so much more in him."

"And the older brother?"

"He was always treated well. And he was invited to the party. Not once did the father reject him. He loved him too. It's never too late to change. Or forgive."

They were quiet for a moment. Abigail glanced over at Tony, who was avoiding her eyes. Did Grandma know more than she let on?

"Tony told me he's looking for a painting you want," Abigail said.

Grandma smiled and closed her eyes again. "Yes, Abigail. It's a miracle painting. That's a story about forgiveness, too."

"The painting is of your mother?"

"Yes. Has he ever told you the story?"

"Not all of it."

"Well then. Settle back and I'll tell you."

Chapter Fifteen

Abigail sat back in her chair and watched as Grandma closed her Bible. The old woman lay there for a while, her eyes closed, and Abigail wondered if she was asleep. Then she opened them again and glanced at Tony.

"He has his eyes," she said.

"Whose eyes?"

"My father's," Grandma said. "My mother told me that. Tony has Russo's eyes."

Abigail looked across the bed at Tony, who had turned a little red. "Grandma…" he said. The older woman grasped his hand in hers. Then she turned back to Abigail.

"I love this boy," she said. "I raised him, you know."

"He told me. He told me how wonderful you have been to him."

Abigail found herself falling in love with this woman. She had never had grandparents. Her mother's family died when she was young, and she hardly remembered them. Her father was estranged from his parents, and she had never met them. She wished this woman had been her grandma.

"My mother was named Margaret Grace Ventura," said Grandma. "She was very beautiful, much like you are. Only she had dark hair, almost black, and vivid dark eyes. Very large, very beautiful eyes. I remember as a little girl, wherever we went, she turned heads."

Grandma paused and asked Tony for a drink of water. He carefully lifted the Styrofoam cup and put the straw to her lips. She took a few sips and then waved it away.

"During her junior year in college, she went to Paris to study. She was an art student and had won a scholarship to stay there for the entire summer semester. She was so excited and packed up her supplies to head over on a boat. She left behind a handsome young man, whom she was engaged to marry. His name was Peter, and he was going into investment banking. Mother was very happy and planned to return at the end of summer and graduate that December. Then they were going to marry on New Year's Eve.

"In Paris, she stayed with a host family. She just loved them and made friends right away with the family's daughter. She loved her classes, too. Then one breezy, sunny day, not long after she got there, she was strolling the streets up to the Basilica of Sacre-Coeur. She saw a man painting, and she stopped to admire his work. "Incredible," she said to him. He was painting a portrait of a young child as the boy sat for him. Margaret said the eyes were so lifelike she could hardly tell the difference between the painting and the child." Grandma laughed. "Sounds like a bit of an exaggeration to me, but Russo's portraits have always been very realistic." Abigail remembered seeing some of them in the museum when a tour of his work came through the University. They were incredible. But she preferred his work as an impressionist more. The flowers, the waterscapes, the field of daisies.

"She complimented Russo on his work, and he said to her, in Italian, 'Gratzi. Sei bello,' not knowing that my mother spoke Italian. Then he added, in English, *'Did my heart love till now? Forswear it, sight! For I ne'er saw true beauty till this night.'* Quoting Shakespeare! How romantic. But *Romeo and Juliet?* Look how that story ended."

Abigail was surprised at the quotation and looked over at Tony. He glanced down at his hands, refusing to meet her eyes.

"Margaret said it happened then. She looked at Russo and knew, just *knew*, that here was the love of her life."

Grandma stopped and closed her eyes again. "I'm tired, children. Let me rest a minute."

"Should we go?" Abigail asked, not wanting the story to end.

"No, not yet."

Abigail sat back in her chair, quiet. Those were the exact same words Tony had spoken to her that night they met. Was he playing her then? Did he mean them?

She looked over at him again, and he met her eyes. She wasn't sure what to say, so she remained quiet. She heard Grandma's breathing and the clock on the wall ticking. After about five minutes, a nurse came in. "I need to take her blood pressure," she said quietly. "Is she asleep?"

Grandma stirred and opened her eyes. "I'm awake," she said. The nurse checked her vitals and left.

"Where was I? Oh yes, Margaret was in love. She told me she blushed prettily and sat on a wooden box next to him and watched him paint the boy. When he was finished, he took her out for a drink, and they talked about art until two in the morning. Then he walked her home, along the river Siene and back to the place where she was staying. She didn't know at that time that he was married.

"He kissed her goodnight and asked to see her the following night. She agreed, and stole away from a party she was supposed to go to in order to meet him down by the river. This time he took her back to his studio and told her about his wife and daughter. His wife was verbally abusive and critical of his work. He was very unhappy with his marriage. After hours of talking and some good French wine, they made love in his studio."

Grandma smiled at Abigail. "This is the adult-rated part, here. Margaret never gave me the details, but apparently after that night, they met nightly for the three months that she was in Paris. He was quite wealthy at this point in his career. One evening he bought her a ring. He said he wanted to marry her, but he knew he never could publically, so he said his vows to her that night, privately, and slipped it on her finger. He called her "Laurel" after that, as a symbol of his intent."

Grandma grew quiet, resting again. Abigail glanced across at Tony, an eyebrow raised.

"Laurel leaves are laid on the ground at French weddings for the bride and groom to walk over," he said. "They never wilt or lose their green foliage, so are thought to represent eternity and eternal love."

"Romantic," Abigail said quietly.

Grandma smiled. "Yes. One evening, Russo asked if he could paint her. He finished it right before she left to come back to America and promised to send it to her when it dried."

"And that's the painting you're looking for?"

Grandma nodded. "Apparently while it was still drying, his wife came into the studio and found it. She had suspected an affair. She grabbed the painting and was about to destroy it, but he took it from her and fled. She torched his studio."

"She *burned* the studio?" Abigail said.

"Yes. Burned it to the ground. All those beautiful paintings that the world will never see! They could never prove it was her. Anyway, Russo fled with the painting and gave it to a friend. He went back to his wife and denied everything, to protect my mother. If the school had found out, she could have lost her scholarship or been kicked out. Women just didn't sleep around back then. Mom didn't find out she was pregnant until she was back in the states."

"Wow," Abigail said. She imagined the young woman, pregnant out of wedlock and alone. "Did she tell her parents?"

"They disowned her, and of course her engagement to Peter was broken off. She wrote to Russo. He never wrote back, but a sum of money was sent to her every few months. Right before his death, Russo sent her a large sum. My mother worked some, but basically he took care of us. She never saw him again, though." Grandma's eyes looked wistful. "He never got to see me."

"He committed suicide," Abigail said. She remembered the story. Found in his studio with a gunshot wound to his head.

"Yes," Grandma said quietly. "The newspapers said he died of a broken heart, yearning for his love. People have been looking for that painting since then. But many believe it was a legend. His wife did her best to turn it into fiction."

"What happened to the ring?" Abigail asked.

Grandma reached out, took Abigail's hand, and then closed her eyes. "I'll tell you the rest of the story later. I'm tired now." She turned to Tony and opened her eyes again. "Good night, Tony. I love you."

Tony stood and kissed her on the forehead. "I love you too, Grandma."

Abigail stood up and wiped a tear from her eye. "That was a wonderful story. Thank you for sharing it."

Abigail and Tony were quiet in the car as he drove her back to her place. She ran inside and changed into some jeans and a sweater and then joined him back in the car.

"So it's true," she said. "The story of the lost painting."

Tony smiled. "It is. At least that's what I've been told my entire life. Russo is my great-grandfather."

"Did she ever marry?"

"Margaret? No. Grandma said she never loved another man. He was her soul mate, if only for three months. It's hard to believe."

"It doesn't take long to love that deeply," Abigail said. She rubbed the naked spot on her finger. "I was only married for three months."

Tony glanced over at her but didn't say anything.

Soon they were back in town. He parked down the street from the LS&A building.

"Do you have a plan?" Abigail asked.

"Just walk around and see what we can find. I copied the words down that were in Latin on the map. There's a reference to water. Let's start at the fountain."

They approached the fountain in front of the building, which was turned off now in the winter weather. They stood and stared at it for a bit, Tony with his hands in his pockets. She watched him for a minute while his attention was on the fountain, watching the wind flutter the curls peeking out from underneath his toboggan. Finally he said, "Let's go inside."

The building was nearly empty because it was 9:30 at night. Students wandered through on their way back to their dorms or some other gathering space, probably to study. Abigail found herself missing the academic life. She was glad she still worked on the University campus.

"Water," she said. "Any other references?"

"Just the words for water and stone, and then a brief sentence that roughly translated to a head sitting on a chair."

"A head sitting on a chair?"

"Yes, it was a vague clue in Latin, and it was hard enough for me to read it in that language. A head. A bust? The Dean?"

"On a chair," mused Abigail. "So the department chair? I'd say it's the Dean."

They stopped just inside the door as they saw a bust of the Dean.

"Funny," said Tony. He put his hands in his pockets again. He seemed tired to her.

"Are you okay?" she asked.

"Sure," he said. "Just worried about my grandma."

Abigail was about to say something when Tony pointed to a sign that said "Dean's Office."

They followed it and took some stairs down. His office, on the lower level and probably overlooking the courtyard in the back, was locked. All the lights were turned out.

"Nobody's down here," Abigail said. It was kind of spooky in the empty hall.

Tony jiggled the door and then pulled a tool out of his jacket pocket. Within seconds, he had picked the lock.

"What are you doing?" Abigail whispered.

"Shhhhh." He pushed the door open and went inside. "We're looking for an architectural pattern, right?"

"Yes." Abigail pulled her phone out and brought up a photo. "It should look like this." She showed him the floral symbol. Tony took his pen light out of his other pocket and shone it on the walls. They didn't see anything.

"This is where his secretary sits," he said. "Let's go through." He pushed another door open, which lead directly into the Dean's office. Abigail couldn't even begin to imagine the trouble she'd be in if they were found. She'd be fired, for sure.

"I think I might wait in the hall," she said.

"Okay."

She wandered back out and leaned her back against the wall. Her heart was pounding. For what seemed like the hundredth time, she asked herself what she was doing. She was throwing her entire life away for a criminal just because he was hot, that's what she was doing. And his grandma. She thought about his grandma and shook her head. She couldn't let her heart get in the way. That's what got her in trouble before.

She took a deep, ragged breath to calm her racing heart and realized she was thirsty. She saw a water fountain just down the hall, sharing a wall with the Dean's office, and went to get a drink. The water was cool and felt good going down. As she stepped back and wiped some from her chin, her eye caught something. It was a floral symbol on the wall beside the drinking fountain, molded into the plaster. The same one as in the picture on her phone.

"Tony!" she said in a loud whisper. When he didn't hear her, she ran back to the door and almost bumped into him as he was coming out.

"I don't see anything," he said, at the same time she said, "I think I found it!"

She grabbed his hand and pulled him down the hall. "There!"

He shone his light on it and ran his hand across it. A smile slowly spread across his face. "This is it!" he whispered.

"Is it behind there?" Abigail wondered.

Tony was running his hand across the wall. He took his phone and used his sonic app.

It beeped.

"There's something inside the wall!" he said, excitedly. Abigail watched as he scanned back and forth. It was detecting something large just below and to the right of the water fountain. "It's not near the pipes, which would be good in case they leaked, or a plumber needed to be called. It's more here, to the right, near the floor. Hidden."

"Behind plaster."

"Yes, behind plaster."

Tony walked back down the hall, and she followed. They turned the corner into the secretary's office and Abigail waited while Tony walked back to what should be the area behind the fountain in the Dean's office. He touched it. "Plaster."

He stood there, staring.

Then they heard a ding. The elevator door opened, and someone walked out.

Tony bolted, grabbed Abigail, and pulled her through the door and around a corner. They heard footsteps walking quietly by them, going towards the Dean's office. The figure didn't turn on any lights.

"What the—?" They heard a voice.

"Crap!" Tony whispered. "I left the door open!"

Abigail's heart started beating triple time again. Then they heard a voice. "Yes, this is the Dean. I need the campus police. I think somebody has been in my office."

Tony grabbed Abigail's hand and pulled her toward the stairwell. He carefully, quietly opened the stairwell door and pulled her through. Once inside, he closed it quietly.

"Let's go," he said, and they ran up the stairs and out into the lobby. "Did you leave fingerprints anywhere?"

"Just on the drinking fountain," Abigail said.

"They won't be able to pull them. Too many sets from all the students during the day."

"They shouldn't be on file anyplace anyway."

"Mine are," Tony said, but he had his gloves on.

They walked casually back to his car. It took the entire walk before Abigail could breathe normally again. She kept waiting for a police officer to shout "stop!" from behind her. Inside the car, she let Tony close her door, and she wrapped her arms around herself.

"Are you okay?"

"Almost," she said and gave a little laugh.

He started the car and neither of them spoke as he drove her to her house. He parked in front and shut off the engine.

"I'm sorry," he said.

"For what?"

"For almost getting us caught. Again. I was sloppy. Technically it was okay for us to be on that floor. It's the school, after all. It's just not cool to break into offices. I got too comfortable."

"It's okay," Abigail said.

"You shouldn't come back with me next time. I'm going to need to break through that plaster. I have to figure out when is the best time to do that."

Abigail sat there, thinking. She wanted to see the painting almost as badly as Tony did. But she was also now an accessory to a crime. Or a future crime.

"Don't do it that way," she said. "Let's get help. We can tell professionals where the painting is, or where we think it is, and they can help us get it out."

"And they'll take it."

"Not if it belongs to you. They can't."

"What proof do I have?"

Abigail was silent. She looked at her hands. Tony pulled his gloves off and reached over and took hold of one. His hand was warm and strong.

"That's the second time we almost got caught. I want you to stay out of this. I'll call you when I get the painting out. You can go with me to the hospice to show Grandma."

She took her free hand and ran her fingers across his. They were soft hands with a few calluses from working with tools. She remembered the tenderness with which he held his grandma's hand and kissed her forehead.

"Abigail?"

She turned to look at him.

"What are you thinking?" he asked. He looked uncertain. "I've put you in a bad position, haven't I? You're friends with a cop, and now you know about a crime that will be committed."

Abigail leaned toward Tony. His spicy aftershave was intoxicating. She closed her eyes, and before she could stop herself, she kissed him on the lips. He moved in and kissed her back, his grip on her hand tightening. She pulled away and smiled. "Good night, Tony," she said and fled from the car.

———◇———————◇———

What on earth had just happened? Tony watched her run up her steps and let herself into her house. She kissed him. He still felt her lips on his, and the flowery smell of her hair lingered.

He sighed and leaned his head back against the car seat. What was he doing? He was about to break the law and was taking her down with him. No, he wouldn't do that. He wouldn't allow her to come with him when he went in to get the painting.

He didn't want her to see him sitting there, so he started up the car and drove back to his apartment. He was pumped up with excitement over finding the painting and that kiss.

He couldn't figure out which was better.

Definitely the kiss.

But the painting was something he knew how to deal with. According to his sonic scans, whatever was hidden in the wall was about 17 x 24 inches. He'd have to find a tool that would quietly cut through plaster. If he broke through, or used his angle grinder, there would be dust everywhere, which would make a nice canvas for fingerprints and footprints. It would also make a lot of noise.

Maybe he could remove the drinking fountain. It was ceramic and looked like it was plastered in.

Tony sighed as he opened up the door to his apartment, wondering why the man who hid the painting went through such trouble. It couldn't possibly all be to save a pregnant young woman's reputation. Was he planning to give it to Margaret, or to sell it? But he had apparently died before he could do either. Had the man who had stolen the painting and hired him, found out about his trickery and killed him? Fortunately, the mapmaker had left behind clues. And they had led him this far.

Tony was distracted by a blinking light. There was a message waiting for him on his answering machine. He pushed the button.

It was a man's voice, telling him that the medication he wanted was available.

Tony replayed the message and wrote down the information. He had found a drug trial for his grandmother. It was expensive and hard to get her on the list because of her age, but it sounded like they had decided to let her in. He had to make arrangements for it to be delivered to the hospice and administered. He'd call them first thing in the morning.

And he had to pay for it.

He pulled off his sweater, leaving on the T-shirt he had on underneath. In his bedroom, he opened a drawer and moved his socks aside. From the false bottom, he pulled out an exquisitely set diamond necklace. He held it up, and it glinted in the light. It was beautiful. He put it back, shut the drawer, and went to make a phone call. A woman answered.

"Charlotte," he said, in his most charming voice. "Are you ready to put some ice around that stunning neck of yours?"

Her laughter was like crystal tinkling. He could picture her wearing silk pajamas, her nails well manicured, her hair perfect even in sleep. She was the type. He had met her at a fundraising dinner he attended last fall. She was looking for a particular piece, and he now had it. He had acquired it a few months ago.

"More than ready, darling," she said.

"I'll buy you dinner tomorrow night. The Apricot Lounge. Say...8 p.m.?"

"Looking forward to it."

"You know where to wire the money?"

"I do. I wrote it on the palm of my hand that night, remember?"

"It's still there?"

"The memory of your touch is still there, darling. That's all I need."

"I'll see you tomorrow night."

Tony smiled and hung up the phone. Then he stretched, changed his clothes, and went to bed.

Chapter Sixteen

Abigail was floating on air the next morning. Between nearly being caught for breaking into the Dean's office (although, she told herself, *she* didn't break in, *Tony* did) and the feelings that came from being so close to Tony once again, her emotions were bubbling over. That romantic story that Grandma had spun had only made it worse.

She knew she was in trouble. There was no way she should let Tony get close to her. She could think of two very clear reasons to keep him away: one involved jail and the second one involved the fact that he might break her heart and she'd end up like...well, like last time. She didn't want to think about that, so she pushed it down.

She had prayed about it a lot last night, mostly because she had trouble sleeping. Why had she allowed herself to kiss Tony? The truth was she couldn't stop herself. He was so handsome and so present, and she felt herself falling for him more each time she saw him. She told herself they were just friends, but that wasn't true. What she felt for him was more than friendship. She just didn't know what to do about it. She knew she was messing with him, the way she went back and forth, but last night she hadn't been thinking clearly with all the adrenaline coursing through her. When he took hold of her hand and she felt his warmth, she just had to have more.

Abigail sighed and put her head in her hands, resting her elbows on her desk. It was only 9:10 a.m. and she was already bored with her job. She had maps to file and documents to repair, and she was ready to be done and see Tony again.

Just then a text came in. She jumped and grabbed her phone. It was from Tony and her heart stirred.

Good morning, Beautiful.

She smiled and texted back. **Good morning.**

So...

She waited.

Are we more than friends, then? Or was that just a friendly departure kiss?

She hesitated. Then typed **Maybe we should get together again as an experiment. Then I can decide for sure.**

Experiment? I like that!

She laughed.

How about dinner? I have some place special I want to take you. It'll have to be Thursday night. I have to work tonight.

She felt a stab of disappointment at having to go a day without seeing him.

Work? Without ME?

Not THAT work. I'm still pondering that.

Oh. She typed. **Thursday is fine. Pick me up at home?**

Her phone rang, and she jumped. "Hello?"

"Hello, Beautiful." It was Tony's deep, musical voice. "I thought all this texting was silly. I needed to hear your voice."

"After you determined if it was safe?"

"Exactly."

She smiled. "About that kiss..."

"Yes?"

"Tony...I don't really know what I'm doing." She twisted a loose strand of hair that had fallen out of her bun.

"That makes two of us. We'll just take it slow. I promise."

There was a moment of silence. She could hear him breathing. *He's a thief,* she told herself. *You're headed for trouble.* But her heart didn't seem to care.

"So I guess I'll see you Thursday night." Her voice was shaky.

"I'll make it worth the wait. I promise."

She waited until he hung up and then turned off her phone and put it in her purse. She wrapped her arms around herself. It was going to be a long two days to wait.

Tony arrived at the restaurant early that evening and sat so he faced the door and could see Charlotte come in. She was dressed elegantly, as usual, and he watched her flirt with the young man at coat-check and the host as he led her to the table.

Tony stood as she approached, and he pulled out her chair.

"Charlotte, you look beautiful as always," he said, kissing her on the cheek.

"And you are your usual, handsome self," she said, letting him slide her chair in as she sat. He sat back down across the small table from her. She was somewhere in her forties, he wasn't sure where, but she was beautiful. Her blond hair was up and showed off her earrings, which looked like 2-carat diamonds, the real thing. She could afford them.

"So good to see you again, darling," she said. "I'm excited to see what you brought me."

"Let's order drinks first," Tony said, picking out a chardonnay from the wine list.

The waiter brought them their drinks, and Charlotte started talking about her latest work. She owned several businesses, and they were all doing very well.

"I'm going to a fundraiser next month, which is what I wanted the new necklace for," she said, seductively tracing her finger along her neckline. "Do you think it will look good on me?"

"Charlotte, everything looks good on you," Tony said.

She smiled and sat back. "You still have the charm," she said. "Maybe we can extend the evening a bit?"

Normally he wouldn't have hesitated, but suddenly the only woman he wanted was Abigail. Charlotte was fun, and he had enjoyed the few nights they spent together. But he realized that now he wanted more than a friendly romp. He smiled at her. "Not tonight, Charlotte. I need to go straight home after this."

"Long day?"

"Something like that."

She watched him for a moment and then put on a slight pout. "Men don't usually turn me down, Tony. I'm rich, I'm athletic, and if I'm not mistaken, satisfying. I don't think you had any complaints last time."

"None at all," he said. "You are all three of those things, if not more."

"Then what is it?"

Tony hesitated. "I just need to get home."

She studied him across the table. "You're in love," Charlotte said suddenly.

"What?"

"You're in love. Someone has stolen the heart of the thief," she said quietly. "My hat's off to whoever this woman is."

Tony neither confirmed nor denied her suspicion but instead took a sip of his wine.

"I knew it," Charlotte said. She smiled. "Well, we can still enjoy our dinner. It's enough for me just to sit and stare at your gorgeous face for an hour or so. And to await what you have for me. You did bring it?"

"Of course," he said, reaching into his jacket pocket. "I don't think you'll be disappointed."

Abigail decided to run some errands since she had the evening free. She briefly thought about visiting Tony's grandma, but that seemed weird. She had gotten strangely attached to the elderly woman in just two visits and wanted to see how she was doing.

She could just ask Tony.

She texted him, and he replied that Grandma had been fine at lunchtime.

We have a new trial medication for her, he typed. **I'll tell you about it tomorrow night. Gotta go.**

She made herself a light meal and then decided to pick up some groceries. After that, she would do a bit of laundry before bed.

She couldn't find her savings card in her wallet and remembered she had left it in her other purse when she switched bags last week. She walked into her closet, where her other purses hung on the wall. She lifted it off its hook and the purse underneath it fell as well.

She hadn't used that bag in a few years. She should get rid of it. She picked it up and was about to hang it back on the hook when she caught sight of a hospital bracelet inside it. It was the one she had worn when she was discharged, and she had cut it off of her wrist in the car on the way home. Her hands started to tremble. She picked it up and read it. *Abigail Chartwell. Winston Psychiatric Hospital.* She swallowed hard and stuffed it back inside the old purse. She tried to push the memory down, but it persisted, and she had to look at the bracelet again for a moment. She fingered the plastic bracelet and then closed her fist around it.

She heard her therapist's voice in her head: *Just breathe in and out. Focus on the present.*

Her heart pounded fiercely, and she looked around for something to focus on. Her scarves. Purple. Red. Blue. Aqua. She didn't really look good in the aqua one.

Breathe.

She touched a scarf. Silky. She took another deep breath and felt her heart rate slowing. The panic was receding.

She got herself a glass of water and decided to get going. She hadn't had a panic attack in a long time and didn't want to hang around thinking up another one.

Abigail drove the few miles to the grocery store. She didn't like to shop downtown because the prices were higher, so she always drove an extra ten minutes to the Fresh Mart. It was in a different part of town, just on the outskirts.

She was done in less than an hour. On her drive back through town, she decided to stop at the ice cream store on the corner to pick up a pint for tonight. She could have gotten one at the grocery store, but this particular ice cream shop had homemade flavors, and their chocolate peanut butter cup was the best.

Since it was a weekday evening, she found a spot easily, right in front of the Apricot Lounge. She got out and put some coins in the meter. She should only be five or ten minutes.

The white lights wound around the trees along the street twinkled above her head, giving her the feeling of being in a magical wonderland. She wondered what Tony was doing right now. He said he sometimes worked private homes on his off hours, so he was probably painting somebody's mansion.

She turned, and that's when she saw him through the window. Inside the Apricot Lounge, Tony was sitting at a table with a blond woman. He was dressed in a black suit with a white shirt and looked very handsome. He was talking, and the woman was laughing. She held out her hand, and Tony took it and gently kissed the back of it.

Then he handed her an envelope. She looked inside and tucked it in her purse. She smiled sweetly across the table at him and put her head on her hands, staring into his eyes. Her dress was very low cut.

Abigail couldn't peel her own eyes away from the scene. Her heart started pounding, and she felt her stomach churning. She felt like she was going to throw up.

Forgetting about the ice cream, she climbed back in her car and drove home. She hardly saw the streets as she turned down them, and at home, she mechanically put her groceries away. She then walked upstairs and curled up in her bed.

He had lied to her. She had trusted him, and he had lied.

Why had she been so stupid as to think he was anything to her but a distraction? She was caught up in the excitement of finding this painting and had let her feelings take over, something she promised herself she'd never, ever do again.

Warm tears fell down her cheeks, dampening her pillow. She turned her face into the downy softness, surprised at the strong feelings she was having.

Now she was crying harder. Why had she let her guard down? She was obviously only someone fun for him. Another conquest. She didn't need this. Or him. He was trouble, one way or another.

She felt her heart beating quickly and worked to still her breathing. For a while, she laid there, thinking only of breathing. The cat purred softly next to her head. As she began to calm, she turned over and wiped her tear-stained face with the back of her hand.

"He was with another woman," she explained to Cocoa, who was watching her with curious, worried eyes.

But he said he was working.
But he kissed that woman's hand.

She thought about the painting and how much she wanted to see it.

"His grandma would be so thrilled if we found it," she told Cocoa. "And I think we have. I think we've found it. I really want to see it."

For a moment, her resolve wavered. What if Tony had been working tonight? She'd just have to figure out a way to know for sure.

Chapter Seventeen

"Grandma," Tony said quietly, leaning over her. "Grandma, it's Tony. I have some good news."

She fluttered her eyes and opened them. "Tony," she said, weakly. She took her hand out from under the covers and grasped his. "My dear boy." She gave his hand a little squeeze.

He didn't like how she looked today. She wasn't her usual, perky self. They said she hadn't eaten breakfast, and her lunch tray sat by her bed. Jell-O, chicken soup, some saltines.

Soft foods. He wouldn't eat that either. He thought he should have brought her a chocolate shake.

"Hi," he said again.

"Shouldn't you be at work?" Grandma said. She kept hold of his hand.

"I'm here on my lunch hour," Tony said. "My boss understands. He's letting me flex my hours a little bit. I'll just have to work later tonight."

"How's your girl?"

"Abigail? We're going out tonight. I have an amazing evening planned for her."

But he was a bit worried about Abigail. He had tried to call her twice this morning and had texted her several times. She hadn't responded to any of them.

"What's your news?" Grandma asked.

"I got you a new medication," Tony said, smiling. He had researched online and talked to her cancer doctor. They agreed to try it on her, since she was otherwise healthy for her age. It was a long shot, her oncologist said, but one Tony was willing to take. At $10,000 per dose and no insurance coverage, he hoped it worked the first time. They said it might take two doses to see really good results, but they should know within two weeks if it was going to work for her or not.

"A new medication?"

"Yes!" Tony was excited. "It could give you another year or two. You could go home, Grandma!"

"I am going home, Tony. That's where I'm preparing to go. It's just a bit of a difficult journey."

"No, Grandma," Tony said. He didn't want her to talk like that. "I want you home with *me*." He gave a little laugh and squeezed her hand. "I'm not ready to say goodbye yet, so you need to stick around."

"Tony, I'm old," Grandma said. "Let me die. It's my time."

She looked tired. She gave him a little smile and closed her eyes.

"No, Grandma," Tony said, fighting back tears. He wondered if the humane thing would be to let her go, but he couldn't. He just couldn't. Not yet. "Please try it. Just try it. For me. They can give it to you right here at the hospice. You don't even have to leave your room. It's by injection."

Grandma opened her eyes and looked at him again. He wiped away a tear that had escaped. "Oh, Tony, my dear boy. I'm so sorry you have to go through this."

"Grandma, please."

She smiled again and closed her eyes. "Okay, Tony. For you, I'll try."

"Thank you." He laid his head on her chest. She stroked his hair, like she had done when he was little. "Thank you," he whispered.

"I'm glad you found Abigail," Grandma said. "She's beautiful. She glows from the inside. Her heart is big. I can see a lot of love in her."

Tony sat up. "I think she likes me," he said, a shy smile playing at his lips.

"Think?" Grandma said. "The way she looks at you, I know she loves you. Hang on to her."

"I plan to."

Grandma reached for her Bible, which was on her nightstand, and handed it to Tony. "Will you read to me a bit?"

"Sure," he said, opening it up. "What do you want me to read?"

"I'm working my way through the Psalms," she said. "I find them comforting."

She closed her eyes, and Tony started to read.

Abigail ignored Tony's calls and texts all morning. She remembered he was going to see his grandma on his lunch hour, so promptly at 11:45 a.m. she left and went over to the house he told her that he and George were working at. Tony said the owner wasn't there during the day, so she figured this would be the perfect time to confront George alone.

She found the house on a cul-de-sac a few miles from the University. She got out of her car, which she drove to work that morning so she'd have a vehicle, and pushed her glasses up on her nose.

Squaring her shoulders, she walked up to the front door and rang the bell.

After about a minute, George opened it.

"Abigail!" he said, looking surprised. "Tony's not here."

"I know. I came to see you."

He was quiet for a moment and then a woman's voice behind him said, "Invite her in!"

George stepped out of the way, and Abigail walked in. She stomped the snow off of her boots and unwound her scarf. The house was huge, well decorated, and had a lot of natural light coming in from the big windows around the vaulted ceiling. The whole place smelled strongly of paint.

"Come in," said a dark-haired woman who was sitting at the kitchen table with a half-eaten sandwich in front of her. Across from her was another sandwich, mostly gone, and some pickles.

"I'm Laney, George's wife," she said standing. "I brought George his lunch. We thought we could sneak a little time in together today. Sometimes he works late, so I have to see him when I can." She smiled and held out her hand. Abigail shook it. She seemed pleasant, and Abigail immediately liked her.

"I'm Abigail," she said.

"I know who you are." Her eyes twinkled. "George has told me about how smitten Tony is with you."

George pulled out a third chair, and Abigail sat down. "I'd offer you some food, but this is all we have."

"It's okay," Abigail said, waving it away. "I came to talk. Not eat."

The two looked at her expectantly. She swallowed. Now that she was here, she wasn't sure what to say. She took her glasses off and put them on the table.

"I saw Tony with another woman," she said and then realized how foolish it sounded the moment she said it. "I mean, I know we're not really exclusive or anything. Or even dating, really. But I thought we were. I mean, I thought he really liked me. But he told me he was working last night, and instead I saw him out to dinner in a really nice restaurant with a woman. A blond woman. An attractive, blond woman. And maybe they were just working, but he kissed her. Her hand, but still, it was a kiss."

The words rushed out, and Abigail blushed, feeling foolish. She stood up. "I'm sorry. This is stupid. I'll leave so you can enjoy your lunch."

"No, please sit back down," George said in a very mature manner, which made her feel like a child. "Please, Abigail. So what you're trying to find out is whether or not Tony is cheating on you?"

"Yes. No. I guess he can't be cheating on me if we're not dating, but…" Abigail sighed. "I guess what I want to know before I get into this is can I trust him?"

The answer was obvious to her now that she had the words out. He was a thief. But her heart was still involved.

George and Laney looked at each other across the table.

"Yes," George said. Laney raised her eyebrows.

"Yes, I believe you can," George said. "He really likes you, Abigail. I haven't seen Tony like this over a girl before. Ever. I don't think he'd do anything to mess it up."

Abigail looked at Laney. "What do you think?"

"He's crazy about you," George interrupted. "I don't want to put words in his mouth, but I'm pretty sure he really likes you. I wouldn't worry."

"George," Laney said. "Be fair." She turned to Abigail. "Tony is the nicest guy you'll ever meet. He's funny, charming, smart, and handsome. He turns the head of girls everywhere we go. And he can also use that charm to turn their hearts. Tony can walk into a restaurant with us for dinner and walk out with the waitress. He can stand in line at the post office and end up with a date with the woman in line behind him. He's very likeable. And fun. George could be right. Tony could be ready to settle down with you. From what George has told me, he's crazy about you, and honestly, none of the women he has had before have lasted this long."

"I've only known him a week or so."

"Exactly," said Laney.

Abigail thought about that for a moment. "I see."

"There was Darci," George murmured.

"Darci." Laney waved the thought away with her hand. "She doesn't count. That wasn't love. That was lust. And we never liked her."

"Laney, we shouldn't be having this conversation." George looked uncomfortable. "Not without Tony. I don't feel right about this."

"We're not talking bad about Tony," Laney said. "But she needs to know. He's a player. But he's also one heck of a wonderful guy, so if you're the girl who lands him, you'll be one lucky woman."

Abigail picked up her glasses and started chewing on the frame. "Okay," she said. "Thank you."

"Any other questions?"

"Yes. Why would he meet a woman for work?" She looked at George.

After a moment of silence, George shrugged. "Maybe someone who wants him to paint her home or her office space?"

"Wouldn't he tell you about that?"

"Not always," George said. "I work a second job as a handyman, so I don't always have the time to work odd jobs with him at night."

Abigail nodded and then looked at her watch. "Thank you." She turned to Laney. "Thank you both. I need to get back to work. Please don't tell Tony I was here."

She hurried to the door and let herself out.

It didn't make sense that he would meet the woman for a job, so he had to be on a date. He was obviously flirting when she saw him through the window. She bit her lip. She felt better for having talked to George and Laney. She could see it, the playboy in him. The mischievous eyes, the smooth talk, the handsome face. He could easily melt someone's heart. He had melted hers.

But she couldn't allow herself to be hurt. Not again. She had to stay away from Tony before that happened. She decided not to make a big deal of it. She would tell him that she had reconsidered their relationship and decided that it wasn't right. She couldn't date a thief, and she wouldn't see him again. Then she could go back to her life as it used to be, safe and uncomplicated.

It twisted her stomach when she thought of how far she had let this relationship go. She was breaking into places and stealing a map from the library – for *him*.

What had she gotten herself involved in?

Tony texted her again after lunch. This time she replied.

I can't go out tonight.

Why?

She didn't want to tell him over a text. He *had* been nice to her. She could at least let him down in person.

I can't talk now. I'm at work.

Can we talk later?

She paused. She didn't want to face him tonight. She decided to ignore him for now and stall. **Gotta go.**

She turned off her phone.

She wasn't surprised when he showed up at her door at 7 p.m. She had thought about leaving, about not being home, but she didn't want to be mean to him. She at least owed him an explanation.

She opened the door, and he was standing there with flowers. She was still dressed in her work clothes, her hair up. She had her glasses on.

134

"For you," he said, holding them out to her.

She kept her hands by her side.

"Tony," she said. The air was cold. She thought of asking him inside, but was afraid she wouldn't want him to leave.

"Uh-oh," he said when she didn't take the flowers. "What have I done?"

"Nothing. But I've been thinking. I can't see you anymore. I just can't. This is crazy. I don't want to date. I never wanted to date. And then you came and I got all...you made me..."

Tony raised his eyebrows.

"Feel?" he supplied the word for her.

She frowned. "I'm not interested. I'm just not. I prefer to be alone."

Tony's arms dropped to his side and one of the flowers fell out onto the snowy porch. "What did I do? One moment you were kissing me. Now, you don't want to see me? Ever again? Not even as friends?"

"That's right. I'm messed up, see? You don't want to get involved with me."

"I think I have a right to decide that."

They stared at each other for a moment. Cocoa came to the door, and Abigail brushed her back with her foot. "No. You don't."

"Abigail," Tony said. "If this is about you losing Nick...I can't promise I will never die, but I can promise I will never hurt you."

That was too much. Abigail felt the anger surge up in her.

"You already have. Now go, Tony. Good luck with finding the painting, and I truly am sorry about your grandma. She's a sweet lady. But go and don't come back. Oh, and I need that map returned."

She tried to close the door, but Tony put his foot in it. "Abigail, please. What did I do? How did I hurt you?"

"Who was that woman you were with last night? The blonde? You said you were working." The words were out before she could stop them.

Tony looked caught. He took a deep breath, as if weighing his words. "Where did you see us?"

"In the Apricot Lounge. I was going to the ice cream shop and there you were."

"I *was* working."

Abigail gave a humorless smile. "Working is one way of putting it, I suppose. Is that how you get what you want? How you get your painting jobs? Or were you wooing her so you could get inside her house as a painter and then steal something like you did Darci's ring? You 'work' your painting clients?" She knew that was unfair, but she was hurting. She felt so stupid for ever letting her guard down.

"I was working my *other* job," he said quietly. "I had something to sell, and she wanted to buy it."

Abigail was silent for a moment. That had never crossed her mind.

"Oh."

She felt the hot tears sting her eyes. "Well, all the more reason to never see you again. You're a thief, Tony. A thief. What kind of a life is that? Now go!"

Her voice was angry, and she saw the hurt in his eyes. He held her gaze for a moment and then turned and walked down her steps. She closed the door and leaned against it. She could feel the cold through her back. She heard him start his car and listened as he pulled away. Then she cried.

Chapter Eighteen

Tony drove around town aimlessly. The flowers had fallen out of their wrapper and were sitting on the floor of the car beneath the passenger seat. He had really screwed up this time.

He pulled into his parking lot and slowly walked up to his apartment. He let himself in and flopped down on his couch. He had hurt her. He promised her he would never hurt her, and he had. That's what he got for a life of dishonesty.

But he had never *intended* to hurt her. That's the last thing he wanted to do.

He picked up his phone and texted her.

I'm so sorry. Please let me explain.

He would tell her that he was quitting. No more lies. No more stealing.

But what about his grandma? How would he pay for her treatments? He pounded his fist into the pillow on the couch in frustration.

He wasn't expecting anything, so it startled him when his phone beeped with a reply.

I can't trust you. Please leave me alone.

I can explain.

No explanation necessary. We were not exclusive. You have been a good friend. I just need some space.

Why was Abigail this upset over him meeting with Charlotte? Were her feelings for him really that strong?

Tony tried to call her, but she sent it to voicemail.

"Abigail, please let me explain. Let's talk."

He hung up. Then she texted him.

Good night, Tony. It has been fun. Please give your grandma my best wishes, and when you are

done with what you borrowed, please return it. You can mail it to me. Don't come back to the library.

She was cutting him off completely? It sounded like it. She didn't even want to see him at work.

Abigail, please.

His text went unanswered. For the next hour, he waited for her to answer. He thought of going back over to her house, but that would be pushing it. He didn't want to hurt her. Not again. But he needed to talk to her, to explain.

That's when he thought of Pauline. Yes, that was it. Pauline!

He got on his computer and did a search on "Paulines" in the city. There were thirty-four. Who knew it was such a popular name? And what if the phone was under her husband's name? He went to the library's database and tried to log on. The security wasn't too tight, and within an hour, he had broken into their employee database. They really needed to beef up the security in the place if those maps were as valuable as Abigail said.

The University's records showed a Pauline Smith working at the library but had no home address. Smith? Couldn't she have a more unique name? He searched for Smiths in the city, and the number was even larger than the number of Paulines. But when he put them together, he came up with a Drew Smith married to a Pauline Smith on Cleveland Drive.

He wrote down the address and logged off, erasing any ties that would trace back to him.

He'd go see her.

Pauline's house was a bungalow in a cute little subdivision near campus. He stood on her porch, hand raised to knock. He hadn't really thought about what he wanted to say. Oh well. He'd have to wing it. He knocked. When nobody answered, he rang the bell.

A porch light came on above his head, and Pauline pulled aside the curtain on the door and peeked out. Then she disappeared, and he heard the locks give.

"Tony!" she said. "What are you doing here? Is Abigail okay?"

He heard kids crying inside. "I was hoping you could tell me that."

Pauline turned. "Can you kids be quiet, please!"

She brushed some hair behind her ears. "It's late. They're tired."

"I'm sorry," Tony said, suddenly realizing how bad an idea it was to stop by this late. It was 9 p.m.

"Why are you here?"

"I'm..." He wasn't sure what to say. "I'm worried about Abigail. Look, I'll go. This was a bad idea." He turned to leave.

"No, come in. They're usually in bed by now."

Tony stepped inside. There were toys on the floor, and a big, yellow dog came over to greet him, wagging its tail. It had a bonnet tied around its head.

Pauline reached down and pulled the hat off the poor dog. "Drew? Abigail's friend is here. Can you finish putting the kids to bed?"

"Sure thing, honey!" Tony heard a voice from upstairs. "Get in here and brush your teeth, kids, or no TV tomorrow!"

There was a thundering of feet above his head and things got quiet.

"Here, sit down," Pauline said, moving a laundry basket of unfolded clothes off the couch. "Would you like something to drink?"

"No. I'm okay," Tony said.

"Is Abigail okay?" Pauline repeated, her eyes wide.

"She is. I guess. She's mad at me and won't answer my calls."

Pauline crinkled her eyes. "Oh, Tony, I'm sorry. What happened?"

Tony told her the story George had told him.

"I tried to apologize, but she won't talk to me. The thing I don't get is why she's so upset. It doesn't make sense."

Pauline was quiet for a minute, twisting the corner of an afghan in her fingers. "How much do you love her?" she said, finally.

Love? Tony had never used the word love before. But he knew the instant Pauline said it that he loved Abigail a lot.

"Never mind," Pauline said. "Your eyes say it all. And you're here asking about her."

She sighed. "I can't tell you a lot. Let's just say that after Nick died, Abigail shut down. You're the first guy she has shown any interest in. She won't even go out with us, for fun. "

"Me?"

"Yes. You and only you. Which is the only reason I let you into my house this late at night to discuss my friend when I should probably stay out of this." Pauline looked long and hard at him. "She hasn't dated at all in six years."

"It really hurt her when he died," he said. "That's understandable."

"It did. She took it hard."

"I would imagine anyone would."

Pauline looked at him for a moment, as if weighing how much to tell him. "The thing is, Tony, she *really* took it hard. She blamed herself. She blamed him. She really loved him. They were inseparable from the time they met."

"How did they meet?" he asked. He wanted to know more, wanted to keep the conversation going.

Pauline smiled and got a far away look in her eyes. "She said she was sitting in the library with a stack of books, studying for finals. He walked in and sat across from her because it was the only seat. She looked at him and *knew*. And he was thinking the same thing, because he slipped her a note across the table. That started a conversation, which got them 'shushed,' which got them both laughing. They were asked to leave the library. So they went out for pizza and fell in love."

"Did you meet him?"

"Yes. She started working at the library before they were married. He was wonderful. Smart, witty, always smiling. He stopped by all the time and brought her flowers or candy. If she wasn't there, he left a note. They had a fun, flirty romance. She was different then."

"And then he died."

"Yes."

"And you said she took it hard, but I get the idea there's more to the story."

Pauline resumed twisting the yarn on the afghan's fringe. From upstairs, they heard Drew herding the kids to bed, little footsteps running down the hall and voices giggling.

"This really isn't my story to tell," Pauline said. "She's doing well now. But she's lonely. You're good for her, Tony. Don't let her get away without a fight, okay?"

Tony gave her a little smile. "I'm not sure if there's anything I can do to reach her. She's shut me out, it appears."

"You don't seem to me like a man who gives up easily," Pauline said.

Tony thought about that. "I don't want to hurt her."

"You won't. And please don't mention this conversation. I had no right to tell you these things. I just care about her. She's my friend, and I see how she lights up when you come around. I want her to be happy."

"Me too," Tony said.

Chapter Nineteen

Abigail almost took the day off work to hide from Tony but decided that was stupid. She was happy with her job and wasn't about to let him mess up her life.

But she couldn't think.

"Are you okay?" Pauline asked when she brought a fried bagel by around 10 a.m. It was cinnamon sugar.

"Thank you," Abigail said, taking it and setting it down on a napkin. She wasn't hungry. "Yes, I'm okay. Why do you ask?"

"You're just awfully quiet," Pauline said. "I mean, more than usual."

Ms. Scott, the library director, came by then. "Abigail? I was cataloguing this morning. We seem to be missing a map in the local section. The drawer is empty."

Abigail felt her stomach sink. She should have guessed Ms. Scott would notice something missing. "I sent it out to be cleaned," she lied.

"Can you log it in? We really need to be more careful."

"Yes. I will. I'm sorry," she said. Mrs. Scott thanked her and left. She had to get that map back in the library. But that meant seeing Tony.

"And you're so pale," said Pauline.

"Pauline, please. Leave."

"Look." Pauline came around the desk so she was facing Abigail. "Tony stopped by last night."

"Here?"

"No. At my house."

"At your *house?*"

"He's worried about you. He says you aren't returning his calls. I told him I don't want to get involved."

Abigail frowned. "Good. So don't."

142

"Abby." Pauline hardly ever called her that; it was Nick's name for her. But she wanted her attention. "He seems like a nice guy. What happened?"

Abigail pulled her phone out and looked at the time. "You know, I do think I'm hungry. I'm going to call Martha and invite myself to lunch. If Tony stops by here during his lunch hour, tell him I don't want to see him." She closed down the file on her computer that she had been working on.

"Okay," Pauline said. "I'll cover for you during lunch. I'm sorry I got involved. It's just that he showed up on my doorstep. He looked desperate."

Abigail wanted to turn to Pauline and get more information. She wanted to know what Tony said and what Pauline had said back. But why? The best thing to do was get him out of her head.

To distract herself, she quickly pulled out her phone again and called Martha to invite herself to lunch. Martha was just making up some chicken salad.

"Sounds good," Abigail said. "See you in a little bit."

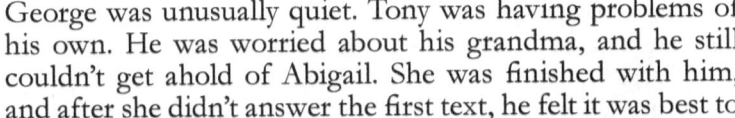

George was unusually quiet. Tony was having problems of his own. He was worried about his grandma, and he still couldn't get ahold of Abigail. She was finished with him, and after she didn't answer the first text, he felt it was best to leave her alone. Tony tried to make conversation with George, but George said very little and seemed extra interested in the details of his job.

"Did you and Laney have a fight?" Tony asked.

"No, nothing like that," George said.

Then more silence. George was closing the paint cans and stepping on the lid of each one, making sure it was sealed. He was avoiding Tony's eyes. Tony was about to question him again when George stood up and looked at him.

"Tony, she told me not to tell you, but she was here."

"Who was where?"

"Abigail. She stopped by here during lunch yesterday."

Tony thought about that. "But she knew I was going to see my grandma at lunchtime."

George stood there, waiting for Tony to catch on.

"Oh," he said. So she was avoiding him. But what did she want with George?

"Tell me why she was here," Tony said.

George sighed a dramatically heavy sigh. "I told her I didn't want to talk about you," George said. "But Laney thought she should know."

"Know what?"

"Things."

"What things?" Tony asked quietly.

"Apparently she saw you in the Apricot Lounge with an attractive woman on Wednesday evening. She said you were flirting, and you kissed this woman's hand."

Tony closed his eyes and stood there with his hands in his pocket. He took a deep breath and blew the air out in a long sigh. "And you're just now telling me this?" He had been so distracted with thinking about his grandma yesterday afternoon he wasn't even aware if George had been acting strangely.

"Were you on a date?" George asked.

Tony looked up at his friend. "No," he said quietly. "I was with a client. She wants me to do a job for her."

"I told Abigail you took paint jobs in the evenings sometimes. So I was right! I knew you wouldn't cheat on her! Or would it be cheating? You guys *are* together, right?"

"I like to think so. Now I'm not so sure."

"So it wasn't a date."

"No."

"But you kissed her hand." George didn't usually get this personal, but Laney would want to know details.

"I might have been flirting a little."

George sighed. "Tony, don't mess this up. You're crazy about Abigail. I know you are. She'd be good for you."

"What did she ask you?"

"If she could trust you."

"What *things* did you and Laney tell her?"

"It doesn't matter."

"I think it does," Tony said. He rubbed his forehead with his hand. He was getting a headache.

"Laney told her what a wonderful man you are and what a catch."

Tony narrowed his eyes. "And?"

"And..." George sighed. "And she might have mentioned that you're a bit of a player."

"What? Geez, George!"

"I told her not to say anything. It wasn't her place. But you know Laney."

"Oh geez," Tony said. "No wonder she's so upset with me."

"She is?"

"Yes. We were supposed to go out last night and she canceled. After telling me off."

"Man, I'm sorry."

Lunch was chicken salad sandwiches on croissants with cantaloupe slices on the side. Martha had baked up some of her scrumptious blueberry muffins, and they were sitting on the kitchen counter, still warm.

"Martha, how on earth did you do all this just since I called you?" Abigail asked.

"The muffins were already in the oven," she said. "And I had the chicken boiled up yesterday. All just good timing." Martha wiped her hands on her apron and sat down. "It may need a little salt," she said, handing Abigail the shaker.

"You always make everything seem so easy," Abigail said, salting her sandwich and then picking out a few pieces of cantaloupe.

The back door opened, and Jimmy stepped in, shaking snow off his hat.

"Jimmy! I didn't know you were coming!" Abigail said, getting up to give him a hug. He took his boots off and walked over to Martha, pecking her on the cheek.

"Martha called and told me you were coming to lunch. I was in the neighborhood patrolling and figured I'd stop in. I could smell Martha's muffins clear over on State Street."

They blessed the meal and then made small talk. Abigail relaxed. It felt good to be someplace safe doing something familiar.

"How's that guy of yours?" Martha asked.

"What guy?" Abigail said stiffening. Oh well. Couldn't forget the real world forever.

"That Italian guy you were telling us about."

"Oh, Tony," said Abigail. She wanted to turn this topic around. Fast. "He's okay. His grandmother has cancer though."

"Oh dear," Martha said. "How bad?"

"Bad, I think. She's over in Dove Hospice."

"That doesn't sound good."

"No. She's really sweet."

Abigail told them what little she knew about his grandma and then Martha relayed a similar story about a woman in church who had terminal cancer.

"Enough of this sad talk," Jimmy said after a few minutes. "I don't want to go back to work depressed."

"How's work going?" Martha asked.

"It has been a busy week. Oh! Remember the Stewart and Cross Law Firm? It was broken into the other night."

Abigail felt her stomach clench. That was the firm she and Tony had broken into.

"That law firm that Jonathan has?" Martha asked.

"Who's Jonathan?" Abigail asked.

"He's a guy I went to school with," said Jimmy. "His grandfather started it."

"Did they take anything?" Martha asked.

Abigail stared down at her plate, trying to focus on cutting her melon off the rind. She couldn't look at them.

"No. But it looks like they were after a painting he has behind his desk, or at least that's what triggered the alarm. I have no idea why. It's not worth that much."

"Who knows what drives the minds of youths these days," said Martha. "That's probably who it was—kids."

"Maybe," Jimmy said, chewing thoughtfully. "But it's more likely it was a professional. The job was neatly done until the end. It looks like the unexpected alarm made them leave quickly."

146

Martha shook her head.

"Are the muffins ready?" Abigail interrupted. "I have to get back to work."

"Of course, dear." Martha got up.

"Bring some of that Irish butter," Jimmy said. "So anyway, we're thinking this guy is the same one we've been chasing for a few years. He was always untouchable before. He's very smart, knows how to turn the security off, and gets in without breaking stuff. But he got sloppy at the law firm, and possibly once before."

Jimmy glanced over at Abigail. "We're thinking maybe it was the same guy who broke into the library."

"Oh?" Abigail realized her voice sounded higher than normal. "What makes you think that?"

"Just the way he works." Jimmy cut off a slice of butter, broke his muffin in half, and spread it on. "Mmmmm. This is why I married you, Martha."

"Oh, honey, you married me for more than that," Martha said, winking at him. Abigail felt the chicken churning in her stomach and thought she might throw up. It was all she could do to sit there and try to relax as she ate her muffin. They talked about other stuff for the next five minutes or so and then Jimmy pushed his chair back and got up.

"I've got to get back to the office," he said. "I'll see you tonight." He kissed Martha and put his hat back on.

Abigail glanced at her watch. "I have to get back too," she said. "Can I help you clean up?"

Martha brushed her away with her hand. "No. Scoot. You two get back to your jobs. I've got this."

"Thanks, Martha." Abigail gave her a quick kiss on the cheek and put her coat on.

"Bring that Tony of yours around sometime," Martha said. "I'll cook him my chicken pot pie."

Tony took a long lunch and went back home to figure some things out on his computer. He needed to figure out a way to get the painting out of the LS&A building without anybody seeing him. Since it was a university campus, there were always people up and around. Anybody could walk by at any moment. It's not like he could rappel down from the ceiling—there were no skylights. There weren't even any windows in that corridor. He'd have to go in through the doors like a normal person and walk to the spot. But how do you break apart plaster without making a lot of noise? And he'd have to watch out for the water pipes.

He searched the Internet for a while but was distracted. Not good. He had already lost an entire day on the search.

There was something else weighing heavier on his heart. He needed to make it right.

The bus ride back to work was only ten minutes, but it gave her time to settle her nerves. Abigail returned to work feeling both worried about Tony and somewhat sleepy from all the great food. She was hoping for a slow afternoon.

Instead, Tony showed up at her desk with a dozen yellow roses. Pauline was standing beside her, and at her friend's gasp, Abigail looked up.

"Hi," Tony said.

Abigail frowned. "What's the occasion?"

"Does there need to be an occasion?"

Tony offered her the flowers, but she kept her hands on her desk. He was wearing a gray sweater over faded jeans, and his hair was curling from the dampness of the snow. He had on a black wool coat, unbuttoned, which had remnants of snow on the shoulders.

Pauline cleared her throat. "I...um...have some filing to do." She walked back into the stacks.

"You're making me look like an idiot," Tony whispered, attempting humor. "Please take the roses."

Abigail raised an eyebrow. "You *are* an idiot."

He fought a smile and lost. "You're right about that." Then he pulled a small package about the size of a bracelet box out of his pocket.

"Here, I brought you a gift," Tony said. "I think you'll like it."

"Did you steal it?"

"Wow. What did I do to deserve that?"

"Stole."

"Abigail, can we go somewhere and talk?"

She didn't meet his eyes. "I don't have anything to say."

He set the box on the desk. "It's not jewelry. And it's not stolen. Open it."

Curiosity got the best of her, and she picked it up. It was light, and she tore the white paper off it. Inside was a key.

"It fits into the padlock on the locker next to yours in the break room. Go see what's in there." He leaned closer to her. "The cameras are in a loop. You have an hour." He laid the roses on the desk, put his hands in his pockets, and walked out.

Abigail watched him leave and stared for a moment at the doors where he departed. But she knew she didn't have time for contemplating anything. She glanced around to make sure nobody was approaching her desk. Then she headed for the break room.

Thankfully, it was empty. It smelled of warmed-up leftovers and stale coffee. She saw the padlock immediately, and opened it easily with the key. She took the tube in her hand and discreetly (she hoped) brought it close to her side. As she did, an envelope fell out of the locker. Yellow, the size of a greeting card. There was no name on it, but she didn't have to think twice to know whom it was for. And from.

She grabbed it and walked out, back into the stacks.

"Abigail?" Ms. Scott said.

She froze. Took a deep breath. "Yes?"

"I need to talk to you later this afternoon about acquiring some new maps. Michigan State needs a place to house some ancients, and we need to figure out if we can take them."

"Sure," Abigail said, trying not to look like she was carrying a recently stolen item.

"There's a lot to consider," Ms. Scott mused. "Plan for about an hour."

After she left, Abigail went back to the map's spot and pulled the drawer out. She pulled on some gloves, figuring it had been handled enough recently without them. She carefully removed it from the tube and rolled it out. As she put it back in its glass drawer, she looked at it carefully for those hidden blue messages. She couldn't see them. She took it over to the desk and rolled it out under a light. Nothing. Then, not wanting to handle it anymore in case someone asked what she was doing, she put it back in the drawer and pushed it shut. She took a long, deep breath.

Then she went back to her desk and put the yellow envelope on the desk. She took a bite of the cinnamon sugar bagel and chewed, thinking. She should just throw it away and be done with it. But she couldn't really justify that. Tony had been nothing but a friend, had promised her nothing, and had done nothing to hurt her. She couldn't really justify her sudden anger at him. She sighed again and looked at the roses. They lay on the desk where she had left them. Yellow. Symbolic for friendship. She knew Tony well enough to know he was sending her a message. He was saying he'd respect her space, but he still wanted to be friends.

She sighed a third time and opened the card. Inside was a handwritten note.

Let me take you out tonight and explain. No ties. No expectations. Just friends. Please.

That's all it said. She closed her eyes. There was no denying she missed him. He was so unique, smart, and creative. He was the first person since Nick who made her feel alive. But he was a thief, her close friend was a cop, and she was treading on thin ice. Somebody was going to get hurt.

"Abigail?" It was Pauline. She was holding a vase filled with water. "For the roses?"

Abigail smiled at her ruefully and accepted it. She unwrapped the roses and put them in, taking her time to arrange them. Pauline was still standing there.

"Yellow is for friendship," Pauline said quietly.

"I know," Abigail said.

"Abigail?"

"I don't want to talk about it," she said, meeting her friend's eyes.

For once, Pauline let it go. "Okay," she said and gave her a squeeze on the shoulder. "Friends is okay. I just want to know where he stands in case he comes back."

"I'll let you know tomorrow. Let me sleep on it."

Pauline left to finish her work. Abigail picked up her phone and held it in front of her, hesitating. Then she texted **YES. 7 p.m.** and sent it to Tony.

Chapter Twenty

He picked her up promptly at 7 p.m. He came in quietly, not putting on airs or quoting Shakespeare. She was buttoning up her coat and looked up when he walked through the double doors. He was still wearing the same sweater and jeans he had on earlier but looked freshly shaved.

"Thank you," he said quietly. She nodded, catching a scent of his aftershave. She set the alarm and then pulled on her gloves before they went out into the cold night air.

Neither of them spoke for a moment. "Do you want to go see my grandma first?" he asked. "Or are you hungry?"

"No, I'm not hungry," she said, although she was starving. A small part of her heart jumped at the prospect of seeing his grandma again. "Let's stop in and see her."

They didn't talk in the car. Abigail felt foolish for her actions the other night and foolish for agreeing to go out with him again, neither of which she wanted to talk about.

Grandma was asleep and not responding when they went in. They sat on either side of her bed. Abigail looked over at Tony who had taken his grandma's hand in his. He was gently rubbing his thumb on her soft skin, caressing the back of her hand.

"I think I did this to her," he said quietly.

"Did what?"

"I talked her into trying a new drug therapy. It was just an injection, but she spiked a fever about an hour after they gave it to her and has been sleeping ever since." He looked up at Abigail. "She didn't want it. She just did it for me."

Abigail looked at the sleeping woman. "She loves you," she said.

"Yes."

They sat there quietly for about a half hour. Grandma kept sleeping. Finally, Tony said, "Let's go." Without waiting for Abigail, he walked out of the room, his shoulders back and his step suddenly determined.

———◇———————◇———

Tony was his usual chipper self in the car.

"Are you hungry?"

"Starved," she admitted. She wanted to ask him how he was doing after seeing his grandma, but he seemed determined not to think about it. She understood about pushing down unwanted feelings.

"Good. We're about to go eat."

He turned on the radio to a local pop station, and the mood lightened considerably.

"Where are we going?" Abigail asked.

"It's a surprise," Tony said. "But I think you'll like it."

He parked on a side street not far from the library, and they got out. It was cold and dark out, and the wind was picking up. Tony opened the trunk of his car and pulled out a picnic basket and a blanket.

"A picnic?" Abigail pulled her coat closer around her.

"Come on," he said.

She followed him up to the doors of the Astronomy building.

"What—?"

"The planetarium," Tony said.

Abigail looked at the hours posted on the door. "It's closed."

"That's not a problem," Tony said. He put the picnic basket on the crook of his arm and pulled his phone out of his pocket.

Abigail crossed her arms. "We are *not* breaking into this building," she said, feeling anger rise up in her. Who did he think he was, gallivanting around the town like this, just helping himself to wherever or whatever it is he wanted? She had broken enough rules because of him and wasn't about to break more.

"I don't intend to," Tony said, sending a text. "There are some grad students here for the evening, watching the stars," he said, nodding to the clear sky above them. "Micah will let us in."

"Micah?"

"George and I painted here last year, and I made some friends. I come here every now and then when it's too cold to stargaze from my rooftop."

Before Abigail could take that in, the door opened, and a tall, gangly guy with a mess of dark hair motioned them in.

"Micah, meet Abigail," Tony said. "Abigail, Micah."

He looked to be in his early twenties and was wearing an open flannel shirt over a T-shirt that read "I need my Space."

"Nice to meet you," he said, pushing his glasses up on his nose. They followed him down a nearly dark hall. "I have it all set up for your—uh—date."

"It's not a date," Tony said. "She's just a friend."

"Whatever, dude." Micah pushed open some doors, and Abigail found herself inside the dome of the planetarium. Only the red glow from the exit signs illuminated the dark space. Rows of upholstered reclining chairs circled around the middle, filling most of the room. Tony took her hand and led her to the open floor space at the center.

Micah went to the controls and pushed a few buttons. Soft music came on, something classical, and then suddenly the entire dome filled up with stars. "I'm heading back upstairs," he said.

"Wow," Abigail breathed. It was beautiful. She looked up over her head and all around her and saw familiar constellations and the Milky Way. It was breathtaking, even though she knew it was only from a projector.

"You've never been in here?" Tony asked, giving her hand a little squeeze.

"My dad brought me here once, when I was little," Abigail said. She remembered the day. Her mom had a conference to attend that weekend, so it was a daddy/daughter day. Just the two of them. "I want to show you something special," her dad had told her. The planetarium was newly renovated then, and they had a special showing of the stars of the world.

154

She was mesmerized and had talked about it with her dad for months after. He had promised to bring her back, but they had never returned.

Tony let go of her hand and spread the blanket out. He sat down and motioned for her to do the same. He opened the picnic basket and handed her a plate.

"I'm afraid it's all cold," he said. "We have some potato salad, which admittedly I picked up from the deli, along with the fried chicken, also cold." He opened up the containers so she could help herself. "And to drink, we have some ginger ale. Cold."

"It's perfect," she said, taking the plasticware he offered and scooping out some potato salad.

She looked across at him and then back down at her plate. "I'm really sorry for getting mad at you back there at the door and jumping to conclusions that you were going to break in."

Tony shook his head. "No apologies necessary. It was a valid reaction, considering how we've spent our last few times together."

Abigail took a long, deep breath. "It has been quite a trip."

"Yes, it has."

They ate in silence for a little bit. Abigail kept looking around her at the beauty in the "sky" above. The food was delicious. This was quite possibly the best picnic she had ever been on. The evening was so perfect—the atmosphere, the food, the intimacy of being the only ones in the dome. She remembered Laney's words about how Tony could charm a woman.

"I bet you bring all your girls here," she said, giving a little laugh.

"No," Tony said. "You're the only person I've ever brought here. Ever. Usually I just come by myself to think."

Their eyes met.

"Tony—"

"I know," he said. "I don't expect anything, Abigail. You've made it clear we're just friends. Only I'm not so sure now we're even that." He raised an eyebrow.

"No. Yes."

"That woman you saw me with," Tony said, setting his food down.

"You don't have to explain—"

"Yes, I do." He ran his hand through his hair and then met Abigail's eyes again. "She wanted a necklace for an event she was attending, a big fundraiser. So I sold her one."

"A stolen one."

"Yes."

Tony had a look on his face. Abigail wasn't sure, but she thought he looked ashamed. Maybe regretful. "What if somebody at the event recognizes the necklace?"

"Not likely. Most of the events she attends aren't on the up and up. Some are charity fundraisers, but others are black market auctions. Half the ice in the room is probably hot."

"Oh."

"She's a client I've worked with a few times in the past. Usually she wants jewelry, but one time she wanted a museum piece for an online auction on the dark web."

"Oh." Abigail said quietly. "Sounds...scary."

"Maybe," Tony said. "I don't deal with that stuff or go to the events. I just get her items now and then."

She was quiet, unsure what to say. Here he was telling her secrets that could probably get him put away for life, and yet she felt closer to him for opening up, for trusting her.

"You hate me," Tony said.

"No," she said. "No. I don't hate you." She put her fork down and rubbed her forehead with her hand. "I went to lunch today at Jimmy and Martha's."

"The cop?"

"Yeah. He said someone broke into the Stewart and Cross Law Firm. They think it's the same person who broke into the library. He said the thief is getting sloppy for some reason."

Tony was quiet. He looked down at his plate and moved his potato salad around.

"I didn't say anything," Abigail said. "But Martha had made this wonderful lunch and baked her blueberry muffins. Jimmy came home just because he knew I'd be there. I can't go on lying to them, Tony."

"I'm so sorry," he said. He put his fork down. "I've put you in a terrible spot."

But Abigail wasn't listening. "And I know why you're getting sloppy. It's because of me. I'm going to be the reason you get caught, and I couldn't stand seeing you go to jail. And I can't stand not telling Jimmy what I know. This just isn't working for me, Tony. I just can't."

They were both quiet. Above them, the stars blinked, as if in time to the music. "The heavens and earth sing to the Lord," Abigail said. "That's in the Psalms. What a marvelous universe. How big it is. And we are so small."

She looked across at Tony, who was looking at his plate. Then he looked up and met her eyes.

"What if I quit?"

"Quit what?" Abigail asked.

He shook his head, as if searching for the right words. "Stealing. Breaking into places."

Abigail watched him for a minute, uncertain of what to say. Wondering why he was suddenly willing to give up a life that had proved so lucrative to him and that he obviously enjoyed. She didn't want to be the reason.

"Why?" she asked.

"Because you make me want to be a better man," he said.

The door to the dome burst open. "Guys, there's this awesome meteor shower going on tonight," said Micah. "You want to take a peek from the telescope?"

Tony grabbed a bag of chips, and they ran up the stairs with Micah, leaving the rest of their picnic behind. Tony's other friend, Ian, and a woman he didn't recognize were sitting up in the observation deck. The room was dark except for a penlight that the woman was taking notes by, and a small opening in the dome for the telescope. Ian turned on a dimly lit computer screen, which showed a broader version of the nighttime sky above them.

"Who wants to look first?" Micah said, peeking through the large telescope himself to adjust a setting.

Tony's hands were trembling, and he was glad of the darkness. "Ladies first," he said. He watched as Abigail put her eyes to the lens and wondered if he could do what he had offered. For her. For a woman who he wasn't even sure was interested in him. He had noticed earlier that day in the library that her wedding ring was back on her finger.

"Sometimes you have to wait a little bit, but we're getting several a minute," Micah said.

"There!" Abigail gasped. "I see one!"

Tony smiled at her excitement, and gazed upward through the small opening to see if he could see anything with his naked eye.

"Tony, look!" Abigail stepped back so he could put his eye up to the lens. The sky was quiet for a moment and then he saw one streak across the sky.

"Make a wish," Micah said.

"It is not in the stars to hold our destiny, but in ourselves," Tony said.

"That's a quotation. Not a wish," Micah said, taking a sip of his Mountain Dew.

"Not more of that Shakespeare crap again," said Ian. Tony tossed him the unopened bag of Doritos he had carried up with him.

"Here, Ian. I brought you some nerd food." He put his eye back to the lens.

Abigail laughed. "I made a wish," she said. Tony took his eye away from the telescope to look at her.

"Oh yeah? What did you wish?"

"She can't tell or it won't come true," Micah said.

"Who are you, the wish master?" said Ian. He popped some Doritos in his mouth and then passed the bag to Micah.

The woman who was taking notes finally spoke. "You guys are ruining the moment."

Abigail just smiled and put her eye back to the telescope now that Tony had moved. They stood there, taking turns with the grad students watching the falling stars shoot across the sky. Tony could feel her excitement.

"There's a bird in orbit," said Micah, wiping Doritos dust from his fingers and coming over to the lens.

"A bird?" Abigail asked.

"Satellite," said the woman. "Look."

She saw it moving across the sky and took a closer look through the lens. "This is really cool," Abigail said.

She kept her eye to the lens for another moment, seemingly entranced.

"Look," she said quietly. He smiled and waited for her to step away before he entered the space she had been in.

"What type is it?" Abigail asked.

"Probably a communications satellite," the woman said. "Sometimes you can see the name of the company who owns them on the side."

Tony felt Abigail move next to him. He could smell her floral-scented shampoo and feel her skirt brush against his leg. He noticed his hands were still trembling.

"Can I see again?" she asked.

He stepped back. "I didn't see any company logo," he said.

"Maybe it's turned the wrong way," Abigail said.

It wasn't too long before it was out of their sight. Abigail looked at her watch.

"Oh my gosh, it's after 11 p.m.!" she said. "I have to work in the morning."

"Me too." Tony smiled. "Thanks, guys. This was awesome."

"I have to let you out," Micah said.

They followed him back down to the dome, where they gathered their picnic items and put their coats back on. Micah let them out and locked the door behind them.

There was no wind blowing, and the night had grown still. Students hurried across campus, probably on their way back to their dorms from studying. Tony opened the car door for Abigail, and she climbed inside.

"I'll drive you home," he said, because he couldn't think of anything else to say.

"Okay." She folded her hands in her lap. He wanted to reach across and take one, but he didn't. Instead, he concentrated on the road and the short distance back to her house.

Her porch light was on, and Tony saw the cat in the living room window. He turned to Abigail.

"Well? Did you have fun?"

"Yes," she said. Her eyes were shining. "I actually did. And thanks for bringing the map back today." She hesitated. "Why don't you call me tomorrow?"

Tony nodded and said good night. He watched her walk up to her porch and let herself in before he pulled away.

Before he went home, he stopped to see his grandma. The hospice was quiet, the hallways darkened. Alice, the night nurse, was at the desk.

"How is she?" he asked.

"She's doing better. Her fever broke, and I think the Tylenol is helping. She doesn't need anything stronger."

He nodded and hurried to her room.

"Tony," his grandma said weakly as he pulled a chair up beside her bed in the darkened room. "Hi, honey."

"I didn't mean to wake you."

"No, I wasn't asleep. I was just lying here thinking. I had the nurse open the drapes to my window. Have you seen the falling stars?"

"I have. Abigail and I went to the astronomy building this evening. The grad students I know there let us in, so we got to see some of them up close."

"Beautiful," Grandma said.

"They are."

"I was talking about Abigail."

Tony smiled, remembering the way her red hair fell around her shoulders tonight. How he had wanted to touch it! "She is."

They were quiet for a moment, looking at the window on the other side of Grandma's bed.

"There!" Tony whispered. "Did you see it?"

"Yes," Grandma said. "I love the stars. Remember when you were little and your mom used to take us up on the roof of her apartment to look at them?"

"That was fun," Tony said. "Dad would sometimes make popcorn."

He felt the familiar pang that he still got when he thought of his lost family. It was so many years ago, but sometimes it felt like it was yesterday.

"Do you love her?"

Her question startled Tony and brought him out of his thoughts. "Abigail?"

"Yes, Abigail."

"I don't know. It's too early to tell."

"No, it isn't. I believe in love at first sight. Don't you?"

Tony sat back in his chair. "You're perky and full of questions tonight," he said.

Grandma waited.

"I guess."

"You *guess*?"

"It's complicated."

"That doesn't mean it's not good. I'm happy you've found someone. It's about time."

"So tell me how you really feel," Tony said. His heart lifted to see his grandma acting like her own sassy self tonight. "Besides, I found someone once before."

"Darci? That skinny little dancer?" Grandma raised her hand in a dismissive wave. "Pfft. That wasn't love. That was lust, although I can't imagine what you saw in that thin wisp she called a body. I never liked her."

Tony smiled. "No, you didn't."

"She wasn't the one for you. I've never seen you light up around a woman the way you do around Abigail."

"Well, it's probably a one-way connection. I think Abigail just wants to be friends."

Grandma closed her eyes. "Tony, go home. We both need our rest."

"Okay." He reached over and gave her a kiss on the cheek. "I'll stop in tomorrow."

Grandma smiled but didn't answer. Tony watched another star fall from through the open curtains and then left to go home.

Chapter Twenty-One

Abigail curled up in the cool sheets and pulled the comforter over her. It felt good to be in bed. She was tired but happy, relaxed after the evening with Tony and the stargazing. She hadn't had that much fun in a long time. Then again, she didn't go out much.

She thought of all the fun things she used to do when she and Nick were dating. He had driven their car into the country once, and they went to a park and ate peanut butter and jelly sandwiches. He had switched on the car stereo and they slow-danced in the grass. Because they were graduate students, it was all they could afford to do at the time. She smiled. It was a great memory, and she hadn't thought of it in a long time.

Cocoa jumped on the bed and curled up next to her, purring. She closed her eyes to the comforting sound and felt the rumbling against her shoulder. It was good Tony had brought the map back. She thought about the map and wondered why it didn't lead them on the entire trek to find the painting. Why was it only half the picture?

And what was so special about this particular map that the library decided to keep it? Weren't there other old maps of the city? This one had the early streets and the early sewer line, but she didn't understand why the man who hid the painting chose this particular map to put the details on.

The images of blue lines came into her mind.

"The sewer lines," she said, sitting up and spilling the cat onto the floor. "That's it."

Cocoa complained and circled again, trying to find a new spot to lie down.

"The answer is in the sewer lines," she told her, as Cocoa looked into her eyes.

The clock on her nightstand read 12:08 a.m. She could hardly wait until morning.

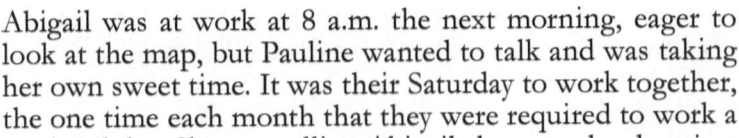

Abigail was at work at 8 a.m. the next morning, eager to look at the map, but Pauline wanted to talk and was taking her own sweet time. It was their Saturday to work together, the one time each month that they were required to work a weekend day. She was telling Abigail about a school project that her son had.

"I mean, he's in *kindergarten*," she said. "I think they expect too much."

"Mmmm." Abigail agreed. "Well, Pauline, I have a lot of work to do."

Pauline was re-arranging the yellow roses. "So, is he a friend?"

"What?"

"Tony. You told me you'd tell me today if I could consider him a friend or not."

"Oh, yes. He's a friend. He's fine," Abigail said, glancing at her watch. "I really have a lot of work to do."

Pauline's eyes narrowed. "It's a library. How much work do you actually have that is so pressing?"

Abigail could not believe the audacity of this woman. Couldn't she take a hint? She tried another route. "Maybe I want to text Tony, and I'm waiting for you to leave so I can have some privacy," she whispered.

Pauline smiled. "Well, why didn't you say so? I'll be downstairs filing."

After she left, Abigail went back to the section where the map was kept. She pulled on some gloves and opened the drawer, carefully taking the map out. She was just about to unroll it when she spotted the camera up on the wall. She pretended to check the reference number on it and then put it back and checked a few more reference numbers on other random drawers just to be safe. Now she was acting paranoid. She went back to her desk and called Tony.

"I have a totally inappropriate question," she whispered when he answered.

"Sounds fun."

"Can you loop the cameras? For about an hour? Or even a half hour?"

There was a pause. "Not from here. I'm at work, and I need to be at my computer. I can do it at lunch. Why?"

"I have an idea."

"Abigail…"

"No. It's nothing terrible. I'll tell you more later. Just text me when you're ready. I gotta go."

She hung up just as Ms. Scott came over to her.

"Do you have time to rework the Greek stacks with me?" she said. "We'll have to quit by 11 a.m. I have a lunch meeting and will probably be gone late into the afternoon."

"Perfect," said Abigail, not believing her luck.

"What?"

"Perfect. I meant perfect timing. I have a slow morning."

And the morning *was* slow. It seemed to drag forever, and then Ms. Scott was late leaving for her meeting. After she was finally gone, Abigail used the time to do some research on the library computer. The more she read, the more excited she became. Finally, Abigail got a text from Tony.

It's done. Be careful.

She texted him a smiley then checked to see where Pauline was. She wasn't in sight, so she must be at lunch. Abigail went over to the drawer and pulled the map out. She laid it down on the table, spreading it out. She was right. The light blue lines of the early sewer system ran along the same path they had traveled the other night. This was really two treasure maps in one. First, you had to find the clue in the lawyer's painting, which led to the LS&A building. Then you had to use the map again to get in to the LS&A building. If you couldn't go through the doors, you went in from beneath.

Brilliant!

She carefully rolled the map up and put it in one of the tubes they used for transporting maps to and from cleaning. She pulled up her thick sweater, glad for her baggy clothes, and once again stuck it in her waistband. It was uncomfortable, and she was trying to figure out how to get it out of the library. Maybe she could put it inside her coat. She pulled it back out and went to get her coat out of her locker near the break room.

"Abigail?"

She nearly jumped out of her skin at the voice. It was Pauline.

"Geez," Abigail said. "Walk a little more loudly next time."

"Sorry," said Pauline. "I'm ordering from Taco Tim's. I came to see if you want a burrito or something."

"No," Abigail said. "I'm fine."

Pauline glanced at the tube. While it wasn't unusual for Abigail to be carrying around maps, she felt she needed to explain.

"It needs to be cleaned. I accidentally spilled something on it. Please don't say anything."

"Oh no!" Pauline whispered. "Is it one of the French ones?"

"No," said Abigail. "Heck no. I'd just turn in my own resignation if it were. It's just a local map."

Both of the women sighed in relief. Abigail grabbed her coat.

"Okay. I'm going to order then," said Pauline. "I'll see you later."

Abigail pulled her phone out of her pocket and disappeared back toward the break room.

"Is that it?" said a voice behind her. She spun around. It was Tony. "Did I scare you?"

"My nerves are shot," she said. She glanced around. "I need to get this cleaned."

Tony eyed the tube. She smiled and motioned for him to follow her over to her desk.

"Are the cameras still off?" she whispered.

He glanced at his wristwatch. "Yep. You have a good half hour."

"Let's go," she said, grabbing his hand and pulling him toward the door.

She put the tube up against her and pulled her coat closed with her other hand. "Let's get some lunch," she said, in case anybody was listening.

The sun was shining for once, and Abigail had to shield her eyes against the glare off the snow.

"My car is over here," Tony said.

She got in. It was still warm from his drive over, and the sun coming in helped. "I figured it out," she said excitedly. "This is really two maps in one." She explained how the first map, the one they found under moonlight, was meant to lead them to the lawyer's painting, which in turn gave them the clue to go to the LS&A building. She pulled it out of the tube and unrolled it. "These here," she said, tracing her fingers along the light blue lines, "these are the lines to the early sewer system. It's no longer in use. I checked. But the tunnels are still there. They are just closed off to keep the riffraff out."

"And the alligators."

"And the alligators," she said, smiling. "So if you follow this line," she traced her fingers along the old sewer system, "it ends here." Her finger landed on the LS&A building. "I did some research. The old sewer line runs inside the building and guess where it ends?"

Tony raised an eyebrow.

"Right under the Dean's office."

Tony whistled. "That means there's another way to get to the painting!"

"Exactly!"

Tony laughed out loud. "You're brilliant!"

"I know," she said, smiling.

"Wow. So what is the next plan, my lady?"

"Let's check it out tonight."

"No. You don't need to steal anything."

"We're not stealing. We're exploring."

Tony's eyes lit up. "I can't pass up a good exploring opportunity," he said. "What time should I pick you up?"

"Late. Maybe 9 p.m.? The opening to the sewers that we could use is behind a shoe shop. I'm thinking it will be closed by then, as well as the other little shops. It should be pretty quiet in that part of town."

"Sounds good," Tony said.

For a moment, Abigail thought that he was going to give her a hug. But he only smiled at her. She rolled the map back up and put it in the tube.

"Here," she said, handing it to him. "Keep it safe until tonight."

"What if someone notices it's missing?"

"I'll check it out of the library as being cleaned. Pauline saw me take it. Nobody will question it. It's my job."

Tony nodded as Abigail opened the door.

"Parting is such sweet sorrow," Tony said.

"But we shall meet again, before tomorrow." Abigail smiled, closed the car door, and ran back into the library.

Chapter Twenty-Two

Tony showered, shaved, and dressed in some fresh jeans and a long-sleeved black cotton shirt. He packed his bag with the tools he thought they might need and made sure his phone was fully charged. Then he went to pick up Abigail.

She was ready and had her coat on when he knocked on her door.

"Let's go!" she said. She seemed excited and started talking as soon as they got inside the car.

"So the best entrance, from what I can figure, is behind the shoe shop on Taft Street. There's an alley that runs alongside there and supposedly an old manhole cover, if it's still there. If it's not...well, then we have a problem. But I think it should be. They upgraded the sewer system. This one is no longer in use, but it's still there. I mean, what do you do with underground tunnels? You can't just fill them in. Although I guess actually you could."

Tony laughed.

"What?" She turned to look at him.

"You haven't talked this much the entire time I've known you," he said. "Are you a bit pumped up about this?"

"Well, yes. This is what I do for a living, Tony," she said with fake sincerity. "I research and analyze old maps and documents. I have an advanced degree in this. You have *your* talents. I have mine." She arched an eyebrow at him.

He laughed again. "I'm glad you're so excited about crawling down into an underground tunnel, which is probably filled with spiders."

"You don't scare me." She smiled, and her whole face lit up. She didn't have her glasses on, and he noticed again how green her eyes were.

He parked a few blocks down, and they walked until they reached the alley. Abigail was right. It was pretty deserted in this part of town. Tony kept an eye out for anyone who might try to rob them. You just never knew. He also scanned the buildings overhead and saw several cameras covering the street.

"I thought you were against stealing," he said again. He was excited about what she had discovered, but a bit nervous to have her involved.

"I don't plan to steal. We're just looking."

"We're trespassing."

She glanced at him. "This is city property. I pay my taxes."

Tony let it go. He had to admit that he certainly had caught her enthusiasm. He smiled again, thinking how close they were to finding the painting, and shoved his hands further down into his pockets to keep them warm. It was cold outside and very dark.

"Here," Abigail said, and he followed her farther into the alley. She seemed to be counting steps. Then she clapped her gloved hands together. "I was right!"

There it was. An old manhole made of cast iron. Abigail reached down and gave it a tug. It didn't budge.

"It's probably stuck," Tony said, unzipping his bag. He pulled out a crowbar and pried at it. It took a lot of effort, and he was working up a sweat when it finally came loose. It popped up and made a clang on the alley street. Tony and Abigail both looked around, but apparently no one had heard—or cared.

Tony shone his light down inside the hole. The walls glistened with frozen moisture, but there wasn't any standing water. Large cobwebs were strewn across the rungs of the metal ladder leading down.

"Ladies first," he said.

Abigail hesitated. "I don't mind going last," she said eventually. She looked over at him.

He carried the lid over to a dumpster and hid it behind it. Then he secured one of his ropes to the top bar that the ladder was attached to. "I don't want to get trapped down here," he said. "Becoming part of the University's catacombs isn't in my future plans. If the ladder gives way, this should hold."

Then he brushed away the first few cobwebs and began climbing down. The floor was damp, and as he shone his light around, he could see that it wasn't really that cobwebby at all. The tunnels were musty, and there was some green slime growing along the floor. Other than that, they were pretty clean.

He glanced up. "Coming?"

He heard her sigh, but she made her way carefully down the ladder. He had to give it to her—she had guts. She jumped the last few feet and landed lightly beside him.

"Let's go," she said, unrolling the map.

He pulled out a compass and they slowly, carefully made their way along the tunnel. It was cold, but they were protected from the wind, at least. They made a right turn and then a left. At each intersection, Tony marked an arrow in chalk. Leaving breadcrumbs.

"Tony?" Abigail said, breaking the silence.

"Hmmm?" He glanced at her map, and they made another right turn.

"How much was that necklace worth? The one you sold to that woman at the Apricot Lounge?"

Tony wasn't expecting that question. Apparently that night was still bothering her.

"Ten grand," he said.

"Did she pay in cash?"

"She wired it."

Abigail was silent for a moment. "But can't the money be traced?"

"No," Tony said. "Not this account."

They had come to an intersection. The tunnel branched off into three separate areas. He heard a noise, and a rat scuttled by. Abigail jumped.

"Why did you sell it to her? I mean, what do you use that much money for?"

Tony cleared his throat. It made him uncomfortable to talk about this topic. "This is going to sound like a line, but I used it to buy medicine for my grandma."

As they walked, he told her about the drug trial and how it was experimental and not FDA-approved. "It will take two, possibly three injections and they are $10,000 apiece. But this cancer strategist I'm working with thinks it has a good chance of helping."

"Wow," Abigail said. She was silent for a few minutes and then quietly asked, "How much money do you have in that account?"

"Not much anymore. Only about five hundred dollars."

They stopped to look at the map again.

"It should be just up ahead." Abigail glanced at him. "So did you mean what you said, that you would quit stealing?"

He met her eyes. "Yes."

"But why? I mean, why now all of a sudden?"

Tony hesitated. There was so much he wanted to say to answer that question, but he didn't want to push her. Instead, he said quietly, "If I did quit, what would that mean for us?"

They walked about another thirty feet ahead, and the tunnel dead-ended. Abigail stopped. "Us?"

Then her eyes traveled behind him and down to the map.

"According to the map, we're right under the Dean's office," Abigail said.

Tony shone his light around on the walls and then up to the ceiling. "There," he said. Above him was an image stamped into the concrete. The flower symbol they had been following. He glanced back down at the map and read the Latin out loud. "Plantavit flos sub capite, et defensis puellis adaquavit bene, which loosely translates into 'The flower is planted under the head and watered well.' But don't quote me on that." He smiled. "This is it. We've found it." He felt a thrill of butterflies in his stomach. Finally.

Abigail looked at it. "But it's concrete or...something very hard."

"Yes."

"Did you bring a sledge-hammer?"

"I brought something better," he said and pulled out a small hand tool. He had used this in another job when he had to break through the wall of a museum. "It's like a demolition hammer, only lighter and smaller. It does a marvelous job on plaster, and I think it might work on this as well, since it's so old."

But then his phone rang. They both jumped.

"You get a signal down here?" Abigail said.

"Apparently so," Tony said, fishing it out of his pocket. When he saw the caller ID his heart skipped in his chest. It was the hospice.

"Hello," he said, feeling his voice shake.

"Tony? Your grandma is having trouble breathing. You need to get here right away," said the nurse.

"I'll be right there," Tony said and ended the call.

He looked at Abigail. "I heard," she said. Tony glanced up at the flower above him one last time. *So close.*

"Come on," he said, "Let's get out of here."

They ran down the tunnels, and by the time they got back to the opening, they were both out of breath. Tony let Abigail climb up first and then he hauled himself up, carrying his bag of tools. He pulled his rope free, and Abigail was already rolling the manhole cover over toward him. They put it on and headed for the street.

When they were almost to his car, Tony saw a cab and flagged it down.

"Go home," he said. He needed to do this himself. He needed to be with his grandma. Just the two of them if this was it.

"Tony," Abigail said.

"Go," he said. "I need to be alone right now."

He left her there and ran to his car. As he started it up, he saw her getting in the cab and realized he had never asked her if she had fare for the ride. Running his hand through his hair, he sped to the hospice as fast as he dared. The last thing he needed was to get pulled over with all his tools in the passenger seat beside him.

"Alice!" he said, bursting through the doors.

She was at the desk, waiting for him.

"You're in time, Tony," she said. "This way."

She led him down the hall, as if he didn't know his way by now. His grandma was there in bed, gasping for breath, even with two little tubes in her nostrils giving her oxygen.

"She was doing so well yesterday," he said. The new medicine had been working. He ran his hand through his hair again.

"We're doing everything we can," said Alice. "We have her on oxygen. We've called her oncologist and the cancer strategist you're working with."

Tony sat in the chair beside the bed. "Grandma?" he said. She reached her hand toward him, and he grasped it. There was fear in her eyes.

In hospice, they didn't usually engage in life-saving measures, only comfort ones. But since his grandma was on the new trial drug, it had been agreed that they would do what they could to get her home.

"It's okay," Tony said. He was scared. He had never gone through anything like these past few months. His life had gone along more or less smoothly. He didn't know what to say or do for her, but it was obvious she was struggling.

"Can you give her something to make her more comfortable?" he asked.

"We need to talk to the cancer doctor first. Since this is a drug trial, it's risky to mix stuff. We have a call in to him. I'll be at my desk in case it comes in."

Tony continued to hold her hand, fighting the rising fear inside him. He thought about the painting and how close he had been to it after all these years. If he had only had one more day. He leaned in toward her.

"Grandma," he whispered. "I think I found the painting."

She squeezed his hand, but right now he could tell she was just struggling to survive. He squeezed it back and shut his eyes, willing with all his might that his grandma would be okay.

He wished he had someone to call. Being an only child, and never having been in a serious relationship except for the brief six weeks with Darci, he was used to doing everything solo. He even kept his close friends at an arm's length. It just seemed easier because of what he did. But now he was wishing he had someone.

He thought of Abigail and wondered why he had sent her home. It was the stubborn man in him, probably. Needing to do it himself, yet again. But he had already shared so much with her.

He took out his phone and texted her with his free hand. **I'm sorry. I'm just used to doing things alone.** Abigail immediately replied. **How is she?** **Not good.**

Do you want me to come?

He hesitated. He did. He wanted her there. He wanted to hold her hand, look into her eyes, and have her tell him it was going to be okay, that his grandma was going to come home tomorrow. But he knew that wasn't true. And he didn't want to cross her boundaries. He couldn't lose Abigail too, and if he started making stupid emotional moves, he would.

He texted her back. **No. Not yet.**

Alice came back into the room. She was carrying a syringe. "We heard from her oncologist. This will help her relax." Then she turned to his grandma. "This will make you sleepy, but it will ease your breathing up. Okay?"

Grandma nodded, and Alice inserted the needle into the IV and pushed the golden fluid into the tube. Within seconds, his grandma's eyes fluttered and closed. Her breathing was still labored, but she was no longer struggling. They watched her for a few minutes and she seemed comfortable.

Alice put a hand on Tony's shoulder. "She should be okay tonight. I'll call you if there's any change. Why don't you go home and get some rest?" Tony shook his head.

"I'll make out the recliner for you then," she said. She left the room and returned with a blanket and pillow. Tony wearily moved to the recliner and accepted them. It was just after 1 a.m.

He texted Abigail to let her know the immediate emergency was over and then closed his eyes and tried to sleep.

Chapter Twenty-Three

Abigail put her phone on her nightstand, relieved Tony's grandma was resting well. It was after 1 a.m., but she still wasn't able to sleep. She kept thinking about the painting and why it was in the Dean's office. Even more curious was why the lawyer had his own painting alarmed. Was he afraid it would get stolen? She was no art curator, but she didn't imagine his painting itself was worth much.

Unless the lawyer knew it had clues in it to the missing Russo.

She got up and pushed her feet into her slippers to protect them from the cold wooden floor. Then she pulled her robe around herself and went over to her laptop. Logging in to her university account, she typed in the name of the current LS&A dean. It came up with his photo and credentials. She went to the bottom of the page and found a link to the previous dean. She clicked on it and up came a photo of a man with wavy red hair and a bright smile. There was a list of former deans. She did some mental math and clicked on the dean who sat on the chair close to the time the painting came up missing. Up came a black and white photo of an elderly man with a short, neatly trimmed gray beard and spectacles. She read his bio and stopped short in the second paragraph. She read it again.

Gasping, she sat up straighter in her chair. He was an art fancier and an avid collector of Russo's work. Upon his death, his estate had donated several privately owned Russo paintings to the university's Museum of Art.

Abigail paused. Those would be the ones she saw hanging in there on her visits to the museum. She read on.

"...came to an untimely death when he was found murdered in his office."

Murdered?

The site didn't say anything more. Abigail did a search on the dean's name and some news articles came up. She scanned them, reading quickly for information. Apparently, his secretary found him when she came into work on a Monday morning, face down on his desk in a pool of blood. He had been stabbed deep in the chest. No motive was discovered, and the killer was never found.

Abigail sat back, thinking. Wondering. What if he had found the painting and was hiding it and someone—perhaps a treasure hunter?—had been trying to get him to reveal the information? Did the current dean—or any of the other deans, for that matter—know about it? She doubted it.

But she bet that lawyer did. What was his name? Stewart?

She searched his name and address and came up with a staff photo of Jonathan Stewart on his firm's website page. She looked at the picture. He was probably in his late fifties, gray, tall, and thin. He looked kind. She clicked on his bio. Apparently he was the city attorney, representing government matters for the city, but he also handled some small crime within the city limits. He and his wife had been married for thirty-four years and had two grown children and three grandchildren. He attended church, volunteered at the children's hospital, and was also involved in other charities, mostly for children. He seemed like a really nice guy.

She left the law office's website and did a web search on him. Nothing much of interest came up. Nothing that could tie him to the painting.

It was 3:20 a.m. Abigail closed her search engine and turned off her laptop. She wanted to get to bed. She lay there for a few minutes thinking about how to piece it all together, but sleep soon found her, and she didn't wake again until 9 a.m.

Chapter Twenty-Four

"She's going to need another injection very soon," said the oncologist. "Her body is fighting the cancer, and she needs the other boost now."

Tony stood at her bedside Sunday morning, his hands in his pockets, and nodded. Then he motioned the man outside to the hallway.

"I can pay you in a few days," he said. He was tired. He hadn't slept well in the recliner, and the morning sun seemed unusually bright in the hall.

The oncologist shook his head. "I'd love to do it that way, but the pharmacy we order it from wants the money up front. I need it to order the medication."

"How long?"

"If you can get me the cash today, I should be able to get it delivered here by tonight or Monday," said the oncologist. "They're open seven days a week. But it's Sunday. I doubt you can get that from an ATM."

Tony sighed and shoved his hands deeper into his pockets. "I'll try to get it to you tonight."

"Call me, no matter the time," he said, handing Tony his card. "I want to get another injection into her as soon as we can."

He left, and Tony wandered back into the room. Grandma was lying down, but her eyes were open.

"Tony," she said. "Come here."

"How are you feeling?" He took her hand and sat down on the edge of her bed.

"Pretty tired." She closed her eyes, as if the words took a lot of effort. "I have to tell you something."

She motioned for him to lean in closer to her.

"Grandma…" Tony said, but he did as he was told.

"That's my boy," she said, reaching up to touch his face. "Now listen carefully. I have something I want to give you, and I need to tell you where to find it."

Abigail saw Tony's text that his grandma was doing better, and he was heading home to rest. She decided to go to church instead of over to the hospice.

She was tired and running a little late, but Jimmy and Martha had saved her a seat, as usual. She slid into the pew beside them.

As they were singing the last refrain of the entrance hymn, Tony stepped in the row to stand beside Abigail. She looked over at him, startled, and he gave her his smile, the one that melted her heart. She smiled back at him and saw Martha and Jimmy looking over at him out of the corner of their eyes.

When they sat down, Abigail whispered, "You came."

"Yes," he said. "I figured I needed to put in some time with God."

"Is Grandma not doing well?" Abigail whispered. Tony shook his head.

She wanted to reach over and take his hand, but she was very self-conscious of the Stouts sitting next to her. She couldn't help but notice the smile playing at Martha's lips, and when she dared a glance at her, the older woman looked at her and nodded, giving a little thumbs up that Tony couldn't see. Abigail felt herself blush and then leaned over to Martha and whispered, "We're only friends."

"I know." Martha got a mint out of her purse, popped it in her mouth, and focused on the front of the church.

Maybe Tony would take *her* hand. Then it wouldn't be her decision. But why would he? They were only friends. She had made that very clear.

The sermon that morning was on the prodigal son, the story Tony's grandma had been reading the other day. The one about the boy who leaves home and spends all his inheritance partying. He returns, brokenhearted to his father.

178

"The son said to him, 'Father, I have sinned against heaven and against you. I am no longer worthy to be called your son.' But the father said to his servants, 'Quick! Bring the best robe and put it on him. Put a ring on his finger and sandals on his feet. Bring the fattened calf and kill it. Let's have a feast and celebrate. For this son of mine was dead and is alive again; he was lost and is found.' So they began to celebrate."

Abigail thought about Tony and wondered if he worried about his grandma forgiving him if she found out what he did. She herself certainly had reservations about what he did. That made her think of Jimmy, and suddenly she was a little bit worried about the two of them sitting so close together.

She swallowed hard, and then pulled a piece of gum out of her purse. Her mouth had gone dry.

She sat there, conflicted. Her heart was soaring that Tony had come to church. And yet, here she was, pretty much living a lie by sitting with him—a criminal—while Jimmy sat just on the other side of Martha. The policeman and the criminal in the same pew.

But Jesus forgave all, didn't He? What was forgiveness, anyway? It was letting go. It was looking forward and saying that you were going to forget the past and move on. Tony had told her that he would quit stealing. What if he had been serious? Then could she forget what she knew about his past and move forward? Jimmy would never have to know.

She wasn't sure she could live with that. It would be like living a lie.

But she couldn't tell Jimmy either. She sighed heavily and realized how loud she must have been. Both Martha and Tony looked at her.

"Sorry," she whispered.

The pastor was wrapping up the sermon. One more song and they could get out of there. She wanted to introduce Tony to her friends, but on the other hand, she didn't know if she could survive it. She'd tell them she had to leave early for her yoga class.

Tony sat there, listening to the sermon on forgiveness. He was wrestling with decisions that had kept him up all night and were only strengthened this morning when he talked with the oncologist. He was feeling lost, so he had decided to take Abigail up on her offer to come to church.

It had been a long time since he had attended church. He went every Sunday while he was growing up and even attended the Sunday school classes before service and the Vacation Bible Schools where his grandma had taught during the summer. He had been raised to love Jesus. He tried to remember when going to church no longer seemed important to him. Probably when he moved out on his own. At first, he attended with his grandma, but then it seemed less important. As he had started dabbling in criminal activity, he kept late nights, so Sunday mornings became a time to catch up on his sleep. His prayer time had dwindled as well. For a while, he kept up the nighttime prayers his grandma had said with him, but as he became a teen, he got distracted and busy. By the time he was out on his own, he barely prayed at all. His life had been going along so well he didn't feel the need to ask God for anything. It was only recently, since his Grandma had been ill, that he was focusing on God again.

Abigail sighed loudly, pulling him out of his thoughts. He glanced at her and she apologized. She seemed uncomfortable, and he wondered if he should have come. He figured that was Jimmy sitting two people down from her. Abigail brushed her hands down her dress, smoothing it out. She looked beautiful this morning, with her hair down loose around her shoulders and her green eyes free of the bulky glasses.

It was time for the closing prayer. He bowed his head with the rest of the congregation and prayed with all his heart for God to help his grandma.

The pastor gave the benediction, and they were dismissed. Tony stepped out of the pew and waited for Abigail to follow.

"I'm so glad you're here," she said. Her eyes shone, but he could tell she was nervous.

"You invited me," he said.

Abigail turned to the older woman, who Tony assumed was Martha, and introduced them. "Martha, this is my friend Tony."

Tony reached out his hand to shake Martha's, but she came forward and embraced him in a hug. "So nice to meet you," she said.

"And this is Jimmy." Abigail's voice was bright, a little too high.

"Nice to meet you," Jimmy said. Tony reached forward and gave Jimmy a firm handshake.

"There are donuts in the hospitality room," Martha said.

Tony looked at Abigail again, who looked petrified. "I need to get going," he said. "My grandma is sick, and I need to check up on her."

"Yes. And I have yoga class," Abigail said. "I need to go home and change."

"Yoga class?" Tony imagined her in yoga clothes.

"We heard about your grandma," Martha said, pulling Tony's attention back to her. "Jimmy and I are praying."

"Thank you."

Tony followed Abigail out. When the two of them were at her car, they stopped.

"I'm sorry," he said. "This was probably a bad idea."

"No, it wasn't. I'm really glad you came." Abigail was standing by her car, the snow falling lightly on her shoulders, getting caught in her hair.

He stood there staring at her for a moment, wanting to bring her into his world, wanting to tell her about the choices he was battling with.

"The sermon," she said. "That was the same story your grandma was reading the other day."

"Yes," he said. "The prodigal son."

"Whose Father forgave him."

Tony didn't want to pull her into his world. She was so perfect the way she was. She had a job she loved and a family with Jimmy and Martha. Now she was breaking into buildings and hanging out with a thief. Before she met him, he doubted if she had even cheated on a parking ticket.

"I need to go, and you need to get to your yoga class."
Tony reached past her and opened her car door for her.

"What about the painting?" She lowered her voice. "Let's
try again tonight."

"Maybe," Tony said. "I'd like to. I'll call you."

"Okay. Tell your grandma I said 'hi.'"

"I will."

He watched her get in her car and waved as she pulled away.

Chapter Twenty-Five

Tony paced his apartment. He was at a loss about what to do. He poured himself a glass of pop from a two-liter he had in his fridge and put a straw in it. Then he opened a package of cookies, which he toyed with but didn't eat. For the first time in his life, he didn't want to do what he was about to do. But he couldn't think of another way.

Finally, feeling defeated, he picked up his phone and dialed the number of a man he had dealt with in the past.

A rough voice said hello.

"It's Tony." He fiddled with the ice in his glass, moving the straw around and stirring.

"Tony?"

"I've got a piece for you. It's worth fifteen thousand dollars on the black market. I'll sell it to you for ten."

There was a long pause, during which Tony took a sip of his pop to calm his shaking hands.

"What's the piece?"

He described it from memory. An exquisite rose outlined in tiny diamonds set in gold, filled with small, pink rubies.

There was another long pause. "Not interested. Maybe in a month or so. Call me then."

"Look…" Tony toyed with his straw some more. "I'm really in need of some cash today."

"*Today?*" The man's deep baritone laughed heartily. "I can't do anything today. Heck, I don't keep that kind of money just lying around the house. Besides, it's my granddaughter's birthday."

Tony tried again. "It's the perfect present!"

"She's three."

After he hung up, Tony sat down at his counter. He looked around at his kitchen, clean and simple, just like the life of a bachelor. For a moment, he let himself imagine a woman's touch. Maybe some floral print towels hanging from the stove handle, a scented candle on the counter. A framed photo on the window ledge.

He rubbed his forehead. What was the matter with him?

He dialed another number. When she answered, he put on his best charm.

"Charlotte," he said.

"Darling," she crooned.

"I have something for you."

"I love surprises!"

He described the piece to her.

"Sounds beautiful."

"Fitting for you, then." He took a sip of his pop.

"How much?"

He told her the price. "I can meet you tonight."

"Tonight?" Her voice took on a sultry tone. "You want to bring it to my place?"

He hesitated. He had her on the hook, and she was about to bite. He needed the money.

"Charlotte…"

"Oh, that's right. You're in love." He heard the playful teasing in her voice. There was no disdain.

"Maybe."

"Okay. I'll take a look at it. No strings attached. If I like it, I'll wire you the money."

He hesitated again. "I need cash."

"Tonight?" She sounded surprised.

He took another swallow of pop. "Yes."

There was a moment of silence. "Is this as beautiful as you say it is?"

"Don't you have that fundraiser to go to next month? The one where Fabio DuPres is attending?" He knew her soft spots.

She sighed. "Look, you rascal. I need to go. Get the piece and call me. We can talk details then. Miss me."

She hung up, and he stood there for a moment. He decided to go see his grandma one more time.

Abigail sat at her kitchen table and ate a yogurt. She needed
some light protein before yoga class. She had been so excited
to see Tony show up at church this morning. Until she started
thinking. By the time the sermon was over, she had concocted
every way possible for things to go wrong and for Jimmy to
figure out who he was. That was one of the problems with
being an avid reader of fiction. Her mind was always coming
up with possibilities.

She pulled her hair up, changed into her yoga clothes,
and grabbed her mat. It was only a ten-minute drive to class,
and she found a parking spot right away.

A sign on the wall read "No street shoes," so she started
removing her shoes in the lobby like she had done every
Sunday for the past few years. Sunday was the perfect time
to take a class. It was uncrowded. Most people wanted to stay
home in their jammies.

As she slipped her shoes off, a familiar looking woman
walked out of the studio. It took Abigail a moment, but she
recognized her as the blond woman she had seen Tony with
at the Apricot Lounge.

"Excuse me," Abigail heard herself say.

"Hello," the woman said. Abigail suddenly remembered
Tony had called her Charlotte. "Have you taken the hot yoga
class? This is my first time here, and it is soooo amazing!"

"No," Abigail said. She preferred to earn her sweat.

Charlotte looked for her coat and pulled it on. "Do we
know each other?"

"I think we have a mutual friend," Abigail said, smiling.
She wasn't sure what she was doing, but suddenly she needed
to know what Tony was to this woman.

"Do we?" Charlotte pulled on her boots. She was beautiful
and filled out her yoga clothes in a way that Abigail figured
most men would probably find appealing. Even with a fine
sheen of sweat on her, she looked glamorous. Her blond hair
was pulled back in a ponytail, and her makeup was still perfect.

"Tony." Abigail watched her face carefully. There was
no reaction.

"I don't know a Tony," Charlotte said, her smile disappearing as she laced up her snow boot.

"He did a painting job for you. I saw you with him in the Apricot Lounge the other night."

For a moment, there was nothing and then Charlotte smiled again. "Oh, that Tony! He's a looker, that one." She gave a deep, hearty laugh. "Yes, he did some work for me." Her eyes narrowed and traveled up and down Abigail, giving her a good look for the first time. A smile crossed her lips.

"You're *her*," Charlotte said.

"What?"

"You're the woman he loves."

Abigail blushed, hating her fair complexion, which colored so easily. "No."

"Honey, you don't have anything to worry about." She lowered her voice. "I invited Tony back to my place, and he refused. Men don't typically refuse me."

Abigail looked at her and figured there was probably some truth to that.

"He's all yours." Charlotte finished tying her lace and put her foot down on the floor. "Try the hot yoga class next week. And tell Tony I said 'hi.'"

She swept out the door.

Abigail stood there for a moment. Tony *loved* her? Did he actually say that or was Charlotte assuming things? Was Tony willing to give up both stealing *and* playing around? For *her*? She had never asked him to. She didn't think she wanted to be the reason for him to, either, but she had to admit it gave her a thrill in her stomach to think that he was willing to change that much for her.

But Nick had changed too. He had wanted to transfer to another graduate school, but she was happy here with her program. So they had decided to stay and get married. She wondered if they had moved if there would have been less stress and less fighting that last week of his life.

"Abigail! Good! I thought I was late!"

Her teacher's voice brought her out of her thoughts. The woman hurriedly kicked her boots off. "Come on!"

Abigail followed her up the stairs, glad that for the next hour she'd be so busy trying to balance and breathe that she wouldn't have time to think about Tony.

Chapter Twenty-Six

Abigail went home, showered, and dressed in jeans and a soft green cotton jersey. She blow-dried her long, thick hair, which took longer than she wanted, but she was cold. She had to go out again tonight for dinner at Jimmy and Martha's. She was sure they'd have lots of questions about Tony, so she was somewhat dreading the visit. What was she going to say?

She would stick with the basics. He works as a painter. He has a sick grandma. She makes great lasagna. Stuff like that.

Abigail's feelings for Tony were growing, and she had to admit that her conversation with Charlotte only made them stronger. But at the same time, she knew she couldn't get involved with him unless he gave up the criminal life. That would be the only way.

She put on some light makeup and noticed she had an hour before she had to leave. She picked up the book she was reading and sat down on the couch. Cocoa curled up next to her. She was just getting comfy when the doorbell rang.

"Who could that be?" She scratched Cocoa behind the ears and got up, setting her book on the table next to the front door. She peeked through the hole. It was Tony.

She opened the door. He was standing there with his hands in his pockets, wearing his long black coat. He had a white scarf wrapped around his neck.

"Can we go for a walk?" he said.

No theatrics. No Shakespeare. Not even his charming smile.

"Is everything okay?" Her mind first went to his grandma.

He gave her a shrug. "My grandma is sleeping."

"Let me get my coat." She reached into the closet and grabbed it, took her door keys off the table by the door, and joined him on the front porch. He turned and started down the porch steps. She kept step beside him on the sidewalk, digging into her pockets for her gloves.

"What's wrong?"

He glanced at her and then looked ahead again. "I just needed someone to talk to."

"Oh."

They walked about a half block, and she waited. Finally, he spoke again.

"The thing is..."

"Yes?"

He sighed. Whatever it was, he was having trouble saying it.

"I want to quit, you know, what I do. The stealing. I know that's what you want."

"What I want is not important," Abigail lied.

Tony turned to look at her. "It is to me."

Abigail pushed her hands deeper into her pockets. "Oh." She thought about what Charlotte had said to her earlier. *He loves you.*

"But I think I need to do one last job."

"The painting?"

"No. Something else. I need more money for my grandma's medicine."

Tony explained to her what was happening to his grandma and the costs of the medicine. "They need it now, if we're going to have any chance of saving her life."

"That's a lot of money," Abigail said. "Where would you get something worth that much?"

"That's not important. There's a store. I know when it's empty. That's all you need to know."

Abigail walked in silence beside him, weighing her words. A small dog barked at them through a window as they passed.

"Do you think your grandma would want you to help her if she knew how you were financing it?" Abigail kept her tone soft, not wanting to place blame or judgment.

"No." He sighed. "But she doesn't need to know. Just this one last time."

"But doesn't she possibly need *two* more injections?"

Tony was quiet for a while. They turned another corner and walked down another half block. When he spoke, his voice was very quiet "Yes."

"There has to be another way," Abigail said. "We know where the painting is. I can find some people through the art museum to help us get it out. It will be obvious it belongs to you, and you can sell it."

"That will take too much time. She doesn't have that kind of time."

"We can borrow the money then. I have friends. I can ask around." She realized then that she was embracing the problem as hers as well. Using the word "we" instead of "you." "We'll find a way."

They turned another block, and Tony was quiet until they got to Abigail's house. She got butterflies in her stomach when she thought of him breaking into a store. What if he got caught? Worse yet, what if he got shot?

At the porch steps, Abigail turned. "Are you asking me for permission?"

He gave her a little half-smile. "Maybe. But I think I already know your answer."

It had started snowing. The wind was picking up. He looked so alone standing there, so fragile and different compared to the charming, self-confident man she had grown to know.

"Why don't you come in and warm up," Abigail said, not wanting him to leave.

He nodded. "For a few minutes," he said. "But then I need to go. And don't you have dinner at the Stout's tonight?"

Abigail looked at her watch. "I've got time."

Tony followed Abigail up the steps, wondering if he would see her again after tonight. He soaked in the sight of her, her long red hair cascading out from under her white snow hat, her slim figure wrapped in her thick coat, in case this was their last time together.

She unlocked the door and walked in, but the cat decided to greet Tony. Abigail lunged for her to stop her from going outside and bumped into the side table by the door, knocking everything off. Her purse spilled on the floor, and a book fell beside it, its pages fluttering open and the bookmark falling out. Meanwhile, the cat took advantage of her stumble to sneak out the still-open door. Tony scooped up the frightened feline and brought her inside, closing the door behind him.

Abigail knelt down on the floor and shoved the contents back into her purse. "I need to clean this thing out," she said, laughing. "What a mess!" She closed the purse and reached for the book.

Tony saw something on the floor by the front door and picked it up.

"Here, you forgot this..." His voice trailed off when he saw what it was.

Abigail saw it at the same time. She hastily grabbed it from his hand and closed her fingers around it. It was a hospital bracelet for the psychiatric ward. *Her* hospital bracelet. Tony read it before he realized what it was.

She swallowed and attempted a smile. "I'm crazy," she said.

"I doubt that," Tony said. Abigail closed her eyes and swallowed hard again. She seemed to be breathing quickly.

"I changed purses the other day and it fell out. It was from back when Nick..." Her words stopped. She took a deep breath. Then another. She seemed to be hyperventilating.

"Abigail, are you okay?"

When she didn't answer, Tony went into the kitchen and ran a glass of water. He handed it to her, and she took it in her free hand and drank a few sips. Her other hand was still grasping the plastic bracelet.

Tony knelt down on the floor beside her. "You don't have to explain anything to me. Just take a few slow breaths. It's okay." He wanted to put his arms around her, but he wasn't sure if she would want that.

She nodded, and he sat with her while she regained control of herself, slowing down her breathing. After a few minutes, she met his eyes. "After Nick died things were hard. Then one day I went to bed and didn't get up again. I just couldn't. It

191

was all wrong, how he was suddenly taken from me. I mean, we were *newlyweds*. We were supposed to have years together. Decades. Have kids."

Tony was quiet. Cocoa rubbed against Abigail, comforting her. Abigail set down her glass and petted her, still holding the bracelet in a death grip in her other hand.

"Can I see that?" Tony asked. He reached his hand out. He wanted her to focus on something else.

She shook her head, clutching it against her chest. "I was in for six weeks. Major depression, they called it. They put me on suicide watch, and Martha stayed with me for another six. It took every ounce of strength I had to crawl back out from under that darkness into my life."

His heart went out to her. To love that much and hurt that badly. But there had to be more to the story. He remembered how hesitant Pauline had been to talk to him about it.

Abigail looked at him, her big eyes wide. "It was my fault."

Tony wasn't sure what she meant. "What?"

"Nick's death. It was my fault. If I hadn't needed that milk so badly, he wouldn't have gone out." Her eyes took on a distant look. "I was so angry that week. I was working a lot of hours, plus we were tight on money and we had been fighting. That morning before I left for work, he said he missed the "us" we used to be." She gave a short, humorless laugh. "*Used* to be. Like we were married for more than three months."

She looked at Tony again. "That was hard too. People would be all sympathetic when they heard. But when they asked 'How long were you married?' and I told them, they'd get this look, like oh well, at least you didn't have time to get attached. So then I started telling myself that to get through the day. 'Well, we weren't married that long.' Like it didn't matter.

"So when he said that morning that he missed us, I told him that if he'd just do his part around the apartment, we'd be fine. I had tried to shower and had to plow through his dirty laundry, and there were all these little hairs in the sink from where he shaved and I was angry. I was angry that morning and I was angry when I came home that night, even though he had grocery shopped. But there was no milk. I got angry over hair in the sink and no milk. How stupid is that?"

Her eyes filled with tears. "I loved him, Tony. I loved him so much, and I got him killed."

She started to sob. Sitting there on the floor on her knees, clutching the bracelet to her chest, she closed her eyes and cried. "It's my fault."

"No, Abigail, it's not your fault," Tony said. She was rocking back and forth, the tears streaming down her face. Tony moved toward her and pulled her into his arms, holding her against his chest. He stroked her hair with his hand. "It's okay," he said. "It's okay." Her whole body was shaking with emotion.

She cried hard for a few minutes. He sat there with her, stroking her hair. Slowly, the sobs quieted down into sniffles, but she kept her face against him. He continued to hold her.

"It's not your fault. You were being human, like we all are from time to time. You didn't make him go out. You didn't send the ice storm. You weren't the driver who plowed through the intersection. I wasn't there, Abigail, but I don't believe you'd ever wish harm on anyone. It just happened. The timing was awful, and yes, it would have been easier on you—or maybe not—if you had kissed and hugged before he left, but that's not how it happened. That's only how it happens in movies."

Her crying had stopped.

Tony looked over at the book that was lying on the floor, its pages open. It was Shakespeare's *The Winter's Tale*. A story of lost love and regret.

The pages were open to scene five. King Leontes was lamenting the fact that he had killed his beloved wife, but Lord Cleomenes was telling King Leontes that he needed to end his long years of penitence. Tony smiled at the relevance. Was it coincidence, or the hand of God, that had left this book open on the floor at this scene?

"Do as the heavens have done, forget your evil; With them forgive yourself," he quoted softly into her hair.

Abigail was quiet for a moment and then slowly lifted her head. "What?"

Tony nodded toward the book. "Look," he said.

He reached for it and pulled it over to where they were sitting. Abigail pulled away from him far enough so that she could look at where he was pointing.

"Oh," she said quietly.

"Do as the heavens have done, forget your evil; With them forgive yourself," he quoted again. "God, or fate, has left you a message. Don't you think you have punished yourself long enough? Abigail, you need to forgive yourself. And you need to forgive Nick. He would have never left you on purpose. No man in his right mind would leave you. It was an accident. It just happened."

She looked at the book, and slowly a small smile played on her lips. She looked up at Tony. "All this time, I was worried about *you*. About how you needed to forgive yourself. About how you needed to let go of the past and move forward and that God would forgive you. But it's *me*. The sermon on forgiveness, your grandma telling us this story, and now this book. It's God telling me to forgive."

"And to accept forgiveness," Tony said. But she had touched a soft spot with her words. Yes. He needed to forgive himself as well.

But after tonight.

He handed Abigail her water glass, and she took another sip. Then she looked at her watch and stood up, rubbing her hand across her eyes. "I should go before Jimmy sends out a search car to look for me."

Tony stood, picking the book up and setting it back on the table. Abigail was pale but seemed well. "Are you okay?"

She nodded and wiped at her eyes with a tissue. "Come with me to dinner."

He wanted to. He wanted to so badly it hurt. But he had something else to do tonight.

"I need to go. Maybe next time."

Abigail nodded.

'Tony?"

He stopped at the door and turned to look at her.

"Don't do anything you'll regret."

"I won't," he said because he wanted to make her happy, but he couldn't meet her eyes when he said it. He had to save his grandma. How could he regret that?

Then he went outside, shutting the door behind him. Walking down those steps and leaving her was one of the hardest things he had ever done. He wanted to go back in and tell her how much he loved her and that he'd do anything for her. But he had something else to do first, and after that, she would never want to talk to him again.

With a heavy heart, he opened his car door and climbed in. He glanced at the house but her door was closed, and he didn't see her in the window. He pulled away, looking once more at the house and then focusing his mind on what lay ahead.

Chapter Twenty-Seven

Abigail stood inside the door, holding the plastic bracelet in her hand. She looked at it, but this time it didn't fill her with the dread it had when she saw it in her closet the other day. She must have stuffed it in the wrong purse at the time.

She sighed heavily, thinking of what had just transpired. It was like a weight had been lifted. She had loved Nick and had loved him well. She knew they had a great courtship and a great marriage. The problem was they were young newlyweds getting used to a shared life not their own anymore. There were bumps. That was only natural. But she knew in her heart that they had loved each other deeply.

She could look at this from a different side now, as if she were looking in a window that night. Nick had been angry too. To try to appease her, he had gone to pick up groceries. When she complained anyway, it was only natural that he got angry. But she had tried to stop him from going out that night.

She remembered trying to stop him and him leaving and shutting the door with a slam. She wondered if he had been angry at her while he drove. What were his last thoughts? Was he grumbling about her? Was he regretting his abrupt departure? Would they have made up when he got back home, when she told him the milk wasn't important and he told her that he only wanted her to be happy? She would never know.

Now it didn't seem to matter as much. What had happened was in the past. Nick would want her to move on, as Martha and Pauline had told her time and again. At only thirty, she had her entire life ahead of her.

She went to her closet and pulled down a box. Inside was a notebook—she had been asked to keep a daily journal while she was healing. She tucked the bracelet inside the notebook, right in the middle, and smoothed it down before shutting the book. Then she closed the lid and put it back up on the shelf. She would keep the bracelet not as a symbol of how she had failed Nick, but as a symbol of how much she had loved him and how hard it had been for her to let go.

Then she went to the bathroom to wash up. As she was drying her face in the mirror, she smiled at herself, a little happy with what she saw. She would start over. Tonight. Right now. And it sounded like Tony would too. She'd speak to Jimmy and Martha tonight about how to pay for his grandma's medicine and then she'd call Tony with the answer, no matter how late it was. She suspected that Jimmy might know of places where people could go to get help in this city of theirs.

She pulled up to their house, only ten minutes late, wearing only a light foundation on her face, some mascara, and the comfortable clothes she had changed into after yoga. She felt light and happy.

Jimmy greeted her at the door, and she could smell Martha's pot pie as soon as she stepped inside.

"You look relaxed tonight," Jimmy said. "Martha hopes you can stay late. She wants to beat you at a game of cards."

Abigail laughed as he led her through the living room to the kitchen. She helped carry the food to the table and clasped Jimmy and Martha's warm hands as they blessed the meal. Her heart felt full of love. She was so lucky to have them.

Tony stood in the lobby of the hospice and ran his hands through his hair. His grandma looked horrible when he checked on her.

"She really needs that injection," the oncologist said. "She doesn't have much time without it."

Tony nodded. "I'll have the cash tonight. I'm working on a transfer with my bank right now."

He felt numb during the drive home, but once he opened his door, he went into autopilot. He changed into his black clothes and packed his bag, making sure his rope was in there and that his phone was charged. He had to come in through the ceiling if this was going to work. He looked at his watch.

Only 8 p.m. It was way too early to be doing a job like this, but he didn't have much choice. At least with the winter hours, it was already dark.

He opened his computer and took one last look at the building's specs, memorizing what he needed to know. Then he powered it down and turned on the lamp by the couch so he wouldn't have to return to a dark apartment.

If he made it home.

"Father, deliver me," he whispered, praying to a God he had ignored for so long. "Please."

Taking a deep breath, he closed the apartment door behind him and went to his car. He didn't have the same thrill running through him that he usually did for a job. The excitement, the adrenaline, the rush. Instead he felt a heavy weight and a sense of loss.

He circled the block. It seemed empty. Not much happening on a Sunday night in a university town. He parked a block away, grabbed his bag, and walked, pulling his jacket around him against the cold. A bitter wind blew through the streets, promising snow after midnight.

The jewelry store was up ahead. Tony stopped and looked up toward the roof. The coffee house next to it had camera surveillance on the street. He didn't want to get caught on film, so he turned down the alley and spotted a fire escape. He tossed his rope up. When it caught, he effortlessly climbed up, his bag on shoulder. The jewelry store was highly alarmed—rightly so—and he couldn't just break in through a door or window. He'd have to come in from above. He climbed up to the roof of the three-story building and then walked across until he found an entrance: a steel door leading inside the building that contained the jewelry store, the coffee shop, and a men's clothing store. The lock took him a few minutes before he was able to jimmy it open. He slipped in and quietly shut it behind him.

The stairwell was dark, so he took out his penlight and turned it on. He headed down two flights of stairs and then opened another lock to let himself into the men's clothing store. Quickly and precisely, he cut a wire near the door. The cameras inside the building were already disabled—he had taken care of that from his computer at home. Remembering the specs he had pulled up, he found the vent just above the dressing room, pried off the screen, and pulled himself in. He hated tight spots. He hurriedly crawled several feet until he found a similar grate. This one he had to cut open because he couldn't get to the screws from the inside. It was sloppy, but he didn't have a choice. They'd notice it tomorrow.

Then he was looking inside the jewelry store. There were three cameras, which he had disabled. There was a perimeter alarm, which he didn't need to worry about since he was already inside. But there should be a third alarm system, as most jewelry stores had, and it was troubling him that he couldn't locate it. It didn't show up on the security specs he had found, and he couldn't see any laser beams or other signs of an alarm. He took an aerosol can out of his bag and sprayed the hair spray into the air, but it just filtered down to the ground, not highlighting any beams he couldn't see with his eyes. Nothing.

Slowly and carefully, he lowered himself into the room. He was near the back, behind the main jewelry case. There were two cases along each wall, and in the middle of the room a small, glass case containing the rose pendant. He planned to simply take the rose pendant from the case and get out.

He moved slowly and expertly across the carpeting and then took his time looking at the glass case. It should have tiny wires around it that might trip if it were lifted or perhaps a sound sensor to detect breaking glass. He couldn't identify anything, only locks. Taking his glasscutter out of his bag, he cut a hole big enough for his hand to fit through. Using a suction cup, he put the piece of glass on the floor beside him. Then he reached his hand inside. Nothing happened.

Maybe this was going to be easier than he thought.

Abigail had a full house. She had won the first two hands and it looked like she was going to win a third. She yawned. It was nearly 9 p.m.

"I need to go home," she said. She didn't usually stay this late, but she was enjoying the comfort of being with her friends. Dinner had been excellent. They had asked about Tony, as she knew they would, but had moved on shortly to other topics of conversation. Perhaps they were respecting her privacy.

She had thought about Tony on and off all night. Jimmy knew of two different places they could ask for help for his grandma's medication. If that didn't work, Jimmy could ask around the precinct. Maybe raise a little. All told, he figured he could help them find something by late tomorrow.

"I think I have you this hand," Jimmy said. He was about to pull a card out of his hand when his phone rang.

"Hello," he said absently. Then he set his cards down abruptly, face up. Abigail saw that it was a pathetic hand. He had been bluffing. "Okay. I'll be right there. No. Keep the sirens off. Maybe we'll get him this time."

Abigail's heart jumped in her chest.

"What is it?" she said, as Jimmy pushed his chair back and got up. He was grabbing his coat.

"Gotta run, ladies. Sorry. There's a break-in at Waldorf Jewelers."

And before she could ask any questions, he was gone.

Waldorf Jewelers. Suddenly, she knew in her heart that it was Tony. He hadn't been able to wait for some reason or another, and he went after the steal. A surge of anger swept through her, followed quickly by fear.

"I've gotta go," she said, jumping up and throwing her cards on the table.

"What on earth...?" Martha said, pushing her own chair back.

"I'm sorry, Martha. I need to go. I can't—"

She didn't finish her sentence. She grabbed her coat and stuffed her feet into her boots.

"You can't what?"

"I'm sorry," she apologized again and shut the door behind her, running down the steps. The wind had picked up, and it blew open the front of her coat, chilling her instantly. She jumped in her car and started the engine. The steering wheel

200

felt freezing cold to her bare hands. She turned on her phone and asked her GPS system where Waldorf Jewelers was located. Then she sped along the roads, taking them too quickly as she followed the directions, barely able to see as her windows fogged up. She had to get there before Jimmy did.

Chapter Twenty-Eight

Tony took the rose pendant in his gloved hand. His hands were steady now, his practiced concentration guiding him through the steps. He took a moment to look at it. It was beautiful, its exquisite diamonds and rubies layered in just the right way to catch even the dim security lighting in the store.

The lighting.

Tony looked up. From where he stood, several beams of light shone down from innocuous looking light fixtures above him, capturing him in a web of crisscrossed patterns.

He swore.

Just then, he heard a click, and the front door burst open. There was Jimmy, standing with a gun pointed straight at him.

"Freeze!" Jimmy's voice was firm, loud.

Tony was glad for his mask. Slowly, he raised his hands above his head. His escape was the vent behind him, or if he remembered correctly, there was a back door. But he'd need to get behind the rear case first. And that didn't look like it was going to be possible. Five other officers had entered the store and were standing with guns pointed. There were probably more out back.

"You brought the whole posse," he said.

"Don't move," Jimmy said, "and keep your hands up."

The wind was whistling loudly outside, but Tony thought he heard something else out in the night air. So did Jimmy. "What is that?" Jimmy asked his men.

The door burst open, almost knocking Jimmy down, and a woman Tony instantly recognized as Abigail shouted, "Stop!" and raced past Jimmy. Someone grabbed her arm, but she took her fists to him, and he was so surprised he let go.

"Abigail?" Jimmy's voice was surprised, angry, and scared all at once.

"He isn't armed!" she said, putting herself in between Tony and the men.

"Grab her!" Jimmy said, the anger winning over.

Someone reached for her.

"Abigail, no!" Tony said as he started toward her. But someone shouted and the guns aimed higher. He realized too late that by saying her name, he had probably implicated her.

"Lower your weapons!" Jimmy shouted to his men. "That's Abigail. *Now!* Put them down before somebody shoots her!"

Abigail backed up until she was right up against Tony. He could feel her coat brushing his legs, could smell the soft floral scent of her hair. He kept his hands raised and his voice quiet. Suddenly he was very afraid for her.

"You need to stop," he said. "You don't need to get involved in this."

"I'm already involved," she said. "Go. You can leave out the back door. Hurry before they go around."

Jimmy was the only one with his gun still raised. "Abigail, what is this? Step aside. You're obstructing the law."

"Jimmy, put the gun down. He's unarmed."

"How do you know?"

"Stop," Tony said. "Please stop." He started to lower his hands again and to step in front of Abigail, but Jimmy waved his gun, motioning Tony to freeze. He kept his hands up, his mind working. He had to get between her and the guns. Or better yet, get her out of there completely.

"You can't take him away, Jimmy," she said. "You can't. He's a good man. He's not armed, and he's not going to hurt anybody. Just let him walk away, and I promise I will explain everything to you back at the station. You can take me in. Look! Here I am, blocking justice." She threw her arms up, and one of the officers raised his gun back up, his eyes wide. Things were getting tense in the room. Tony's heart raced. She was going to get herself killed. To save him.

"That's enough," Tony said. "Please, everybody put your guns down before she gets shot. I'll come with you." Slowly, he reached for his mask and pulled it off over his head. He could feel his curly hair sticking up in the dry static of the room.

"No." Her voice came out as a sob.

"Tony?" Jimmy's voice registered confusion. As he looked from Tony to Abigail, understanding came into his eyes. "Ahhh."

He had suspected.

"Abigail, I need you to move away."

He nodded to one of the officers, who started to slowly move behind Tony. Shortly, the exit behind him would be blocked.

"I'll go with you," Tony said. "I'm surrendering."

"No! I love him!" Abigail's voice was firm and then grew louder. "Jimmy, I love him! You can't take him away from me! I will *not* lose him like I lost Nick!" Her voice was frantic. She reached behind her head and took Tony's hand in hers. It was cold; Tony could feel it through his gloves. Then suddenly she turned and was kissing him, and he was lost in her hair, her smell, and the wonderful feeling of touching her. She placed both her hands on his face and pulled him into her. He was immersed in her warmth and her softness. He had never felt so alive. His hands started to lower, to hold her, but he knew the only way to keep her was to let her go.

"Abigail," he whispered, kissing her back and then slowly pulling away.

"No." She clung to him, her hands moving from his face to the front of his jacket. "No. Don't leave me. Please."

Tears were streaming down her cheeks, and he felt his own eyes filling up.

"I have to. This is no life for you. I can't go on like this. It needs to end."

"No...you can still run."

"Not really."

She glanced around and saw that they were surrounded. Then he did put his hands down and he put his arms around her one last time, his hand at the small of her back, pulling her against him. He kissed her, as he watched one of Jimmy's men move in behind her quietly. He closed his eyes briefly, drinking in the feel of her, committing it to memory. Then he opened them and saw that the man was nearly upon her. "I love you," he whispered and then stepped back, breaking her grasp. She reached for him again, but Jimmy's man grabbed her arms and pulled her away from him.

"No!" she screamed, her voice hysterical. "Let him go! Jimmy!" She tried to beat the officer off her, but this time he had her tight.

"Abigail, I'll be okay," Tony said, his heart breaking at the sight of what he had done to her. "I'll be okay."

Jimmy put his gun away and approached him. "I'm sorry," he said quietly. Then loud enough for the others to hear, he began to recite Tony his rights as he handcuffed him.

But Tony's eyes were on Abigail. She had crumpled to the floor and was rocking back and forth, sobbing. Two officers were near her. A third one picked Tony's bag up off the floor and went to get his rope.

"Abigail," he said, softly, when Jimmy was finished.

She looked up, her face tear-streaked, her eyes swollen.

"Visit my grandma. Don't let her die alone."

She nodded. He tried to give her his charming smile, but it felt dry and forced. A tear escaped his eye. "I'm so sorry. I said I wouldn't hurt you, but that's exactly what I have done."

"Let's go," Jimmy said. He handed Tony over to his officers. "Take this guy down to the station and book him. I'll be along shortly. I need to talk to Abigail. Matt and Delvin, I need you two to gather evidence here at the crime scene."

The last thing Tony saw before they pulled him through the door was Jimmy kneeling beside Abigail and putting his big, strong, fatherly arms around her.

Jimmy, scowling, led Abigail through the station and into his office, shutting the door behind them. He sat in his swivel chair.

"Take your coat off and sit down." Jimmy motioned toward the metal chair on the other side of his desk.

"No, I think I'll leave my coat on," said Abigail stubbornly, but she decided to sit because her legs were feeling wobbly.

"Would you like a cup of water?"

"No."

"Coffee?"

"No."

Abigail had stopped at the restroom on their way in and saw that her face was red and blotchy and her eyes were swollen from all the crying. She self-consciously rubbed at her nose and then folded her arms across her chest.

"So nothing?"

"No. I'm fine." Which wasn't true. She thought she might throw up.

Jimmy looked at her from under his thick, gray eyebrows. He was still scowling. Most of the concern he had for her well-being had diminished on the car ride over. She knew he was angry now.

"We'll send someone to get your car and bring it here."

"You told me that already."

"Hmmmm."

He stood up and began to pace. "So what were you thinking?" When she didn't answer, he asked again. "By stepping closer to him? I told you to move away from him and you—you—you *kissed* him!"

Abigail had never seen Jimmy this upset. "He wouldn't have hurt me."

"You don't know that. He could have grabbed you and used you as a human shield."

"He wouldn't have. Never." She folded her arms tighter across her chest. She knew her actions and words seemed ridiculous, but she knew in her heart she was right.

Jimmy stopped behind his desk and leaned forward. "That's the same man who was in the library that night, isn't it? That's when this all started."

Abigail closed her eyes and remained silent.

"Abby? Isn't it?"

"I plead the fifth."

Jimmy huffed, crossed his arms, and began pacing again. "All of this time, you have been aiding and abetting a criminal. Abigail, I could have you arrested for withholding information! You brought him to church. We invited him to dinner! And all of this time you knew. You *knew!*"

206

He turned to look at her, and she dropped her eyes to the floor. She sniffed and reached into her coat pocket to dig out a tissue, and when she pulled it out, her phone came with it, clattering to the floor. She picked it up, checked the screen, and put it back in the pocket.

"Abby?"

He was sitting back at his desk now. The anger had suddenly left him.

"You lied to us. Martha and me. We have always thought of you as..."

Abigail swallowed and looked back up at him. "As what? A goody-goody? As someone who would never do anything wrong?"

"As a daughter."

"Oh." Abigail felt her eyes filling again and dabbed at them with the tissue. Guilt was crushing down on her, tightening her chest. But so was fear. "Jimmy, I'm so sorry. I don't know what happened. I just fell in love. Tony is a good man. He really is."

Jimmy sighed and sat back in his chair, clasping his arms behind his head.

"What's going to happen to him?"

"I don't know. He will probably have a rap sheet a mile long once we start filling in the blanks, including this latest. Did he break into the law office?"

Abigail lowered her eyes.

"Never mind." Jimmy said. "The less you say, the better. I'm going to let you go because I love you, and so far the only thing we have on you is disrupting an arrest."

"He's trying to save his grandma." She looked at Jimmy again.

"I told you I'd try to help with the money. Of course, that was before I knew he was a criminal."

"I want to pay his bail."

"It hasn't been set yet. That takes time."

"Can I see him?"

"No."

Abigail slid the damp tissue into her pocket and was about to protest when she felt the cold metal of a phone. Only this time it was in her left pocket. She took it out enough to take a quick peek and realized it was Tony's cell. He must have dropped it in her pocket when he hugged her. Her fingers felt something else metal. Small, delicate. She ran her fingers over it and realized it was a piece of jewelry. She needed to get out of there.

"I want to go home."

Jimmy looked at her long and hard. "Are you okay?" he asked gently.

She nodded. "Jimmy, I love you and Martha. I really do."

"I know you do, kid." He stood up and walked over to his office door, opening it. "Your car should be here by now. Let's go. You need some rest."

Abigail took the few extra minutes to drive to the hospice before heading home. In the parking lot, she put her hand in her pocket and pulled out the piece of jewelry. It was a beautiful rose pendant, surrounded by tiny diamonds and filled with rubies. It must be worth a fortune. At least the ten thousand Tony needed. She carefully put it back, deep in her pocket.

Her hands were shaking as she opened the door and walked in. A woman was standing behind the desk. Her nameplate read "Alice."

"I'm here to see..." she realized she didn't know Grandma's name. "Tony's grandma."

"Of course. You must be Abigail."

"Yes. How did you know?"

"She has talked about you quite a bit." Alice smiled. "You can go on in. She's probably asleep but she's doing okay."

Abigail felt a big rush of relief at those words. She didn't want to have to tell Tony that his grandma had died. Alone.

The room was dark except for a small nightlight on the wall. She could see Grandma's eyes, and they were closed. She quietly sat down in the chair beside the bed and was surprised to see them flutter open.

"Hi," she said quietly.

"Abigail." Grandma reached for her hand. Her breathing was heavy, labored. Abigail held the soft hand. It felt very weak, but warm.

"I just wanted to check on you."

Grandma gave her a little smile. "Where's Tony?"

"He couldn't come this time." She wasn't sure what to say. The last thing she wanted to tell her was where Tony was.

Grandma was quiet for a moment. "He wouldn't stay away if he didn't have to. Not now." She paused. It was hard for her to breathe. "He finally got caught, didn't he?"

Abigail didn't respond right away. Did she know? How much should she tell Grandma? Why did she come here?

"You shouldn't talk," Abigail said, giving her hand a little squeeze.

Grandma swallowed with some difficulty, but kept her tired eyes on Abigail. Her chest heaved up and down. "Tell him...it's okay. Let him know that I have...never...been disappointed in him."

Abigail felt tears sting her eyes for the third time that night. "Okay," she said quietly. "He loves you."

"I know. I love him too. He's...a good kid."

Abigail reached for the tissues near the bed and dabbed at the corners of her eyes.

"I love him," she said. It felt good to say the words.

"I know you do." Grandma gave her hand a faint squeeze. "It will be okay."

After that, Grandma closed her eyes. Abigail sat there for a few minutes and then got up to leave, suddenly needing to fix this. Grandma kept sleeping. Abigail needed to get home and figure out how to get her hands on that painting before this sweet woman died.

She needed Tony's grandma to live. She couldn't deal with yet another loss. There had to be a way to get that medicine.

———◇————————◇———

Abigail had only been home a few minutes when her cell phone rang. She didn't recognize the number. "Hello?"

"Hi."

"Tony!" She grasped her phone to her ear, drinking in his voice.

"I'm using my one phone call on you."

"But you need a lawyer!"

"I don't need a lawyer. I had to know if you were okay."

"I'm okay." She realized her voice sounded shaky.

"Really?"

Abigail took a deep breath. "Yes. Really. And I stopped by to see your grandma."

"You are awesome."

"She's doing okay." She could hear him let out a breath. "She asked where you were."

Tony hesitated. "Did you tell her?"

"She knows. She has known all along."

Abigail heard a voice in the background. Then Tony said, "Okay. Just a few more minutes." He waited, Abigail assumed, until the person with the voice left. When he spoke it was in an urgent whisper.

"Listen. My phone is in your coat pocket."

"I know. I found it." He didn't mention the pendant.

"I'm going to give you my password. Go in and find the cancer strategist's number. His name is Scott Weaver. Call him and tell him I don't have the money and see if he can keep my grandma comfortable. There's a few thousand in my personal savings, not the other account, but my personal one. You can use that to pay him."

"Tony—"

"Do you have a pen?"

She looked around and grabbed a pencil and a notepad off her desk. "Yes." He gave her the bank information.

"Now go throw the phone in the river. It has the contacts of all my buyers in there, and if anyone gets it and hacks in, I'll make a lot of enemies."

"I can hide it. Along with the—"

"No. If they find it on you you'll get in trouble." Tony's voice grew softer. "*Are* you in trouble?"

"No. Jimmy says there's nothing to connect me to your crimes. He may have pulled some strings."

"Good." She heard him sigh. "I'm so sorry, Abigail."

"Me too."

"Do you really love me?" His voice sounded small.

She smiled. "Yes, Tony. I really love you."

"Then it's all worth it."

"I was foolish not to realize it sooner."

"You were foolish to love me to begin with."

"That's not true." She gripped the phone to her ear, there in her kitchen, leaning against the wall where they had first kissed. "Jimmy told me I can't visit you tomorrow. That I need to stay away. But I won't listen to him."

"Abigail...I need to do my time. We both know I'm guilty."

She felt the tears coming.

"Tony, I can't wait years to see you again. I need to see you now." She twisted her hair around her finger. *"For where thou art, there is the world itself, And where thou art not, desolation,"* she whispered.

"You've been catching up on your Shakespeare." He was trying to keep his voice light, but she could hear the pain in it. "I have to go. The guard says my time is up."

"Okay. I love you."

"I love you too," he said. Then, in closing, *"This bud of love by summer's ripening breath, May prove a beauteous flower when next we meet."*

She smiled and wiped away the tears from her face. "Bye, Romeo."

"Bye, Juliet."

The phone went dead, and she stood there for a moment, holding it to her chest. Then she went to do as Tony had asked.

She used the password to unlock his phone and started typing the name Weaver into his contacts search bar. Three names popped up before she had typed more than two letters:

Scott Weaver, cancer strategist

Charlotte Weber, client

Dom Weiss, paint sales

She wondered if that was the same Charlotte. If it was...

Suddenly she had an idea. Before she could change her mind, she dialed.

On the fourth ring, a voice, full of sleep, answered. "Hello?"

It was 12:50 a.m. A ridiculous time to call someone.

"Charlotte?"

"Yes? Who is this?"

"This is Abigail. We met at the yoga studio the other day. You know, Tony's girlfriend."

There was a pause, then, "Oh yes. That would explain why you're calling from Tony's phone."

"I have what you want."

She heard bed sheets rustle, as if Charlotte was sitting up. "Where's Tony?"

"He's...um..."

"It doesn't matter. Why are you calling so late? I have a work meeting in the morning." Charlotte sounded irritated and somehow still smooth and sexy at the same time.

"Look. I'll just be honest." Abigail started to pace as she explained the situation with Tony's grandma. "We need the money tonight. She doesn't have much time."

There was a silence. "And where is Tony?"

Since she was being honest she might as well go all the way. "In jail."

There was some swearing on the other end.

"Okay. Look. Are you competent? Can you come to my house without being followed?"

"It's 1 a.m."

"I know. But you can never be too careful. I'm doing this for Tony because he's a good guy. I've got the cash here because I was expecting him and because I always keep some lying around the house. If you can get here within the half hour, it's yours. Bring the pendant."

"Thanks so much!"

"You said she needs two more injections. Isn't that going to cost an additional ten thousand?"

"Yes."

"How do you plan to pay for the second one?"

"We'll cross that bridge when we come to it."

———◇————————◇———

Charlotte lived on the edge of town in a huge mansion with an iron gate across the entrance. She must have been watching for her because as soon as Abigail pulled up, the gates automatically swung open. She drove her car up to the front and got out. The wind was stronger here, and the cold bit into her skin right through her coat.

Charlotte opened the door and was waiting for her. "Come in," she said, ushering Abigail into the front entryway, where a chandelier hung overhead. Charlotte was wrapped in a red silk robe, her blond hair hanging loosely around her shoulders. She looked gorgeous, even when rudely awakened and without makeup.

Abigail pulled the pendant out of her pocket. She had put it in an old ring box that she had in her dresser. She opened it for Charlotte. The woman's eyes sparkled, and the corners of her mouth turned up. "Nice," she said and then handed Abigail a thick manila envelope.

"There's twenty thousand dollars cash in there," she said. "I keep a little extra lying around the house. You never know when you're going to need it."

Abigail started to speak, to tell her that was too much, but Charlotte hushed her. "I know. Don't worry about it. I'm looking at it as a donation. It's Tony, and he's a good guy. Go help his grandma."

"Wow."

"And let me get back to bed."

She turned Abigail around and closed the door behind her. Abigail rushed out to her car, clutching the money under her coat.

The clock on the car's dashboard read almost 2 a.m. when she pulled in the hospice parking lot. She had called the cancer strategist on her drive there, and he was in the lobby when she walked in. She handed him the envelope.

"Is this cash?" he asked incredulously.

She nodded.

"Where did you get it?"

"Probably best not to ask."

He looked at her for a moment, his mouth working soundlessly. Then he nodded. "I'll order the medication. I should have it in a few hours."

Abigail thanked him and left without going to check on Grandma. She had other plans.

Chapter Twenty-Nine

Tony sat on the cold bench in his cell and leaned his head back against the wall. He closed his eyes. He had been in holding cells before, in his youth, but never as an adult. He wasn't finding the experience very pleasant.

At least Abigail sounded okay. That was one thing. But his grandma, she was a different story. He had really messed up this time, and there was no way now she was going to get her medicine. Jimmy had mentioned to him when he first came in that he was trying to find some donations. One group was willing to chip in two thousand dollars, but he'd have to wait until places opened up on Monday morning to call around for more help. But that was many hours away, and the hope of raising the money and getting the medication in time were slim.

He kept vacillating between joy and sorrow. Abigail had told him she loved him, and he realized how much he loved her. He had thought he loved Darci, but his grandma was right. He hadn't. Not really. Darci was someone he enjoyed being with and sleeping with, but he had never had this gut-level feeling of connection with someone like he had with Abigail. She was all he could think about, and he put her safety far above his. When those guns were pointed at them, he didn't even think about getting himself caught and sent off to prison. All he knew was that he had to get them to stop before Abigail got hurt. Turning himself in was the only way.

It was time to quit stealing. He had found something that meant so much more. Maybe she wouldn't wait for him. Maybe he'd be in prison for so many years that she'd grow tired and move on. But having found her, he knew his life would never be the same. She had made him feel something he didn't even know he was missing, and this love he had for her was like breathing for him. He needed it as much as he needed air to live. Just knowing that she loved him was enough.

He closed his eyes, trying to see her face, trying to remember how she felt when he held her. Jimmy wouldn't let her visit, nor would he let Tony have visitors.

"Tony."

He opened his eyes. Jimmy stood in the shadows near the bars of his cell. Tony got up and walked over to him.

"How you doing?" Jimmy had his hands in his pockets. He didn't look angry, not like someone who had just found out that the man who stole his "daughter's" heart was thieving, dishonest riff-raff.

Tony shrugged. "About as okay as can be expected. Look. I'm sorry. I messed up."

"Yes, you did." Jimmy said. "You hurt her. She trusted you, and you hurt her."

Tony dropped his eyes. "I know."

"Where's the pendant?"

"I don't know." Tony had gone over that a hundred times in his head because they kept asking him. "I must have dropped it. It was in my hand, and then it wasn't. I don't know where it went. Honest. I was so caught up in Abigail being there and trying to protect her." He spread his hands. "I don't know. I lost it."

Jimmy nodded silently. After a moment, Tony looked up and met his eyes.

"The sermon this morning was on forgiveness," Jimmy said.

Tony nodded, swallowed. He looked back down at the ground again. This was a good man standing in front of him. He wished he could be half the man that Jimmy was.

Jimmy continued. "Seems to me that God wouldn't tell us something unless He expects us to act on it."

"I need to ask forgiveness," Tony said, looking up. "I know I do. And I'm sorry." He had apologized to Jimmy at least a dozen times. His heart felt like it was going to break in two. There was nothing he could do to deserve this man's forgiveness. He had messed up.

"I was meaning myself," Jimmy said. "I need to forgive *you*. You've hurt someone I care about a lot. But you know what? Just like that prodigal son, Jesus is willing to forgive you and forget about what you've done. So that means I should too."

Tony stared at him, not really believing what he was hearing. "But I...I'm a mess," he said, giving a nervous laugh. "I have this whole history of—"

"Let's not talk about that," Jimmy said. "Probably best for both of us if you keep that past to yourself. The question is, are you willing to change?"

"Yes," Tony said without hesitating. "Yes. For Abigail, I'll do anything."

"How about for yourself?"

Tony was quiet for a moment, thinking. Thinking of Abigail and how she had needed so badly to forgive herself for thinking she had caused Nick's death.

"We're all screwed up, flawed human beings, Tony. None of us is perfect. Being willing to change is what counts. If that's what's in your heart to do, you can be a new man. Jesus can forgive you and give you a fresh start."

"Yes," said Tony. He was embarrassed to feel tears coursing down his cheeks. "Yes. I want to do that. Tell me how."

Chapter Thirty

Abigail sat in her parked car on the street, knowing she had finally lost her mind. The wind was howling and was bitterly cold. She pulled out Tony's phone and dialed the number she had looked up only minutes ago.

After four rings, a groggy voice said, "Hello?"

"Is this Jonathan Stewart?" She had found the lawyer's number online. It took some searching, but she found his home number listed in the white pages.

"Yes?" She could hear the fear in his voice. He was probably wondering what was wrong, who had died in the family that warranted a call this time of night. She imagined him checking the caller ID again to be sure it wasn't a hospital and cringed. But she fired the ammo she had.

"I know where the painting is."

"What?" Momentary confusion on the other end. She was gambling with a hunch. She tossed the bait out.

"The lost Russo you've been searching for your entire life. I know where it is."

"Who is this?"

"That's why you had the painting above your desk wired for theft, right? It's not worth much in itself, but you knew it held clues."

There was a brief silence. The next time he spoke, she could tell he was wide awake. "Is this the person who broke in?"

"I don't want trouble, but I need your help. You're a city attorney, and I assume you took that position so you'd be free to poke around the city and not get in trouble, right?"

"Who is this again?"

"I found the painting, but it's not exactly in a spot I can access without getting into trouble. I don't want to break the law. So if I have a lawyer with me...specifically the City Attorney..."

"Where is it?"

"If I tell you, I need your word you'll let me give it to its rightful owner."

"Why would I do that?"

"Because you stand for justice, and you're a decent guy. You're a family man. You volunteer with children. And you want to see that painting as badly as I do." She closed her eyes and prayed.

There was a long silence and then a sigh. "Okay. Where and when?"

"Now. I'll tell you where to meet me. Bring good walking boots and a flashlight. And come alone."

She gave him the address of where she was parked and then hung up.

She kept the car running because it was cold outside. She checked her watch every minute or so. It took him twelve minutes to get there. He parked behind her as she had instructed and cautiously came up to her car. She got out.

In person, Stewart looked to be around sixty years old, but it was hard to tell in the dark. She shined her flashlight on him, careful not to get it in his eyes, and then shined it back to his car to make sure he was alone.

"Thanks for coming," she said because she wasn't sure what else to say. It was dark and cold, and there wasn't anybody else on the street at this time of night. He could kill her or rape her or worse.

"If I help you, what do I get out of this?" he asked.

"I'll give you all the credit for finding it," she said. "It's world-famous. People have been looking for it for a long time, as you know. You can be the one who finds it. The one who unites it with its owner. You're running for reelection soon for city attorney. Think what a great PR story this will be."

He didn't disagree, but he looked wary. "Are you alone?"

"Yes."

His eyes narrowed, and he glanced in the back of her car. "It's dangerous, you out here like this."

"I know. This is important to me."

"Are you the painting's 'rightful' owner?"

"No. But come with me, and I'll tell you the story as we walk."

He followed her to the alley where the manhole was, and she took a crowbar out of her backpack and pried it open. It was easy this time.

"We're going down there?" Stewart looked warily over the edge and down into the darkness.

"Yes." Abigail swallowed. "You first."

"I'm not getting in that hole."

She was afraid of that. She reached into her bag and pulled the map out. "Hold this," she said, handing him the flashlight so she could unroll the map. The wind threatened to tear it out of her hands. She cursed herself. She should have done this in the car. "Look."

She hoped there was enough moonlight that it worked. And there was. Slowly, the glowing blue lines started to appear on the paper.

"What on earth..." Stewart's voice trailed off.

"It's a secret map. The original cartographer hid it on top of this map of the city. It led to the painting. Well, at the time when the map was created anyway. It led us to the old law building." She pointed to it with her finger. "Which is now a temp agency. We looked in there, and it led us to your office."

Stewart was fascinated, she could tell. She watched the excitement grow in his eyes as he looked at the map. "So it was you who broke in. When I saw the thief tried to take the picture above my desk, I knew it was tied in to the Russo. But how did you get here, to this place?"

Abigail rolled the map back up and stuck it in the tube. "Let's get out of this wind, and I'll tell you." She took the flashlight back and motioned for him to climb the ladder down into the sewer. He hesitated, shrugged, and started to descend. She hoped he didn't fall, but he managed to make it down. She followed him on trembling legs, remembering how Tony had also tied a rope to the top bar, just in case the ladder broke. She didn't have one with her.

"We go this way," she said, motioning for him to walk ahead of her. It seemed darker than it had when she was with Tony.

"So tell me about this painting," he said.

She told him the story of Tony's great-grandmother, Margaret, and her love for Russo. She described how the painting had been sent over here to her and then stolen from the carrier and hidden.

"So the original thief must have died before he could go back and get it," Stewart mused.

"That's what we think. But the clues remained."

"What about my grandfather's portrait?"

"Turn here." She was glad to see the marks Tony left were still there. "Follow the arrows."

She explained how they solved the clues, that they stood for literature, science and the arts, and how they led to the Dean's office.

"Fascinating," he said. "I have looked for years."

"I know. That's why you became City Attorney, right? So you'd have access to explore in places the average person couldn't."

He turned to look at her and smiled. "Yes. I've put a lot of miles into this city, looking. I never even got close."

He walked some more and then turned to look back at her. "You're taking quite a chance tonight, young lady. How do you know I won't hurt you?"

"I have a gun." She had thought to bring it with her at the last moment.

"You have a gun? Are you crazy?"

"Well, I *was* institutionalized a few years back." She smiled at him.

"That's crazy. You know I'm anti-gun. And this is exactly why. A girl like you could lead me down here, shoot me, and leave me for dead."

"A girl like me should never be alone down here with a man she doesn't know *unless* she has a gun."

"Good point."

They turned a corner. "Here it is," Abigail said. She shined her light on the flower symbol.

"Well, I'll be..." Stewart rubbed his hands together.

"This is right under the Dean's office. I'm thinking in the wall behind his bookcase. There's a water fountain nearby too." She pulled out Tony's phone and opened the sonic app. She waved it over the ceiling, and it picked up an object behind the concrete. It was a thin edge, as if it were standing upright, which would make sense if it was hidden inside a wall above them. "There's where it is exactly," she said.

"Wow." Stewart was impressed with the phone app. "How are we going to get it?"

Abigail dug into her bag and pulled out the crowbar. She handed it to him.

"Start cracking."

"What? You want me to tear up city property?"

"Well, yes. That's exactly why I brought you. I'm not going to get into trouble."

He looked at her for a moment, hesitating, and then gave the ceiling a good hit. A piece fell off.

"It looks damp, which is probably why it's soft," he said. "I've supervised a lot of concrete broken up over this city, and it isn't usually this easy."

"And I've been praying."

He hit it again, and another piece fell off. Small debris fell on his shoulders and in his hair. "Is the painting right behind this? I don't want to damage it."

"Probably. Yes. Please be careful."

Abigail leaned back to watch and pulled a granola bar out of her backpack. She hadn't eaten anything since dinner with the Stouts.

It didn't take long to get the first layer off, breaking up the flower symbol. Then, Stewart carefully nicked away at a second layer while Abigail held the flashlight for him. They heard a soft thud as the crowbar hit something that wasn't concrete.

"Bingo," Stewart said. He used his gloved fingers to pry the rest away, which revealed an object wrapped in layers of canvas. It was wedged inside a wall up in the ceiling above them. It must be the inside of the wall she saw in the LS&A building. She could see the pipes from the water fountain.

Stewart reached in and carefully pulled the canvas-wrapped object out.

Abigail's heart pounded in her chest. This was it! This was the painting Tony had spent his life looking for! She was about to be the first person to see it since it had gone missing so many years ago. It felt wrong, somehow, to be here without Tony.

Stewart had begun to unwrap it. There were several layers of canvas and after that, several layers of cloth. He slowly unwrapped the layers, laying them on the ground while Abigail held the flashlight until there was one layer left.

He looked at Abigail. "This is it." He was grinning like a schoolboy.

She started to chew her nail but realized she had her glove on. "Wow."

"Do you want to say anything special?" Stewart asked. "I feel like we're unveiling a masterpiece."

"We are," Abigail said, laughing nervously. "Um. Yes. This is for Tony. May all his hard work be worth it."

Stewart nodded. "To Tony." He unwrapped the last layer.

It was breathtaking. The painting looked as fresh as if it were painted yesterday. The portrait was of a beautiful young woman who strongly resembled Tony's grandmother. She was sitting on a white wicker stool wearing a sleeveless blue dress that ended around her ankles, revealing bare feet. Her long, dark hair was down, falling gracefully around her shoulders, and she was laughing. Joy lit up her whole face. Her hands were in her lap, a ring on her wedding finger. Abigail shined the light on the ring, a light green emerald surrounded by small diamonds.

"She looks so happy," Abigail said.

"This is incredible," breathed Stewart. "Incredible."

"Turn it over."

Stewart carefully turned the painting over. There was something written on the back of the canvas. Abigail read aloud.

"To my darling Laurel,
The light of my life, the mother of my child, the joy of my heart. I do love nothing in the world so much as you."

mrs. chartwell and the cat burglar

It was signed by Antonio Russo. There was a heart drawn next to his name.

Stewart looked at Abigail. "Do you have any idea what this is worth?"

"I do. But it's worth more to Tony's grandmother. I need to get it to her before she dies."

Suddenly aware of the ticking clock, she picked up the cloths, and Stewart helped her wrap up the painting. "Let's go," she said. Just to be on the safe side, she took the painting and motioned for Stewart to lead the way.

When they got to the manhole, she went up first, although at this point she believed Stewart was too excited to think of anything but the painting. But still, she was relieved when they were both standing above ground again.

"I'd like to take it," Stewart said. "Or come with you when you show her. Please. This means so much to me."

"I need to do this alone," Abigail said. "Just me and her. After she sees it, I'll announce that you brought it to me late in the night and got it to us. We can make the announcement in the morning. But now I need to go alone."

"I can't just let you walk away with a masterpiece."

"It's obviously meant for her," Abigail said. "She's the rightful owner."

"Still." He reached for the painting. He would probably never hurt her, but she didn't have time for this. She stepped back and pulled the gun out of her pocket.

Stewart froze.

"Get in your car and drive away," she said, her heart pounding so hard she was sure he could hear it. "You will get full credit, I promise. If not, you can press charges against me for trespassing and tearing up city property."

"With what proof?"

She reached into the bag and brought out the crowbar. He flinched. She tossed it to him. He caught it in his gloved hands.

"With this. It has my fingerprints all over it from when I packed it in the bag."

He looked at her for a moment and then down at the gun. "It seems I have no choice." With that, he got in his car and she watched him drive away. She let out the breath

224

she was holding, put her gun back and got in her own car. It was many minutes before she was calm enough to drive. She watched closely in her rearview mirror, but he didn't seem to be following her. To be sure, she made several turns and crossed her path a few times.

On her way back to her house, she turned down the street that ran along the river. It was dark outside, the moon having set. She pulled over to the side and left her car running while she stepped onto the curb. The river stretched out before her, frozen, the few lights from the city twinkling off its snow-covered surface. Only the middle was dark, as a small unfrozen line of cold water ran south on its path out to larger bodies of water somewhere far away. Always running, it never really froze completely across. She pulled Tony's phone out of his pocket but wasn't sure she could throw that far. She'd have to find a bridge and toss it from there.

She was cold, her teeth chattering now from either shock or the temperature. She'd deal with the phone later.

Back inside the car, she used her own phone to call the hospice. She was relieved to hear they had given Grandma a shot. The oncologist had kept his word and got the cancer medicine into her right away.

"She's sleeping," Alice said. "She got a fever about a half hour after the injection. That's what happened last time. She will be out for several hours. Why don't you try to get some sleep?"

Abigail hung up, feeling elated. She had the painting, and she had gotten the medicine into Tony's grandma.

It was a short drive home. She took her coat off, put the painting behind the couch, and sat on the couch to think. Cocoa rubbed against her legs, and she absently scratched her on the head. Should she take the painting to Grandma tonight anyway? How long would she sleep? She glanced at the front door to be sure she had locked it and set the dead bolt. Stewart didn't seem to be a dangerous man, but she was half-afraid he'd come to get the painting. The potential to make millions did strange things to people. Still, he had seemed more fascinated with the painting and the story than the desire for money.

She got up to get herself a glass of water and felt a bit dizzy. Her legs nearly buckled under her. She was exhausted. All of the emotion of the day and the fear and the loss had taken its toll.

She poured herself a small glass of wine instead and sat back down on the couch. She ran her dirty fingers through her hair as she sipped it. Her nails would never be the same. The canvas wrappings had been filthy. She wanted to talk to Tony so badly. She wondered if Jimmy would let her in to see him tomorrow. But she'd have to take the painting to Grandma first, before the lawyer came around. She knew he'd come.

Her fingers finally stopped trembling, and her eyelids grew heavy. She was coming down from the adrenaline rush and crashing. The clock on the mantel read 4:10 a.m.

She was so tired. She set the wine glass on the coffee table and lay down on the couch. Cocoa jumped up and snuggled in beside her. The purring was comforting. She'd close her eyes just for a few minutes and then maybe Grandma would be awake. Just a few minutes.

She dreamed that she was Margaret, and that Russo was painting a portrait of her. Only he looked a lot like Tony.

Chapter Thirty-One

She awoke with a start. It was 9 a.m., and the first thing that went through her head was that she was late for work. She'd have to call in sick. She looked at her phone. No messages. Then she looked at Tony's phone, hear heart pounding in fear that the hospice had called and his Grandma had died in the middle of the night. Nothing.

First things first. She called the library and told Ms. Scott she was sick and would be out for the day.

Then she called the hospice, her heart in her throat. All was well. Grandma was awake and looking much better.

She hung up and nearly wept with relief, but she suddenly realized she was starving. She'd eat, shower, and then call Jimmy to see if she could go see Tony. After she took the painting in. Before the lawyer came looking for her.

She looked at the time again. Her heart started to pound. She had to relax or this was going to kill her. Maybe she'd take a hot shower.

First breakfast.

Her phone beeped with a text. She jumped. It was Pauline, wondering if she was okay. Word got around fast. She texted that she had the flu and then wondered why Jimmy or Martha hadn't called to check on her yet.

She used the bathroom and brushed her teeth. She looked a sight, with her hair all tangled and smudges of dirt on her face. Her nails were still stained, despite the fact that she scrubbed them with the nailbrush. She'd definitely have to shower before she went out.

Back in the kitchen, she fed the cat and grabbed a bowl and a box of cereal. She was about to pour the cereal when the doorbell rang.

She froze. What if it was Stewart? She hadn't given him her name or contact number, and she had used Tony's phone when she called him, but he could have taken down her license plate. He was smart.

She decided she would look through the peephole to see if it was him. If so, she would pretend she wasn't home. What she saw nearly made her faint.

It was Tony.

She flung open the door. He was standing there, holding flowers, dressed in a black suit with the collar open at the neck. His black wool coat hung on his muscular frame, gathering snow. He was cleanly shaven.

She flung herself at him, wrapping her arms around his neck. She had no idea why or how he came to be standing on her front porch looking like a dream, but she wasn't about to let him go. Ever.

"Oh Tony," she said, kissing his cheek, his neck, his lips. "I missed you." He felt so good against her, and she pulled him in closer.

He wrapped his strong arms around her, kissing her back. "I missed you too," he said, kissing her lips again and running his hands through her hair. Finally, he buried his face in her neck. "I love you."

"I love you too."

The stood there like that for several minutes, just holding each other. Then she invited him inside.

"How did you get out of *jail*? How are you *doing*?" She took his coat for him and hung it on a peg by the door. Then she ran to get a vase for the flowers.

"I'm good," he said, putting the flowers into the vase and helping her arrange them. Her head was spinning with questions.

"How are you here? Jimmy said I wasn't allowed to see you and that you were going down the river without a paddle."

Tony smiled. "Turns out, Jimmy is a very forgiving man. He paid my bail, and I have an arraignment coming up. He advised me to keep the past in the past, so all they have me on is the one robbery at the jewelers. And they can't find the pendant. I must have dropped it last night."

So he didn't know. Well, Abigail knew exactly where that pendant was, but she thought she'd keep that to herself for now.

"So will you get jail time?

"Probably not much, if any. Jimmy made it clear I was going to do a heck of a lot of community service though."

"Wow."

"Yeah. I feel kind of bad. I mean, I really was ready to confess it all, but he hushed me and said if I was truly ready to change, the past could remain the past. No condemnation."

"Jimmy's a great guy."

"He is."

Abigail put her arms around him again. "I just can't believe you're here. I was so afraid I had lost you."

"I'm here." He pulled her against him, his arms holding her tightly.

She closed her eyes, leaning her head against his chest. She could hear his heart beating. She had almost lost him twice. She remembered the guns pointed at him when she ran into the building. But no. He was here. With *her.* Safe.

She felt her own heart rate slowing down to match his.

"Abigail?"

"Hmmmm?"

"Why are you so muddy?"

"Oh!" she said. "I have something for you!" She pulled away from him, grinning. She heard herself squeal with excitement. Where did that come from? "Wait until you see it! Sit down first." She pointed to the couch.

"Um. I'd rather stand." He looked nervous.

"No. You have to sit down for this. It's huge." She waited until he sat. Then she pulled the canvas-wrapped painting from behind the couch and held it in front of him.

Tony's mouth opened. Then shut. Then he said, "Is this—?"

She only smiled. "Open it. Carefully."

Gently, he took the painting from her and set in on the couch. Slowly he unwrapped it, stopping once to glance up at her. Then he lifted the last bit of cloth, and there it was.

His mouth opened again, but he didn't say anything.

"Abigail…" he finally breathed. "This is it. You found it."

She couldn't stop grinning. "I got it last night. I wish you could have been there with me."

He ran his hands along the edges of the painting and then took his time looking at it. "Margaret looks so much like my grandma."

"She does."

He traced his fingers lightly over it. "She's wearing the ring."

"I know. It's amazing. Read the back."

Tony turned it over. When he looked up at Abigail, there were tears in his eyes. "It's real."

"Yes," she said, laughing. "It is. It is, and there's your proof, Tony Russo. You are the great-grandson of the famous painter."

"This is amazing. How did you get it? Tell me!"

"Later. We have to show it to your grandma right now. She's doing better."

"I know. I called to check as soon as I got out of jail. They said she got her shot."

"I know."

"You've had a busy night! Where did you get the money?"

"It doesn't matter. I will tell you everything later. Let me get cleaned up and we can go."

She looked at him, sitting there on the couch, cradling the painting as if it were a newborn. He looked so handsome.

"Tony, did you dress up just for me?"

He looked up at her. "Yes," he said. He set the painting down and stood up. Walking over to her, he took her hands in his. "Jimmy told me I could put my...talents...to use in better ways. I'm going to start a security company. Since I'm so savvy on the ways to get into places, I can help my clients keep the bad guys out by finding the loopholes. I'm giving up the life of crime. Or rather, I'm switching sides. You, Abigail, have made me want to be a better man."

She couldn't quit smiling

"And you, Tony, have saved my life. You've made me want to live again." Her life had come so far these past few weeks. While the past twenty-four hours had been nerve wracking, she had never felt more alive.

"I love you," Tony said. "I loved you the moment I first set eyes on you back in that library. I have never felt this way before. Ever."

Suddenly he got down on one knee. He let go of her hands and reached into his jacket pocket, pulling out a box. He held it out in front of him.

Her heart started hammering again, only this time in a good way.

"This one isn't stolen," he said, smiling. Then he opened the box. Inside it sat a gold ring with a green emerald surrounded by tiny diamonds.

"Abigail Chartwell, will you marry me?"

It was the ring. The ring that was in the painting. She looked into his eyes, those sparking, mischievous eyes that she had fallen for that first night, now filled with love. "Yes," she said, getting down on her own knees in front of him. "Yes, Tony Russo. I will marry you."

Gently, he took the ring out of the box and slid it on her finger. It fit perfectly. Then he leaned forward and kissed her. She felt tears running down her cheeks. She put her arms around him.

Cocoa came up, curious. She rubbed against them and then pushed her way between them. They both laughed, and Tony helped Abigail to her feet.

"This is beautiful," she said, turning her hand and admiring the ring as it reflected the sunlight coming in through the front window. "Where did you find it?"

"My grandma has had it for years, safely tucked away. I don't know why she never showed it to me, but the other night she told me about it. 'Tony,' she said. 'Give this to Abigail when you finally get up the courage to ask her.'"

Abigail laughed. "Shall we go tell her the good news?"

"Yes," he said.

"But let me wash up first!"

Chapter Thirty-Two

Abigail drove. Tony sat in the passenger seat and tried to wipe the smile off of his face. His whole life was changing.

"What are you grinning about?" Abigail said, glancing over at him.

He reached over and took her hand. "You make me happy."

She gave his hand a squeeze. "All of this romance and not a single Shakespeare quote. Where has the Tony I knew gone?"

He thought for a moment. *"'I do love nothing in the world so well as you: is not that strange?'* Not paintings or rings or thievery can hold court against your beauty."

Abigail shook her head. "That's a combination of Shakespeare and Tony Russo. Plus, you stole that one line from the back of the painting. Try again."

She was playing tough. He thought some more and found another one. *"'Hear my soul speak. Of the very instant that I saw you, Did my heart fly at your service.'"*

"Very nice," she said. "What's that from?"

"The Tempest."

"Do you have all of Shakespeare memorized?"

Tony laughed. "No, not nearly." He gazed over at her. Her hair was down and shining in the morning sun, which had decided to peek out from behind clouds. She was beautiful.

And so very smart.

"So how did you pay for the cancer medication?" he said. "Did Jimmy come through with the fundraising that quickly?"

"No." She hesitated.

"Uh-oh," he said. "Is this bad? *'The course of true love never did run smooth.'"*

She smiled at his quotation. "No. Not bad. Just..."

She glanced at him and then back at the road. "I found the pendant. You must have accidently dropped it in my coat pocket when you put the phone in." She pulled her hand away from him, dug her hand into her coat, and produced his phone. "Here. I wasn't able to throw far enough to land it in the river."

He took the phone. "So...you sold the pendant?"

"Charlotte's number is in there. I called her." She glanced at him again and smiled. "Apparently she has a soft spot for you. When I told her what the money was for, she gave me double, so we could pay for both injections."

"I can't pay her back."

"It's a gift."

A small smile crossed his face. "She always did surprise me." Tony ran his hand down his phone. "Pull over up here. I want to toss it."

Abigail parked on a side street near the river. She looked over at him. He glanced down at his phone, rubbing his fingers along the side. "This has some really good apps on it," he said.

"Yes, it does. I used one of them to locate the exact spot of the painting before we beat the ceiling down with a crowbar."

"You still have to tell me this story," he said, laughing.

She reached over and put her hand on his. "Are you really going to toss it in the river?"

Tony met her eyes. "Yes. This represents my old life, Abigail. Clients. Women. The whole mess. I really do want to start over."

A little part of him was sad to be letting go of so much. It had been his life for so long, and he had built up a great clientele, many people whom he genuinely liked doing business with. For one reason or another.

"Let me make one last call," he said. He looked through his contacts and dialed her number. He put it on speaker.

"Hello?"

"You're up early, Charlotte. Abigail and I have you on speaker."

"Tony, I'm a woman with many businesses to run and a score of things to do. Good morning, Abigail. You won't see me at yoga anymore. I've moved on to a different studio. The hot yoga isn't for me."

"Good morning, Charlotte," Abigail said. Tony raised an eyebrow, and she mouthed, "I'll tell you about it later."

"So I thought you were on a bit of a break, Tony. Are you...back in business?"

"Nope. The wheel of fortune has smiled upon me. I'm getting *out* of the business. But I wanted to thank you first. My grandmother is doing very well now that she had her medication. That means a lot to me."

"I'm glad to hear that. But why tell me, darling? I've never met the woman."

Tony glanced at Abigail and smiled. "No? But I heard you contributed to her—"

"I have no idea what you're talking about," Charlotte interrupted. "Not my problem. I need to run, darling. There's a world out there that needs me. Businesses don't run themselves, you know."

Tony shook his head. "No, they don't. Goodbye, Charlotte."

"Good bye, Tony. You and that redhead have a good life. She seems to have straightened you out."

The phone went dead. Tony smiled. Typical Charlotte. A good heart but no strings. He clasped the phone once more in his hand and then opened the car door and got out.

The sun was shining brightly on the river, and he had to squint against the light. He walked to the middle of the bridge on the pedestrian walk and looked down below to where the water was running darkly in between the ice. He held his hand over it and slowly opened his fingers. His phone fell, turning over and over, and landed with a small splash, disappearing into the water. He felt suddenly lighter, as if a weight he didn't realize he had been carrying had been removed.

He turned and headed back to the car where Abigail was waiting for him. On the way to the hospice, she told him the story of how she contacted Jonathon Stewart and together they went after the painting. Then she told him in detail about selling the pendant and what the oncologist had said.

"You did all of this for me?" he said. Since his mother had died, no one other than his grandma had ever gone out of their way for him. It felt good.

"Of course," said Abigail, pulling into the hospice parking lot. Just as she turned the car off, her phone rang.

"It's Jimmy," she said glancing at Tony. He could tell she was worried. She answered it.

"Jimmy!" There was a pause. "Yes he's here with me. Thank you so much, Jimmy. I can't begin to thank you enough."She smiled and waved her ring at Tony. "I want to tell them in person" she whispered. He nodded.

"Okay," she said into the phone. "I'll put it on speaker." She switched the phone over.

"Hi," Tony said.

"I just wanted to tell the both of you that the missing pendant mysteriously appeared this morning at the jewelry store. A courier dropped off a manila envelope, handed it right to the owner. The owner didn't pay much attention, thinking it was just some mail or something he had ordered. Then he realized there was no return address. Nothing. When he opened the envelope, the pendant was inside with a note that simply said:

"I thought you might be missing this. It is being returned on the good faith that you will let this matter rest."

Tony looked over at Abigail. Her eyes were sparkling.

"I won't ask if either of you know anything about this, but the owner decided not to press charges. Looks like you're off the hook, Tony." Jimmy cleared his throat. "However, there will still be an arraignment and sentencing, but you'll probably only get community service. You were, after all, caught in the act."

"Thank you, sir." Tony said.

"Jimmy, thank you so much!" Abigail said.

"I'm just following the law," said a gruff voice. Then he hung up.

"It had to be Charlotte," Abigail said.

"It seems she has a soft side to her."

Abigail reached over and took Tony's hand. It was warm, and she gave it a gentle squeeze. "This means I won't lose you." Her eyes spoke volumes. "This is the best day ever!"

Tony carried the canvas-wrapped painting down the hall of the hospice, his heart pounding in his chest. He stopped outside his grandma's door and took a deep breath.

"She's going to love this," he whispered. "It's just that I've been looking for it for so long I can't believe it's real. I can't believe I'm about to show it to her."

Abigail reached over and took his free hand. "Let's do it."

Grandma was sitting up in the bed looking good. Her color was back, and she was bright-eyed.

"Tony!" she said when they walked in the door. "Oh, you brought the lovely Abigail with you!"

Tony set the wrapped painting on the chair and leaned over to hug his grandma. She was soft and warm as she put her arms around him. He stayed that way a minute, just feeling her, taking in the fact that she was alive and here. Last night in jail, he thought he would never see her again.

Finally, he pulled away and was surprised to feel tears on his cheeks. "I thought I was losing you," he said.

"Not yet. Those shots you bought me are doing a great job. The doctor told me today that he thinks after the third one, I might get to go home." A smile spread across her face. She grasped Tony's hand.

"Really?" he said, wiping his tears away with the back of his hand. "That's a miracle! It really is!"

Grandma squeezed his hand and then reached her hand out to Abigail. "Come here, honey," she said. Abigail gave her her hand—the one with the ring on it. Grandma saw it and then looked up at Tony. "That's my boy." She let go of his hand and pinched his cheek. He laughed. "I am so happy for you, honey!" she said to Abigail. "Come here and let me give you a hug."

Abigail leaned down so Grandma could hug her, her long red hair cascading down across the old woman's shoulders. His two favorite people, together.

"Congratulations to the both of you," Grandma said. "You are so perfect for each other. Abigail, the first day I saw you, I realized you were *the one*. I've never seen that look in Tony's eyes before. You're the one he has been waiting for."

She turned to Tony. "How is it that you're here? Abigail had told me another story. Or was it the medicine messing with my mind?"

"No. They let me out of the slammer," Tony said. He picked up the painting and sat in the chair. Abigail sat across from him on the other side of the bed. "I have to do community service. There's an arraignment. Grandma, I'm so sorry. You must be so disappointed."

Grandma took his hand again, and their eyes met. In it, he saw all the years of love that she had poured into him. An endless well. "My dear grandson, I could never be disappointed in you."

Tony felt the tears welling up again, so he changed the subject. "Grandma, Abigail and I have something amazing to show you. We found it together. Well, she dug through the dirt to get it, but, well, I really think you're going to like it."

Slowly he unwrapped the canvas and then removed the cotton cloths. When it was unwrapped, he turned it around and held it up for her to see.

Her face grew serious and tears filled her eyes. "You found it," she whispered. "It really does exist." With trembling hands, she reached up and took it from him. She simply held it there, staring at it, taking it all in. "She's wearing the ring," she said.

"Turn it over," Tony said. "Read what's on the back."

She did. She read it over several times.

"Tony. This is a miracle. So many miracles today." She traced her fingers across the signature of the famous painter. "This must be worth millions."

"It's worth so much more than that," Tony said. He looked across the bed at his fiancée. "It brought Abigail and me together."

They sat there, the three of them, for quite some time, just quietly sharing in the knowledge of a secret revealed. Then Abigail got up. "I need to call somebody," she said. "I told him I'd give him the credit for the find. He was there helping me. Then, Grandma, after the cameras and the craziness leave, I'll tell you the whole story. Tony's right. If this painting had never existed, our paths might never have crossed."

Tony stood. "I'll be right back, Grandma." He took Abigail's hand, and together they walked to the lobby so she could call Jonathan Stewart and invite him over.

"What are we going to do with it?" she asked.

Tony shrugged. "Maybe we can hang it in a museum. I'm sure the University would love to show it off. It'll be safe there. I happen to know they have an excellent security system."

Abigail laughed and pulled him into a warm hug. He put his arms around her, kissing her on the lips. He couldn't believe how blessed he was.

He pulled back a little and gently tucked some of her hair behind her ear, gazing into her eyes. *"He is the half part of a blessed man, Left to be finished by such as she;"*

She gave him that smile of hers that turned him to mush. *"And she a fair divided excellence, Whose fullness of perfection lies in him."*

Tony smiled. "You really have been brushing up on your Shakespeare."

Her eyes sparkled. "I can't wait to show you what else I know."

He laughed and hugged her tight again. Life was good.

THE END

Follow Tony and Abigail in their next adventure in
Trusting the Cat Burglar: A Russo Romantic Mystery: Book 2.

Acknowledgments

To God be the glory. It was He who gifted me with writing. I am incredibly blessed that I can do it for a living.

A special thank you to my critique group partners, Xanthe and Pam. You are incredibly gifted writers, and I'm sure Cat Burglar is so much better because of you. It was definitely fun! As usual, your diversions into television-related talk kept me coming back, and I doubt I'd be where I am without binge-watching your DVDs. Heck, I'd probably be several books further ahead. LOL! Now if only we could call upon the Tardis to take me to Stars Hollow...

Thank you to my first beta readers, Elise and Peggy. Your insights were incredibly valuable. Without you, my timeline may have been snaggled, which is bad since this isn't science fiction! Also, where DID Abigail get that gun? Good questions. Thank you for taking your valuable time to read Cat Burglar. And Roxanne and Greg—what would I do without you guys? Always so willing to read yet another one of my early drafts when you are so swamped with your own busy lives! I am incredibly grateful!

To my incredible team: Erin my editor, Dallas my formatter, and Lyndsey my cover artist. Thank you for making my manuscript look like a book!

And as always, thank you to the people who hold it all together so I can create: Duane, Zack, Logan, Mom and Dad. I love you all!

About the Author

Pamela Gossiaux is the author of the romantic comedy *Good Enough*, as well as the inspirational books, *Why Is There a Lemon in My Fruit Salad? How to Stay Sweet When Life Turns Sour*, and *A Kid at Heart*. She is also a Christian speaker, writing instructor, and freelancer. She lives and writes in Michigan near a wonderful university town with her husband, two sons, and three cats. Visit her website at PamelaGossiaux.com.

Other Books by
Pamela Gossiaux

Meet Amy Summers, a big-hearted heroine whose simple life gets turned upside down when she finds a winning lottery ticket worth millions…but should she cash it?

Amy Summers has it all: the world's best job, an awesome boyfriend, and a happily-ever-after in sight. Then, in one very bad day that involves burnt toast and a police arrest, she loses everything – except for a winning lottery ticket her ex left behind.

Afraid to cash it, she decides to give up men and become a Bohemian novelist. She takes her laptop to Starbucks and literally bumps into caffeine-free, easy-going Josh Gray, a life coach and very handsome man. (Not that she's noticing.) When he offers to help Amy get back on her feet, she decides to hire him.

Her heart is telling her that he's the man for her, but Josh is big on honesty and Amy has a huge secret that could push him away if he ever finds out.

"Richly meaningful while wildly entertaining, GOOD ENOUGH is a major new book by an exceptionally talented author."
– Grady Harp, Amazon Hall of Fame Top 100 Reviewer

"This story is such a fun read, it is impossible once you have opened it not to be thoroughly captivated by Amy's escapades."
– Susan Keefe, *Midwest Book Review*

"GOOD ENOUGH touches a nerve every woman faces. Are we ever going to be good enough? Gossiaux has written a funny, revenge romance that will have you cheering on the heroine, Amy, until the very end."
—Diana Lesire Brandmeyer, author of CBA Best Seller *Mind of Her Own*

Available at PamelaGossiaux.com